BEYOND A REASONABLE STOUT

Also by Ellie Alexander

THE SLOAN KRAUSE MYSTERIES

Death on Tap

The Pint of No Return

THE BAKESHOP MYSTERIES

Meet Your Baker

A Batter of Life and Death

On Thin Icing

Caught Bread Handed

Fudge and Jury

A Crime of Passion Fruit

Another One Bites the Crust

Till Death Do Us Tart

Live and Let Pie

A Cup of Holiday Fear

BEYOND A REASONABLE STOUT

ELLIE ALEXANDER

Minotaur Books
New York

First published in the United States by Minotaur Books, an imprint of St. Martin's Publishing Group

BEYOND A REASONABLE STOUT. Copyright © 2019 by Kate Dyer-Seeley. All rights reserved. Printed in the United States of America. For information, address St. Martin's Publishing Group, 120 Broadway, New York, NY 10271.

www.minotaurbooks.com

Library of Congress Cataloging-in-Publication Data

Names: Alexander, Ellie, author.
Title: Beyond a reasonable stout / Ellie Alexander.
Description: First Edition. | New York : Minotaur Books, 2019. |
    Series: A Sloan Krause mystery
Identifiers: LCCN 2019018209 | ISBN 9781250205759 (hardcover) |
    ISBN 9781250205766 (ebook)
Subjects: LCSH: Murder—Investigation—Fiction. | GSAFD: Mystery fiction.
Classification: LCC PS3601.L353755 B49 2019 | DDC 813/.6—dc23
LC record available at https://lccn.loc.gov/2019018209

Our books may be purchased in bulk for promotional, educational, or business use. Please contact your local bookseller or the Macmillan Corporate and Premium Sales Department at 1-800-221-7945, extension 5442, or by email at MacmillanSpecialMarkets@macmillan.com.

First Edition: October 2019

10 9 8 7 6 5 4 3 2 1

This book is dedicated to the real women working in craft beer!
Thanks for inspiring Sloan Krause and for paving the way
for a new generation of female brewers to come.

BEYOND A REASONABLE STOUT

CHAPTER

ONE

"CAN YOU HEAR THAT?" I asked Garrett as I dumped a box of fresh Chinook hops into the shiny stainless-steel fermenting tank. The hops were grown here in Washington State and had become highly sought after by professional and home brewers for their spicy pine and grapefruit aromas. Garrett and I had procured the popular hop to use in a new hybrid beer we'd been working on together. Adding hops at this stage of fermentation was known as dry hopping. The process would infuse hop aroma into the beer without any of the bitterness that gets extracted when boiling hops.

"Hear what?" Garrett cupped his hand over his ear.

"Nothing," I replied with a broad smile. "Nothing."

For the first time in many weeks, our alpine village was quiet. I closed my eyes. "Isn't it wonderful? The silence. The sweet sound of silence."

Garrett chuckled. "Didn't you tell me that I shouldn't get

used to it?" He removed a pair of chemistry goggles and pressed them on the top of his head.

"True." I opened my eyes. "But we might as well relish it for the moment." Our small Bavarian village, Leavenworth, had recently hosted the biggest brewfest west of the Mississippi—Oktoberfest. Unlike smaller beer celebrations that might last for a long weekend, Leavenworth's Oktoberfest was a month-long party. Every weekend saw a new round of revelers, the constant sound of oompah music, street parades, and flowing taps. It was an exciting time, but equally exhausting. Many business owners in Leavenworth made enough profit during the month of October to keep them in the black for the re-mainder of the year. Typically, Leavenworth's population holds steady at around two thousand residents, but during Okto-berfest that number swells to two hundred thousand over the course of the month. Each week in October, our cobblestone streets and German-style chalets would be packed with tour-ists from throughout the Pacific Northwest and nearly every continent. I appreciated having an opportunity to showcase the place I loved and our new line of NW beers with visitors from all over the world, but knowing that we had a reprieve from the throng of crowds for a while was a welcome relief.

"If Kristopher Cooper has his way, Leavenworth might be quiet forever," Garrett said, balancing on the ladder attached to one of the massive stainless-steel fermenting tanks. His dark hair was disheveled. He pushed it from his eyes as he hopped off the ladder. Garrett was tall and lanky with a casual style. Today he wore his usual brewery uniform—a T-shirt with a beer pun. Today's read BEER CURES WHAT ALES YOU.

"I hope not." I brushed hop residue from my hands.

There's nothing like the smell of fresh hops, in my opinion. I snapped off one of the hop heads and rubbed it between my fingers. The pungent scent of citrus and sappy pine brought an instant calm to my body. "I can't imagine how anyone in Leavenworth would consider voting for him."

Garrett removed a dry-erase pen from his jeans pocket. "It's a stumper. The craft beer industry has put Leavenworth on the map, and he wants to ban it? It doesn't make any sense."

"Agreed." I scanned the brewery to make sure that everything was clean and tidy. "Every business owner I've spoken with is dumping every dime into Valerie Hedy's campaign."

Valerie Hedy was running for city council against the incumbent, Kristopher Cooper. Kristopher had served as a council member for years, but as of late he had taken a drastic stance against Oktoberfest and every other festival that revolved around Leavenworth's thriving beer culture. He was fed up with the aftermath of these events, citing exorbitant cleaning costs that the city had to endure and claiming that petty crime skyrocketed with the influx of "strangers" in town. He had even gone so far as campaigning to make Leavenworth completely dry. His campaign posters were plastered on every light post and street corner in the village. He had designed them to resemble prohibition-era propaganda. They were easy to spot with their sepia-tone paper and black-and-white lettering with sayings like THAT MONEY YOU SPENT ON BOOZE COULD BUY A KID SHOES and DRUNKS DESERVE JAIL. The poster that turned my stomach every time I saw it had a skull and crossbones and read ALCOHOL IS POISON.

I had wanted to engage Kristopher in a debate over the health benefits of consuming craft beer in moderation. For example, there were promising studies that had indicated that craft beer contained healthy nutrients and antioxidants. Drinking beer in moderation might improve cholesterol levels, reduce the risk of type 2 diabetes, and boost bone density. Not to mention the psychological effects of one of beer's main ingredients—hops, which were a known relaxant.

There was no point in trying to argue with Kristopher. He had taken to picketing in front the gazebo every day with a small group of faithfuls. They chanted, "Prohibition now!" His so-called "temperance" rallies had turned the village into a throwback to the 1920s.

Business owners were up in arms. Leavenworth's economy would crumble without tourists' dollars, but Kristopher was undeterred. He was convinced that the only way to preserve Leavenworth's charm was to outlaw alcohol and shift the focus of festivals like Oktoberfest, Maifest, and the winter light fest to center on German traditions and heritage other than imbibing hoppy beverages.

Garrett and I walked to our shared office, where he made a few notes about recipe adjustments on the far wall. He had created a dry-erase wall to keep track of current beers in production and to brainstorm new flavor combinations. It reminded me of a chemistry classroom with formulas and ratios scribbled in colorful pens. Fortunately, Garrett had taught me how to decipher his notes. To anyone else, the dry-erase board probably looked like the work of a madman.

"Have you heard how Valerie is faring?" he asked, drawing a picture of a hop with a green pen and writing "Chinook" next to it.

The smell of the dry-erase pen was overwhelming. I shook my head and waved away the synthetic scent. "Not exactly. I know she has the support of the business community. Have you seen how many shops have her campaign posters propped in their windows?"

"Yeah, I've been meaning to get one." Garrett sketched out a ratio of hops to grains on the whiteboard. The way he stood in front of the whiteboard reminded me of a professor lecturing to a collegiate class rather than a head brewer at a small craft brewery.

"It's hard to imagine anyone supporting his ideas. Leavenworth's entire way of life would change if Kristopher gets elected. But there is a large contingent of people who are fed up with the tourists." I squeezed the hop cone in my fingers and sniffed it again. "He's not wrong about some of the negative impacts of Oktoberfest. We experienced that firsthand—drunk frat brothers getting cited for public intoxication, red Solo cups littering the street, the fact that you can't park anywhere near downtown from the end of September until now. And forget trying to get a seat at any restaurant."

"Yeah, right," Garrett agreed. "And then of course this past year there was a murder to add in the mix. That probably only strengthens his resolve."

"True." We were quiet for a minute. I figured that Garrett, like me, was lost in the memory of a recent tragedy.

"But what Kristopher is overlooking is that the pros well outweigh those cons." As I spoke, Kristopher's stance sounded even more bizarre.

"You're preaching to the choir, Sloan." Garrett finished his notations. "If Kristopher wins reelection, it's going be more than problematic for Nitro. Catastrophic. We can't exactly run a nanobrewery in a dry town, can we?"

"No." I took one last sniff of the hop and shoved it into my jeans pocket.

"Have you talked to Otto, Ursula, or Hans? Der Keller has to be gearing up for a fight." Garrett snapped the cap on the dry-erase pen and set it on the desk.

I appreciated that he hadn't mentioned my soon-to-be ex-husband, Mac. The Krause family were Leavenworth's original brewmasters. Otto and Ursula (my in-laws) had brought their old-world German recipes and brewing techniques with them when they had moved to Leavenworth with their young boys. Back then, Leavenworth didn't resemble the Bavarian mecca it is now. At the time, the town was in shambles. The railroad and mining industries had gone defunct, leaving the small mountain village without an economy. Thanks to the foresight of two residents who recognized that, with its towering mountains and brilliant blue rivers, the town resembled villages in the German Alps, Leavenworth reinvented itself. Every building downtown was refurbished and designed in baroque architecture. Today, strolling through Leavenworth is as close as one can get to traveling to the German countryside without actually being in Europe.

"Yeah, I spoke with Hans earlier." I readjusted my ponytail. "The Krauses are vehemently opposed to Kristopher's platform, not surprisingly. They're holding an open forum tonight at Der Keller. I meant to mention it to you earlier, but we got so wrapped up in the brewing process. They asked me to extend you an invite, as they would love to show a unified front from everyone in the beer industry."

"Count me in," Garrett replied without hesitation. Then he pointed to a stack of paperwork on the desk. "How are you feeling about Kat? She passed her bartending license, so we can get her working behind the bar now, too."

Kat was our first official hire at Nitro. She had come to Leavenworth during Oktoberfest in hopes of landing a small role in a documentary film that had been shot on-site. Her plans didn't work out, but the good news for her and for Nitro was that she had immediately fit in with Garrett and me. In exchange for a place to stay for the weekend, she had handed out flyers and done menial tasks, like cleaning (the never-ending bane of every brewer's existence). In a flash of brilliance, Garrett had offered Kat a permanent position in exchange for free room and board, plus a small salary.

Kat's bad fortune turned out to be a happy coincidence for us. Garrett and I had been brainstorming new revenue streams for Nitro. He had inherited the historic inn that now housed our brew operations from his great-aunt Tess. But converting the property into a fully operational brewery had come at a hefty cost. He had torn out most of the main floor to make room for the brewing equipment. The back of the property housed our fermenters, brite tanks and filtration system, a small office, and industrial kitchen. The front served as a bar and small dining area. Garrett had yet to touch the upstairs, where there were six outdated guest rooms. He had been living in the master suite and offered Kat one of the open rooms. When she had moved into the vacant room upstairs, inspiration had struck. We realized we were sitting on a gold mine—guest suites.

Hotel and vacation properties were at a premium in Leavenworth. The demand for housing was always high, and especially so during the village's many festivals and celebrations. In a stroke of genius, we decided to tap into those tourist dollars by renovating the remaining four guest rooms with beer themes. It was a symbiotic plan. We could offer brewery tours, provide a complete brewery experience, and serve guests brewery-style breakfasts. Nitro would become a modern guesthouse. Garrett was handy, so he could do most of the work himself. Hans, my brother-in-law and a professional carpenter, had offered his services too. Thanks to the fact that the upstairs was already designed to serve as a bed-and-breakfast, there weren't any major structural changes needed. Most of the work was cosmetic—tearing out old wallpaper, carpet, and lighting, and replacing them with modern beer décor.

"Kat's been doing great. I think she's definitely ready to be behind the bar," I said to Garrett. "We've been having a blast digging through old treasures that your aunt acquired and brainstorming themes for each room."

Garrett was a minimalist. That was a rarity in Leavenworth, especially to me, since I had spent most of my adult life working at Der Keller, where every wall was plastered with German memorabilia and awards. Most of the shops in the village had opted to play up the kitsch theme with wooden nutcrackers, cuckoo clocks, German flags, pewter steins, and basically anything that screamed Bavaria. Garrett didn't subscribe to the fake Germany philosophy. He wanted Nitro

8

to stand out for its high-quality, small-batch beers. It was a refreshing concept in a town dominated by lederhosen and green felt caps with feathers.

On my first day, I had been shocked by Nitro's stark white walls and pristine brewing equipment. I had been impressed that Garrett took sanitation seriously, but the brewery felt like a clean room at a tech company, rather than a welcoming spot to gather for frothy pints and good laughs. Luckily, he had been more than receptive to my suggestion to soften the bar and dining room with twinkle lights, greenery, and a collection of black-and-white photos from the inn's early days.

Kat and I were working on a similar aesthetic for the guesthouse rooms. We intended to repurpose Aunt Tess's photos and incorporate items from Garrett's early home brewing days in his Seattle garage.

"Treasures, huh?" Garrett's hickory eyes locked on mine. "Are you sure you don't mean junk?"

"One man's junk is another's treasure, right?" I grinned.

"I think in the case of my aunt, it's just junk. She was a textbook packrat."

"I suggest you reserve judgment until you see what Kat and I come up with."

"Consider it done. Everything you touch seems to turn to gold. I thought I hired you for your killer nose, but I got a bonus chef and decorator. What other hidden talents are lurking under those brown eyes, Sloan?"

The way Garrett let his eyes linger on mine just for a moment made my heart rate speed up. He was so different from Mac. Mac had always needed to be the life of the party. He thrived on attention. Garrett was more reserved and tended to sit back and watch and listen before inserting himself into a conversation. I wasn't sure if my growing attraction to him was because he was the polar opposite of Mac, or if there was any real depth to my feelings. It was too soon to know. I wasn't ready to jump into a new relationship. I had a lot more work to do on myself first.

"Any self-respecting brewer never reveals her secrets," I replied with a wink.

"Unless it's about the best hop to use in this new test batch."

"True." Our conversation shifted to brewing. We had developed an easy working relationship built upon mutual respect and a love of the craft. My short time at Nitro had been different in every way than my years at Der Keller. There were things that I missed about working for the big brewery, like my in-laws, Otto and Ursula. I missed seeing them daily. They were the only parents I had ever known, and even though I knew that they supported my decision to stay at Nitro, I still felt like I was letting them down. In my darker moments, I was filled with regret and guilt over abandoning them. But when I had brief moments of clarity, I knew that nothing could be further from the truth.

I hadn't abandoned Der Keller. Mac had abandoned me for a twentysomething beer wench with plastered-on jeans and not an ounce of beer knowledge. The dissolution of my marriage had been hard to stomach, but the thought of not being a part of the Krause family was unbearable. Otto and Ursula had assured me that regardless of what happened between Mac and me, I would always be part of their family. They had even made me a partner in the brewery. I appreciated the gesture and knew that they were serious about trying to keep me connected to the family. I just couldn't help but wonder if that would change if both Mac and I moved on. The strangest thing was that, for the moment, I was okay with the uncertainty. I'd spent too much of my life swallowing my feelings. It had been a survival strategy to get me through countless foster homes. I was an adult now, and it was time to tap into every aspect of me, even the parts that I didn't want to see. Working at Nitro was opening me up in ways I had never imagined. Kristopher Cooper's prohibition vision threatened my journey of self-discovery. If our village went dry, I couldn't even begin to think what might happen to Nitro and everything I loved about Leavenworth.

CHAPTER

TWO

OUR SLOW, EASY PACE CONTINUED through the rest of the day. I spent the majority of the afternoon training Kat behind the bar. Bartending (or beertending, as it's sometimes affectionately known) is more than just pouring a pint. Knowledge of craft beer and the brewing process is always a plus when it comes to working at a pub. The best bartenders are well-versed in beer styles, IBUs (International Bitter Units that determine the bitterness of the hops), food pairings, and tasting profiles. Some taprooms have gone so far as to have their beertenders become certified cicerones. A trained cicerone can greatly elevate the beer experience. But the most important skill set of any good bartender is being a good listener. Kat was warm and friendly with the customers. She had a natural ability to ask questions in order to try and match each customer's personal tastes with a perfect pint.

By the time the sun was starting to sink behind the mountains, Garrett and I left Nitro in Kat's capable hands. There were only a few regulars savoring happy-hour pints. Nearly everyone else in town was gathering at Der Keller for a community forum about Kristopher's plan to outlaw alcoholic beverages.

"We'll just be around the block if you need anything," I called to Kat.

Kat's dimples indented as she smiled and tilted a chilled pint glass at an angle. She slowly pulled the tap handle so as not to create too many bubbles and pour a foamy pint.

"Like this, right?" Her curls swung as she turned toward me.

"You've got it." I gave her a thumbs-up.

I was impressed that she had been such a fast learner. I had only taught her the technique for pouring a perfect pint a few weeks ago, and she had already mastered it. Pouring a pint with just the right amount of foam takes practice. Pulling the tap handle too quickly can result in a frothy mess, as can holding a glass upright under the faucet. Kat looked like a pro, closing the tap handle swiftly to avoid overfilling the pint.

"No worries. I'll keep the beer flowing here." Her words received a cheer from two older gentlemen at the end of the bar.

Garrett waited for me by the front door. He had a gray Nitro sweatshirt on and a coat resting on his arm. Evening temperatures had begun to dip near freezing. Snow dusted the top of the surrounding mountain ranges. Soon it would blanket the streets, luring skiers and winter sport enthusiasts to the area for its abundance of outdoor recreation opportunities. We had already created a special advertising campaign geared toward the après-ski crowd. Anyone who brought in a lift ticket from nearby Stevens Pass, Mission Ridge, or even the Leavenworth Ski Hill would get a free appetizer with the purchase of two beers.

"Are you going in that?" Garrett asked, staring at my outfit. "Won't you freeze? They've been saying we're due for the first snow and a windstorm this week."

"I'll be fine." I waved him off. Working in a brewery doesn't allow for a high-fashion wardrobe, which was okay with me. I was happy in my jeans, rubber boots, and long-sleeved black T-shirt. Most days I tied my dark hair into a ponytail and didn't bother with makeup. "My vest and scarf are right there," I replied, grabbing a puffy red vest and red Buffalo plaid scarf from the coatrack.

"You're sure you don't want a coat?" Garrett held the door open for me and gave me a look of concern.

A cool breeze wafted into the pub. "We're only going a block away. Really, I'll be fine."

He didn't argue. Instead he ushered me out the door. "What's the plan for tonight? Have you heard?"

I wrapped my scarf around my neck and tucked the extra fabric into my vest as I stepped outside into the crisp autumn air. "I'm not sure. Hans said that Otto and Ursula want to have an open—yet respectful—discussion about Kristopher's anti-beer platform. There could be ten people attending tonight or hundreds."

Leavenworth was always charming, but there was something magical about our village in the evening glow. Warm yellow lights illuminated the baroque storefronts. The street lamps made the changing leaves on the trees even more golden. I inhaled the refreshing cool air that was tinted with the scents of fall.

Garrett and I rounded the corner and turned onto Front Street. I never got tired of the view. German-style chalets lined both sides of the street. To our left were the gazebo and Front Street Park, where dozens of festivities occurred throughout the year. Crews had already started to wrap the trees and storefronts with thousands of twinkle lights for the upcoming Christkindlmarkt, which would take place Thanksgiving weekend. The highlight of the celebration was the lantern parade, where children would stroll along Front Street holding handmade lanterns and following Mr. and Mrs. Claus to the gazebo to watch the lights come on. The ceremonial lighting would kick off the holidays and was followed by Bavarian Christmas markets where shoppers could purchase authentic German gifts and crafts while sipping on mugs of hot mulled cider. The songs of carolers and hand-bell choirs would ring through the streets. Visitors could take rides in horse-drawn carriages and dogsleds. There would be sledding and tubing for youngsters and downhill skiing and snowboarding for older adventurers.

One of the sweetest traditions during the light festival was the great cookie hunt. Children received cookie maps and could sleuth out locations all over the village to receive special handmade treats.

Leavenworth would bask in the colorful light display through March. The "Village of Lights" experience drew thousands of tourists to our tiny town in the Cascades. Many shops were already decked out for the holiday season with garlands, boxes of colorful presents, and Christmas trees.

"Oktoberfest is barely in the rearview mirror, and people are gearing up for Christmas," Garrett noted as we walked past the window of the aptly named Nutcracker Shoppe. It was a relatively new addition to the village, having opened over the summer. However, the owner had wasted no time getting in the holiday spirit. It looked as if the North Pole had exploded in its front windows. Nutcrackers designed to resemble Santa Claus and Mrs. Claus along with a workshop of elves were on display, as well as traditional German nutcrackers in holiday lederhosen and even a set of reindeer nutcrackers.

Leavenworth was already home to a well-established nutcracker store, so I had been surprised when The Nutcracker Shoppe opened for business. There hadn't seemed to be bad blood between the rival shops, but nutcrackers were such a niche item I wondered if Leavenworth could support two shops.

The shop's owner spotted us and ran outside. "Did you see something you like? I know my sign says closed, but I'd be happy to let you come in and have a look. I'm here late working on the window display and don't mind one bit to have you folks in for a while and see if you like anything. You know what they say, Christmas is nutcracker season."

"Do they say that?" Garrett looked to me.

I shrugged and tucked my hands into my vest pockets. The tip of my nose was cold. Maybe I should have taken Garrett's advice about grabbing a coat.

The shop owner nodded. "Oh, yeah, yeah. Nutcrackers fly off the shelves during November and December. They make great gifts. Think of a holiday party without a nutcracker. Can you imagine?" He made a dramatic motion with his hands.

Garrett stifled a laugh. I almost chuckled too, but quickly realized that the owner was serious.

"How is anyone going to crack open that big bowl of nuts that Aunt Susan brought to the party without a nutcracker? Nutcrackers are the key to any holiday celebration. Mark my words, you might want to come take a look now, because these are going to fly off the shelves during the Christmas markets."

"I guess I never thought of that," I said, trying to catch Garrett's eye. "Sounds like you're getting an early start on the shopping rush."

He nodded with enthusiasm. "Exactly, and that's just your practical nutcrackers. You should see what some of the collectors pay for our custom, handcrafted pieces. See that Santa in the window? He'll sell for over five hundred, and I already have two interested buyers."

"That's great." I tapped my wrist. "We're on our way to Der Keller for a meeting. We should get going."

The shop owner threw up his hands. "Der Keller. Is that for the meeting about that crazy politician?"

Garrett nodded.

"Do you care if I tag along? I'd love to hear what other business owners have to say. It's a ludicrous plan. How could anyone want to turn the town dry? Business will dry up. All of us will be out of work."

"That seems to be the sentiment with many people we've talked to," Garrett said.

The shop owner shut the door behind him, slamming a string of red and green lights in the door. He opened it and tossed the lights inside. "My name is Conrad, by the way. I don't think I've seen either of you in the shop before, but I recognize that beer logo. Nitro. Is that the one around the corner? The non–German pub?"

Garrett and I introduced ourselves as we walked to Der Keller. Conrad was in his mid-thirties to early forties with wiry short curls, glasses, and a high-pitched voice. He didn't strike me as the type to open a nutcracker store, but then again, I had no idea if there was a type.

I didn't have a chance to ask him about what brought him to Leavenworth or drew him to the nutcracker trade because we arrived at Der Keller. The sight of its majestic entrance never failed to give me pause. It reminded me of a ski chalet, with its white stucco, slanted wood-beamed roof, and matching wooden shutters. Flags with the Der Keller family crest (two lions waving German flags) flapped in the slight breeze. The brewery encompassed almost an entire block with a bottling plant, the brewery, and a restaurant with an outdoor patio.

The German theme continued inside with red epoxy floors, hand-carved walnut tables, and a vast collection of beer steins. It looked as if the entire town had assembled inside. The restaurant was packed from wall to wall. People crammed into the bar area and spilled outside, gathering around gas fire pits to stay warm.

"Whoa." Garrett let out a whistle. "I would say there's safety in numbers. If this is any indication of how people are going to vote when they turn in their ballots next week, Valerie Hedy is going to win in a landslide."

"Let's hope so," I replied, scanning the crowded space for familiar faces. "Everyone who is here has to actually turn in their ballot." I spotted Hans on the opposite side of the room. He waved me over. "There's Hans, come on."

We parted ways with Conrad, and I dragged Garrett through the throng of people.

"Sloan, can you believe this turnout?" Hans greeted me with a hug. He smelled of cedar and sandalwood. I knew it wasn't from expensive cologne. Hans owned a small woodworking shop where he built custom furniture. He must have come straight from work because he wore a pair of Carhartt pants, and his tool belt was still tied around his waist.

"I was just saying that to Garrett. Is *everyone* in Leavenworth here?"

Hans clapped Garrett on the back in the way of a greeting. He had been instrumental in helping me get my position at Nitro. For that, among many other reasons, I was forever grateful to him.

"Let's hope the fire marshal doesn't show up," Hans said with a scowl. "I think we're violating every fire code."

He had a point. There was no space to move inside Der Keller's warm interior. I glanced around the familiar space. The restaurant was an homage to Otto's and Ursula's German roots. Banners with the Krause family crest hung from the high-beamed ceilings. In addition to the antique steins lining the wall behind the bar, there were dozens of bronze, silver, and gold medals from beer competitions throughout the world. The smell of beer cheese soup and sauerkraut rolls wafted in the crowded restaurant. My stomach grumbled at the thought of a bowl of Der Keller's signature soup paired with a pint of their award-winning Doppelbock.

Dinner would have to wait. At that moment Mac hopped onto the top of the bar and pounded a spoon on a pewter stein to get everyone to quiet down.

"Oh great," I muttered under my breath.

Hans squeezed my elbow in a show of solidarity.

"Hey! Thanks for coming, everyone. Cheers to seeing so many friends and familiar faces tonight." Mac's ruddy cheeks glowed under the golden lights hanging above the bar. He held a full pint glass. "As you know, we are here tonight to talk about one thing. One important and vital thing to our community and our livelihoods." He raised his pint glass. "Beer!"

The room erupted in cheers.

Mac's cheeks turned redder. "Now, I wish I could be serving everyone a pilsner right now, but as you can see there isn't any room to send our servers out with trays."

"We'll make room," someone hollered.

Mac laughed. He was in his element. "Don't worry, Der Keller will be pouring free beer for the rest of the evening, but first we need to talk about this nasty business of trying to make Leavenworth dry."

A round of boos sounded.

Hans's golden-brown eyes met mine. "Free beer?" he mouthed. "On whose dime?"

"Hopefully Valerie's, but then again . . ." I shrugged. It was a classic Mac move. Unlike his brother, Mac loved the limelight. He was constantly "wining and dining" (his words) potential clients and suppliers.

"That's right. That's right." Mac took a swig from his beer. It dribbled down his chin. "How many of you are business owners or work for a business in the village?"

Hands flew into the air.

Mac wiped his chin with the back of his hand. I wondered if someone had coached him on his outfit. He had on a pair of skinny black jeans, loafers, and a Der Keller T-shirt. His blond hair had been slicked back with gel. Was he trying to change his style, knowing that he would soon be officially free to date whomever he wanted?

"I see that basically every hand in this room has been raised. That means that most or all of us make our living off the tourist trade. How many people pulled in a profit during Oktoberfest?"

Again, nearly everyone raised their hands.

"Exactly! One man and one man alone is trying to end the way of life we know and love here in the greatest little Beervarian city, Leavenworth, Washington—Kristopher Cooper."

A number of people rattled off insults.

Mac waited for the crowd to settle. "I know. The man is on a mission to ruin Leavenworth. I'm not sure what his motives are, but if we allow Kristopher to be elected, I know one thing, and that is that many if not all of us are going to go out of business. You're going to lose your jobs, and Leavenworth is going to become a ghost town."

Someone shouted a comment from the other side of the room. I couldn't hear what they had said, but Mac held up his free hand. "Okay, I know we're upset, but let's not talk about resorting to violence. Kristopher has a right to his opinion. And we have a right to vote him out of office."

Everyone applauded.

"I'm going to turn things over to a couple special guests we invited to be part of tonight, but before I do, I want to thank you for your support. We have a table set up on the patio where you can register to vote if you're not already a registered voter, and Valerie Hedy has a bunch of yard signs, posters, and buttons. Take some for yourself. Post them in your shop windows and front yards and share them with your friends and neighbors. We have a week until election day, and Der Keller is casting our vote for Valerie."

He handed one of the bartenders his beer and then helped a woman, who I recognized as Kristopher's opponent, up on the bar top.

"Ladies and gentlemen, give it up for our next city councilor, Valerie Hedy!" Mac boomed.

Valerie had sensibly worn a pair of khaki slacks and tennis shoes. She was about my age, with short brown hair, thick glasses, and a shy smile. She looked more like a librarian than a politician. "Thank you, everyone. Thanks for that warm welcome." Valerie's voice didn't carry the same way that Mac's had. I had to strain to hear her. "Der Keller has been such a great supporter of my campaign. I want to take this opportunity to publicly thank them for their ongoing involvement in the community and for brewing such wonderful beer."

"Has she ever tasted our beer?" Hans whispered.

I laughed and punched him in the ribs.

"My opponent wants you to fear beer and every other thing that makes our village so unique. He wants to dwell on the handful of negative things that happen during festival season. I think we're all well aware of the recent murder that occurred during Oktoberfest. It was certainly disturbing but, as the police discovered, that had nothing to do with the festival and involved village outsiders. As to Kristopher's claims of petty theft and a handful of drunks, they're things that would likely happen anyway, and while they might be a nuisance, they're not going to tear our town apart. What Kristopher Cooper is doing is exactly that. He's pitting neighbor against neighbor and business owner against business owner. This isn't the pioneering spirit of Leavenworth, it's nasty politics." She paused to catch her breath. "I don't claim to have extensive experience in politics, but I can tell you what I do have—that's a passion for Leavenworth. I grew up here. I've raised my family here. I've built my career here, working as a mediator. I want to put my professional skills to work for you."

People clapped, but the applause was nowhere near as thunderous as it had been for Mac.

"Are there issues that arise during Oktoberfest? Yes. Are there practical solutions? Yes." Val sounded soft. Her smile appeared forced. I couldn't tell if she was nervous or if public speaking wasn't her forte.

She pressed her glasses up to the bridge of her nose and continued. "For instance, we can create a citizen volunteer group to support the city in its cleanup efforts. Would anyone in this room be willing to volunteer a few hours to clean up our gorgeous streets?"

Tons of hands raised.

"Excellent." Valerie folded her hands in a prayer position. "Thank you for your support. I'll be on the patio to answer any questions and talk in more detail about some of my other ideas and plans. I would be honored to become Leavenworth's next city councilor, and I want you to know that should I win,

I will have an open-door policy. You can always come to me with questions, concerns, and suggestions for making our fair city the most wonderful place in the world to live."

Valerie climbed off the bar with help from the bartending staff. Mac made his return. "Valerie Hedy, our next city council member, everyone." He led the crowd in another round of applause. "Our next speaker needs no introduction. She is the face of Leavenworth and Leavenworth's biggest cheerleader."

"Oh no," I muttered.

Garrett raised his brow. "What?"

"April Ablin," I said, rolling my eyes. April was Leavenworth's self-appointed ambassador and welcome wagon. She insisted on wearing traditional Bavarian garb and demanded that everyone else do the same.

I watched April scramble up onto the bar in a German dirndl dress that barely covered her ass. Her makeup looked especially garish under the bar lighting. If April were in her twenties, she might have been able to pull off the frilly green plaid dress with a matching milkmaid's apron in pale pink. But she was pushing fifty. No one else in Leavenworth wore their hair in pigtails and walked around the streets in German clogs. April and I had had numerous disagreements over the years, usually about my lack of enthusiasm for the German culture and lately about Mac. April's way of empathizing over the breakup of my marriage sounded about as sincere as a lawyer chasing an ambulance.

"*Guten Abend*," April said in a botched German accent. I wished that Otto or Ursula were nearby. I knew they were getting a good chuckle out of April's fake accent.

"Welcome, friends, to an evening that will go down in the history books as the night that we banded together to save our beloved Leavenworth." April placed her hand over her heart, closed her eyes, and inhaled deeply. She froze in a moment of dramatic reverie before continuing. "As you know, our way of life is being threatened, and we will not stand by idly and watch it happen. We are fighters. We are Leavenworth! We are the land of Bavaria, a sacred space for all who visit. We are the keepers of tradition, and we stand in the footsteps of our grandmothers and grandfathers who fought for our freedom."

"Freedom for what?" Garrett laughed. "To drink beer?"

"Good God," Hans added. "She's laying it on thick, even for April."

"I would expect nothing less." I sighed.

April was just getting started. She launched into a tirade about Kristopher and how he was a menace to society. She even went so far as to say that he should be banished from town.

"If she keeps talking, the next thing we know, she's going to be reaching for a pitchfork and rallying everyone out to kill him," Hans teased.

Hans wasn't that far off. April fumed. Someone needed to rein her in. Finally, Mac, of all people, hopped up on a barstool and shouted. "Thanks, April. I think we all know what we need to do—vote for Valerie Hedy next Tuesday. Now, who is ready for free beer?"

Applause erupted as Der Keller servers wearing red-checkered *Trachten* shirts with black suspenders and barmaid dresses circulated through the packed space with trays of frothy beer steins.

April shot Mac a nasty look. I had to credit him for having a thick skin. He handed her a beer and moved off into the crowd. My fears about Leavenworth's future were silenced. If tonight was any indication, Kristopher Cooper would soon be out of office, and life in our peaceful beer mecca would return to normal.

CHAPTER
THREE

GARRETT GOT CAUGHT IN A conversation with the owner of the hardware store. I snuck out the minute the meeting came to an end. There was no way I was going to chance bumping into Mac or April.

"I'll walk you out," Hans said, twisting his tool belt.

We squeezed through the crowd. The mood had shifted with the delivery of free beer. Conversations sounded upbeat and jovial. Hopefully, the mood would spill over to election day and everyone would cast their ballots for Valerie. I couldn't see any scenario in which Kristopher could pull out a win.

Speak of the devil, I thought as we exited Der Keller and stepped onto the enclosed patio. Most people had been lured inside by the siren call of free beer, but a handful of locals were gathered around one of the large tables, warming their hands by the fire. I would have continued on, but a commotion broke out. Seated at the center of the table was none other than Kristopher Cooper. I quickly realized that he was flanked by his fringe group of followers.

"What are you doing here? You're not welcome." A shrill voice sounded behind me. Hans and I turned in unison to see April with her hands on her hips.

Kristopher leaned back in his chair and rested his feet on the table. "The last time I checked, Ms. Ablin, it's a free country. I'm enjoying a nice dinner with friends."

April's cheeks puffed out. "I thought you hated beer. If you're campaigning against the craft, what the hell do you think you're doing here?"

Kristopher strummed his fingers on his silver beard. "As you can see, my friends and I are sharing our favorite German fare and ice-cold glasses of sun tea. We believe in keeping our bodies pure and devoid of that poison that you all insist on drinking." The smirk on his face was evidence of the fact that he was taking great pleasure in getting April riled up.

"You are such a hypocrite, Kris." April shook her finger at him. "There are dozens of other German restaurants in the village, and you decided to eat at Der Keller. Tonight. You're not fooling any of us. I know what your motive is."

"And that would be?" Kristopher removed his expensive loafers from the table.

"Valerie's hosting a huge campaign rally inside, and you're here to stir up trouble." April pressed the ruffles in her dress. I shivered at the sight of her bare legs. She had to be freezing.

At the mention of Valerie's name, Kristopher shot a look I couldn't decipher to an older gentleman seated across from him. They must have shared some of kind of code because the man pushed back his chair, gave Kristopher a nod, and hurried inside.

Kristopher made a *tsk*ing sound under his breath. "I hope Valerie isn't misusing campaign funding to get everyone liquored up. It would be a shame to have to report her to the council."

I thought April might attack him. Hans jumped in front of her to stop her from lunging at Kristopher.

Kristopher let out a nasty laugh. "Now, now, Ms. Ablin, that's no way for Leavenworth's *ambassador* to act, is it?" His tone was laced with sarcasm, making his friends laugh.

April tried to free herself from Hans's grasp.

At the same moment, Valerie, along with a large group of her supporters, came outside. She stopped in midstride when she spotted Kristopher.

"Hey, Val. Funny meeting you here." Kristopher stood. He was dressed like a politician in a pair of tailored slacks and a buttoned-up long-sleeved shirt. His suit jacket hung on the back of his chair. No one in Leavenworth wore suits. Swimsuits to float the river or ski suits for winter afternoons on the mountain maybe. Kristopher looked out of place in his fastidious outfit.

"Look, Kristopher, this isn't the time or place to do this." Valerie's voice was strong and forceful, much more so than when she was speaking to the crowd inside.

"Why? Are you nervous? Not up to any illegal campaigning, are you?" The arrogant smile on Kristopher's face made me want to take a swing at him. "It would match the illegal boozing you're fighting so hard for. All those boozy dollars going down the drain. Who needs it more? Six dollars for a pint of the devil's drink. Our citizens are literally pouring their hard-earned dollars down the drain, and I'm going to put a stop to it."

"Save it for the debate." Valerie motioned for her crew to join her as she brushed past us.

Hans still had April by the elbow. I caught his eye. He mirrored my sense of disbelief. I had made it a point to stay out of local politics. In a town the size of Leavenworth, everyone had an opinion. On the rare occasion that I had had to attend a city council meeting for Der Keller, I had been shocked by how many people used the venue as a forum to vent their frustrations over everything from unleashed dogs to demands for regulating the height of trees and shrubbery in the parks. Why Kristopher or Valerie wanted the job was beyond me.

"Not so fast." Kristopher blocked the exit. I guessed him to be in his late fifties or early sixties. He moved with lightning speed. "I came to have a word with you in private."

Valerie shrunk back from him.

"You know what I'm talking about." Kristopher gave her a knowing stare.

Valerie whispered something into the ear of the guy standing next to her, who proceeded to try and push Kristopher away.

"Hey! Hands off!" Kristopher shouted.

A fight broke out. Kristopher's and Valerie's supporters began hurling insults and physically pushing each other around. The commotion must have reached inside because people started pouring out of Der Keller to see what was going on. April, who continued to be restrained by Hans, egged everyone on.

"Get them out of here!" Her high-pitched voice cut

through the mayhem. "He's a *Bedrohung*! A *Bedrohung*. He's ruining our beloved Bavaria."

I had no idea what April meant by *Bedrohung*, but then again, she probably didn't either. She was notorious for creating her own version of German or grossly misusing German words. I watched, dumbfounded, as the fight continued to escalate. Kristopher was outnumbered. His group had backed off the patio but were holding their ground on the sidewalk. No punches had been thrown, just a few shoves and plenty of insults. I didn't understand why he didn't leave. If they stuck around much longer, I had a bad feeling that it might turn ugly.

Nothing like this had ever happened, at least in recent memory. Leavenworth political campaigns usually involved a debate at the Festhalle, where candidates sparred over tax policy or parking enforcement issues. I'd never seen a city council race get violent.

A thunderous clap boomed. Everyone froze. I looked to the sky. No one had predicted thunderstorms.

"Break it up," Mac yelled as he leapt onto one of the tables. He held two beer paddles, or flight boards used for tastings. "Enough. Everyone go home. The show's over." He slammed the paddles together again. The sound was so loud, I pressed my fingers in my ears. However, his startle technique worked. The bloodlust energy in the opposing groups dissipated.

Kristopher gave Valerie a triumphant grin before sauntering away.

Had his only mission been to incite an argument?

Hans released April, who shook him off with a huff. She grabbed Ross, the owner of the Underground, and dragged him with her in Kristopher's direction.

"Should we let her go?" I asked Hans.

He shrugged. "I don't know. I've done my duty for the night."

"That was nuts." I glanced around us. There must have been at least thirty people outside. I was surprised that no one had called the police. The irony, that Kristopher was campaigning on a platform that alcohol was the root cause of public disturbance and distress, wasn't lost on me. Had that been his purpose? Did he want a fight to break out at Der Keller, in order to blame it on beer?

Hans frowned. "Nuts, yes, and I suspect also staged."

"Me too. Kristopher came here to pick a fight."

"He succeeded." He tucked his hands in his workpants. "You want me to walk you to your car?"

"No thanks. It's just down the block." I kissed his cheek. "See you later. Don't go getting any ideas about running for city council."

Hans pretended to gag. I left him and headed down Front Street. When I passed Conrad's Nutcracker Shoppe, I noticed that he, Valerie, and April were continuing to trade barbs with Kristopher. For a minute, I thought about intervening, but instead I crossed the street and faded into the darkness. Kristopher had brought this on himself. It wasn't my job to mediate. Thank goodness the election was just a week away. The sooner I could cast my vote and end the craziness, the better.

CHAPTER

FOUR

THE NEXT MORNING, I AWOKE to a thin layer of frost coating the rows and rows of hops that Mac and I had cultivated together. When we purchased the rambling farmhouse and organic acreage just outside of the city, Mac had visions of creating a hop oasis where he could plant a variety of vines and tinker with ideas for new beer recipes. There was one flaw in his vision. The man had a lackluster palate (if I'm being generous). Much to Otto's chagrin, Mac never developed the ability to discern between notes of wood smoke or dark chocolate. He had never met a beer he didn't like, either. His inability to distinguish flavors didn't come from lack of effort. Mac had attended beer university in his parents' homeland; he had spent countless hours working by Otto's side, listening and watching his father, a master craftsman; and he had ingrained himself in the craft beer culture. He knew almost every brewer, distributor, and hop producer in the Pacific Northwest. The man was a walking encyclopedia of beer, but getting him to distinguish the unique subtleties in a pilsner versus a lager was impossible.

The fact that I could pull out a hint of grapefruit or honey in a beer with my eyes closed had irked Mac to no end. It had been an ongoing source of tension between us. Mac was convinced that I was intentionally trying to make him look weak in front of his father. Nothing could have been further from the truth.

Otto had pulled me aside once after Mac had stormed out of a tasting session. "Sloan, do not let Mac get to you. He is upset, *ja,* but he will be fine. Some people have ze nose. Ze gift." His kind eyes had held my gaze. "Do not give up or hide your talent because of Mac. He will get over it with time."

I appreciated Otto's reassurance, but he wasn't married to Mac. He didn't have to put up with Mac's constant whining over why I could sniff out every subtlety in a beer, or his accusations that I was purposely trying to sabotage him.

I shook off the memory and tiptoed down the hallway toward the kitchen. Alex, my teenage son, was softly snoring in his bedroom. I resisted the urge to go kiss his forehead when I caught a glimpse of him curled in a half-moon, the same way he had slept since he was a newborn. Alex was the reason I had stayed with Mac for way too many unhappy years.

And, for what? I thought, flipping on the kitchen lights. The kitchen was my domain. I had fallen in love with its brick fireplace and views looking out onto our small hop farm. Now that Mac and I had split, what was I going to do with all of this space?

Nothing. That was the answer that had been tossing around my brain for the past few weeks. The farmhouse had been Mac's dream. It was time to figure out my own dreams. I was fairly sure they didn't include a huge farmhouse and the ongoing work of maintaining hop fields. I'd had my eye on a small A-frame house tucked in the forest. It was just the right size for me and Alex. So far, I hadn't done anything more. I had been too busy with Oktoberfest. Or at least that was the story I'd been telling myself. The truth was, I was scared. As much as I knew that I was ready to be done with Mac, I was terrified of being alone.

I decided right in this minute to stop by April Ablin's office on my way to Nitro and arrange a time to see the property. April wasn't my first choice of a real estate agent, but in a town as small as Leavenworth, there weren't many alternatives. The only good thing about hiring April was that I knew she would be cutthroat in negotiations. If I had to work with her I might as well reap the benefits of her annoying, tenacious personality.

I brewed a pot of coffee and gathered ingredients for breakfast. Alex had midterms at school all week, and I wanted to send him off with a hearty morning meal. With the cold weather creeping in, I thought a comforting sweet breakfast of my special French toast with a side of chicken sausages would hit the spot.

I started by whisking eggs, heavy cream, and vanilla. Then I added a touch of salt and a few tablespoons of sugar. Next came my secret ingredient—a cup of dark, stout beer. The chocolaty beer would give the batter a rustic depth. I'd been making pancakes, waffles, and French toast with beer for as long as I could remember. I'd never given away the secret. Instead I just smiled when people raved about the unique flavors on their morning breakfast plates. Maybe beer-infused waffles would have to go on the breakfast menu for our overnight guests at Nitro.

Beer is such a versatile ingredient in cooking and baking. It adds a natural froth to breakfast batters and can be used to enhance flavors in soups and sauces. I use it in almost everything I make. There's no need to be concerned about getting tipsy on breakfast French toast because the alcohol burns off in the cooking process.

Once I had a smooth, dark batter, I dredged thick slices of peasant bread and grilled them in butter. The smell of the sizzling French toast and chicken sausages roused Alex from his bed. He shuffled into the kitchen in a pair of sweatpants and a warm-up jacket. His hair was tousled from sleep.

"Morning, Mom. What smells so good?"

"French toast." I slid a slice onto a plate and dusted it with powdered sugar. "There's a bunch of different syrups and jams that I picked up from the farmers' market on the table. Help yourself."

Alex took the plate. He stabbed a couple of sausages and took his breakfast to our farm-style dining table.

Fall in Leavenworth brought a bounty of local produce, along with homemade jams, jellies, and salsas to our weekly farmers' market. I had picked up apple butter made from Washington's famous Pink Lady apples, Bing cherry preserves, honey, maple syrup, and a black raspberry sauce.

"Geez, Mom, how am I supposed to pick?" Alex motioned to the assortment of sweet accoutrements on the table.

"Have them all." I filled my plate and joined him. "Are you ready for another day of testing?"

He chomped a bite of the chicken sausage. It was also locally produced and packed with fresh herbs like rosemary, fennel, and basil. "I guess."

I thought about broaching the subject of moving but didn't want to stress Alex out during testing week. "You have soccer practice after school, right?"

"Yep. I'll catch a ride home with someone. You don't have to come get me." He slathered his French toast with the black raspberry sauce.

"I don't mind. I'm happy to leave a little early to grab you. It's slow at Nitro right now. I might as well capitalize on that as long as I can." I spread apple butter on one slice of the golden brown toast, and cherry preserves on the other.

"It's cool, Mom. Some of the guys want to grab pizzas and study for our math midterm together. Is it okay if I invite them here?"

"Of course. If you want, I can pick up pizzas on my way home and meet you here." I felt like I was often walking a tightrope when it came to mothering Alex. I didn't want to smother him, but I also wanted him to know that I was here for anything he needed. The teenage years had brought a burgeoning independence. It was heartening to see him developing into such a wise and capable young man, but I knew that he was still hurting from Mac's and my separation. He didn't talk about it much. Every once in a while, I would catch him in the right mood, and he would divulge that it was "weird" that his dad and I weren't living together. Otherwise he kept his feelings bottled up. I knew that he had inherited that trait from me. My only play was to continue to gently nudge him and make sure the line of communication stayed open between us.

"Sure. That would be great." Alex finished every last bite on his plate and went back for seconds.

Keeping the kitchen stocked with a teenage boy in the house required multiple trips to the grocery store each week and buying in bulk. I made a mental note to order extra-large pizzas for Alex and his friends later.

We finished our breakfast and got ready for the day. The sky outside was a brilliant shade of blue. I had a hard time concentrating on the road as we drove into town because the trees were putting on a spectacular show of color. Red, yellow, orange, brown, and golden leaves fluttered in the wind. Organic orchards lush with the last harvest of fall stretched in every direction. The mountains surrounded us in a sea of forest green.

"It's so gorgeous. Can you believe we live here?" I turned to Alex, who was staring out the window.

"Mom, you say that every year."

"I know, but it's so beautiful." I pointed to a red-tailed hawk circling overhead.

Alex scoffed. "Okay, I guess it's pretty great."

"You better watch your step, young man, or you're going to end up grounded," I teased.

"Right, Mom." He knew it was an empty threat. I'd never grounded him, let alone ever needed to punish him.

When we arrived in the school parking lot, I blew him a kiss. "See you later with pizza."

"See ya." He waved and jumped out of the car.

I waited for a minute and watched him join a group of friends. He looked happy. Was he? Was he faking it? If Alex was okay, I knew I would be okay, but if he wasn't . . .

Don't go there, Sloan. If I allowed myself to loop through scenarios where Alex wasn't okay, then I might really start to lose it.

I pulled away from the curb and continued to the village. The season was definitely changing. Leaves drifted from the trees and piled along the side of the road as I made my way into town.

I made up my mind in that minute to stop at April's office before I lost my nerve. Garrett and I kept opposite hours. He was a night owl. I liked the mornings. Brewing in the early hours at Nitro had been a welcome change of pace from Der Keller. The operation at Der Keller was a well-oiled machine with a large staff. I had rarely ever had a moment alone at the brewery. At Nitro I spent most mornings alone. I had come to crave the solace. The gift of time alone with myself had forced me to look inward and confront old demons. I still had work to do, but I could feel myself changing.

Usually by midmorning, Garrett and Kat would join me. Nitro would rev up with their energy. It was a good balance—solitude and collaboration.

Since I knew that neither of them would be up for an hour or two, I might as well talk to April while I had the confidence. Her office was at the far end of the village. The building was a converted ski chalet divided in half with April's office on one side and a vacation property management company owned by my friend Lisa on the other. Lisa was taking a well-deserved three-week getaway to the Caribbean while things were slow in the village. If she were in town I would have opted to work with her instead of April, but desperate times called for desperate measures.

I had no trouble finding a parking space nearby, another sign that Oktoberfest was behind us. The grass was dewy from melting frost as I walked toward April's building. I was glad that I had layered with a long-sleeved black T-shirt and a charcoal gray fleece.

The village sat in a peaceful morning silence. Aside from a handful of workers installing holiday lights and a few business owners preparing their storefronts for the day, things were peaceful. Most of the shops wouldn't open until later.

"Morning," I called to a crew wrapping the trunk of a giant weeping willow with purple lights.

They greeted me with the classic tongue-in-cheek *"Guten Morgen."*

That would make April happy, I thought as I continued along the sidewalk. Chief Meyers's police car was parked in front of April's office, but I didn't give it much thought. April had likely demanded that Chief Meyers arrest Kristopher Cooper on charges of severe detriment to the community after last night's confrontation.

Suddenly, a siren wailed. I jumped and clutched my chest at the surprising and piercing sound. At first, I thought it was the workers playing a joke.

I paused and listened. Sure enough, the sound of police sirens cut through the quiet village.

Something had to be going on. I turned and stared down Front Street toward the gazebo. Blue and red lights flashed. They weren't dainty Christmas lights. They were police lights.

What was happening? Was April hurt? She wasn't my favorite person in Leavenworth, but I didn't want to see her harmed. Could that be why Chief Meyers's car was parked in front of her building?

Without thinking, I hurried toward the office and took the stairs to the porch two at a time. The intricately carved wooden door to April's office was open.

"April, are you okay?" I called, stepping inside the front lobby.

The minute I did, I wished I hadn't. A body was sprawled on the carpet. It had been covered with a sheet, but a red stain the size of a dinner plate spread on the center of the sheet.

That had to be blood.

I covered my mouth with my hand.

Don't throw up, Sloan.

Poor April. She and I weren't exactly the best of friends, but I couldn't believe she was dead. A sick feeling swelled in my stomach. I was staring at a dead body. The body of a woman I had known for years.

"Let's go, Ablin." I heard Chief Meyers's voice coming from the back office.

Huh? I took a closer look at the body and realized the person was much too tall to be April, and he was wearing black loafers.

Okay, well, at least April's not dead. I reached for the white wainscoting to try and steady myself.

This had to be some sort of bad dream.

"Chief, you don't understand, it wasn't me. You can't arrest me! I didn't kill him, I swear. I did not kill anyone!" April's earsplitting voice jarred me back to reality.

Was Chief Meyers arresting April? And who was dead on the floor in front of me?

Chief Meyers led April down the hallway toward me.

"Look, Ablin, the more you resist, the worse this is going to be." She had ahold of April's wrist.

April caught my eye. Her face was wild with fear and confusion. Black mascara had streaked down her cheeks. "Sloan! You have to help me! Tell her. Tell Chief Meyers that I didn't kill him."

"Keep moving." The chief directed April out the front door and into her squad car as two other police vehicles squealed into empty parking space in front of the building.

I followed them outside and stared in disbelief. What was happening? April was being arrested?

Once Chief Meyers had secured April in the car, she came over to me. "Sloan, I'm going to need to ask you to stand back." She pointed behind her to April's office. "This is an active crime scene. My squad is going to secure the area now."

"What happened?" I pressed my thumbs into my hips, trying to keep from sounding as hysterical as April. "There's a dead body inside, isn't there?"

Chief Meyers adjusted the walkie-talkie clipped to her snug-fitting khaki uniform. "I'm afraid that April Ablin is under arrest."

I blinked twice. The flashing lights were making it hard for me to concentrate. Or maybe it was the reality of having just seen a body.

She motioned for two officers to move past us. "There's been a murder, and April's our prime suspect." She glanced to the police car and then back to me. "Sloan, April could use a friend right now."

I could tell from her hard stare that she was talking about me. "Me? April and I aren't exactly friends." Being friends with April would be like drinking mass-produced beer. The thought made me shudder.

Chief Meyers frowned. "Like I said, she could use a friend, and I think you and I both know she doesn't have many."

"What did she do? Who was killed?" I couldn't believe this was happening.

The chief sighed. "Kristopher Cooper. I know that you'll be discreet, Sloan. The news will spread soon enough, but I'd like to keep it under wraps as long as possible while my team does their initial investigation."

Kristopher was dead? My God. I thought about the town meeting last night. Everyone in the room had wanted to kill him.

"Things aren't looking good for April. I'm sure she'd appreciate any help you can offer." With that, she returned to her squad car.

What did that mean?

I had known Chief Meyers most of my adult life. She was intelligent and fair. If she thought that April was involved in Kristopher's death, she must have good reason. April Ablin wasn't on my short list of people I wanted to spend time with, but there was one thing I knew for sure—she was no killer.

CHAPTER

FIVE

MY MIND REELED AS I walked to Nitro. April was a suspect in a murder? Impossible. Or was it? She had been fuming last night. But she couldn't have killed him, could she?

I stuffed my hands into the pockets of my puffy fleece. The frosty morning air made my cheeks sting with cold. Smoke puffed from the top of the chimney on the bookstore. The bookstore was one of my favorite places to steal away a lazy Saturday afternoon. It was tucked on the hillside and looked like an enchanted castle from a brothers Grimm fairy tale. There were carts of books, covered with a plastic tarp, lining the porch. In classic Leavenworth fashion, the bookstore owner left overstock outside at night without worrying it would disappear.

The sound of sirens and the flashing lights had brought the workers to a halt. Shop owners and employees began coming out to the sidewalk to see what was going on.

I walked in a daze, barely noticing the activity. Kristopher was dead. He was currently the most despised man in the village, and he was dead. Could someone who opposed Kristopher's stance on prohibition have taken matters into their own hands? But who?

I certainly didn't want to see our little beertopia turn dry, but I couldn't imagine any of my fellow business owners going so far as to murder Kristopher. Given last night's turnout, it didn't make sense. It was evident that Valerie had the majority of voters in her camp. Maybe someone snapped after Kristopher initiated a fight.

A wave of guilt washed over me. I had walked by when I saw him, April, Ross, Valerie, and Conrad in front of The Nutcracker Shoppe. Should I have intervened? What if one of them killed him?

A line had formed in front of Strudel, the pastry shop. I wondered if news was already spreading or if it was because they were making their famous Bavarian waffles today. The sweet waffles smothered with buttercream and strawberries were so popular that whenever they were on the menu they sold out in a matter of hours. Leavenworth had a reputation for gossip. It came with the territory, living in a small town of two thousand permanent residents. The gossip wasn't mean-spirited, it was simply that news tended to travel fast, whether that news was a murder or delicious waffles.

"Sloan!" a woman called from the back of the pastry line. It was Heidi, who owned the Hamburg Hostel next door to Der Keller. She and I had volunteered together on a number of fund-raising committees. The Hamburg was a boutique property with ten guest rooms. Getting a reservation for the busiest times of year at the hostel required booking months—sometimes years—in advance.

"Morning, Sloan. Have you heard the news?" She pointed down the street in the direction I'd just come from. She was dressed in workout gear. Her black spandex pants were skin-tight as was her neon orange tank top. A warm-up jacket and towel hung over her shoulder.

I wasn't sure how to respond, since the chief had asked me to be discreet. "No. What's going on? Are they serving waffles today? And aren't you freezing?" I rubbed my arms.

"Sadly, no waffles for me." She dabbed her face with the towel. "I'm still cooling down from my morning CrossFit class. You should come. It's a killer workout, but my abs are loving it." Heidi didn't have an ounce of fat on her body. She looked like she could compete in body-building contests, with her chiseled arms and lean, muscular legs.

"You're not exactly selling it by saying it's a killer workout. Although maybe I'll have to join you if I keep finding myself at Strudel every morning." I eyed a tray of almond-paste tarts in the display case.

"Sloan, come on. You're in great shape, and it gives you the biggest endorphin rush. I was telling my instructor that I need a post-workout coffee to maintain the high." She tossed the towel back over her shoulder. "What's the scoop with the police activity? Someone in line said they heard there's been a murder."

This might have been a record for gossip spreading. "Really?" I played naive.

She jabbed the man in line in front of her. I recognized

him, too. I'd seen him with April last night—it was Ross, the owner of Leavenworth's most unusual bar, The Underground. The Underground was literally that. It was a bar that had been constructed in the basement of an old church. To access it, you had to descend a steep set of stairs and then travel through a small underground tunnel.

"Oh hey, Sloan." Ross smiled. He was short, stocky, and completely bald, but with a full, shaggy red beard.

"You're up early," I said to Ross. "I thought bar owners shunned the morning sun, especially after the craziness of last night."

"Yeah, that was something. Kristopher got what he deserved, if you ask me." He motioned to the coffee counter. "I usually don't like to see the sun. I'm more of a stars kind of guy, but that's why I'm here. I need the biggest cup of java they can brew. We had an issue with the electricity last night. I have an emergency appointment with the electrician in a few minutes to try to get things sorted out."

"What happened last night?" Heidi asked.

Ross massaged his shiny head. "The dude went off the deep end. He started a fight at Der Keller after the rally for Valerie. I thought I saw you there?"

"No, not me." Heidi shook her head and then unzipped a tiny pocket on the top of her thigh that was barely noticeable. She pulled out a folded five-dollar bill. "Ross, tell Sloan what you just heard. Maybe it's really true if there was a fight last night."

Ross tried to glance behind us, but both Heidi and I were taller than him. "I heard that Kristopher Cooper is dead. I can't say that I'm broken up about it. The man was a nutcase. Who in his right mind would think it was a good idea to prohibit alcohol in a tourist destination better known as Beervaria?"

How had Ross already heard about Kristopher? I had just left Chief Meyers minutes ago. Gossip couldn't travel that fast. Could it?

"Seriously," Heidi agreed. "I'm surprised someone didn't kill him sooner. Everyone in town hates him. Can you imagine what would have happened to our businesses if he had been reelected?"

I agreed that banning alcohol would have had a tremendously negative impact on every business in town, but I was surprised by Heidi and Ross's callous tone.

"Kristopher had it in for the Underground," Ross said. "I wouldn't be shocked to learn that he was behind our mysterious power outage last night. He's been trying to shut us down for months."

"Why?" I asked as we moved forward with the line. The smell of hand-rolled pastries and coffee made me almost want to go for a second breakfast.

Ross shrugged. "No idea. He freaked out on me when a couple of frat guys got arrested after we kicked them out. They'd had too much to drink at Oktoberfest, so my bartender refused to serve them." He paused. "You know how it goes, Sloan. There's no gray area when it comes to overserving."

"Right."

Heidi put on her warm-up jacket. "Why would Kristopher have been upset about that?"

"One of the guys threw up on his shoe." Ross rolled his eyes. "As if that was our fault. They ran into him on the sidewalk, and one of the guys puked. Kristopher called the police and claimed that we had overserved them. We had video footage of my bartender kicking them out basically from the moment they stumbled in, but Kristopher wouldn't let it go. He said that we were underground for a reason. He had the wildest theories that we were serving minors and running a bootleg operation. He had gone off the deep end."

"I had no idea," I said.

Ross made it to the front of the line. He placed his order. Heidi turned to me. "Well, I guess we won't have to worry about next week's election if Kristopher is dead."

"True." I waited while she ordered. Then I ordered a black coffee for me and lattes for Garrett and Kat. I've always been experimental when it comes to coffee. Much like the process of brewing beer, I enjoyed a variety of coffee styles. Some days I drank my coffee black, other days I ordered a latte. We chatted for a few more minutes while waiting for our coffees. Then we parted ways. I figured that Ross and Heidi were likely venting their frustration over Kristopher, but I couldn't shake the feeling that they had both had a strange reaction to the fact that he had been murdered.

When I arrived at Nitro, the front door was unlocked, and the brewery lights were on. Garrett was filling the mash tun with malt.

"I didn't expect you to be awake yet," I commented, and handed him a latte.

"Me neither. Thanks for this." He took the coffee with a grateful smile.

"Why are you up so early?"

"I heard a bunch of sirens. Is something going on?" Garrett took a sip of the latte. His reading glasses were propped on his head.

I set the latte I had purchased for Kat on the bottom step of the fermenting tank. Then I cradled my coffee in my hands. "There's been a murder."

Garrett nearly dropped his latte. "What?" He caught the coffee at the last minute, but not before sloshing some on his shirt, which read BEER, IT'S WHAT'S FOR BREAKFAST.

I explained about how I stopped by April's office and saw her get taken into custody. Garrett and I had worked with Chief Meyers in a previous murder case, so I knew that I could trust him to keep the information between us. Then I filled him in on my conversation with Ross and Heidi.

"Can you believe they'd already heard? I mean, it had literally only been minutes between the time I saw the chief taking April away and bumping into them."

"Man, that's uncanny timing." Garrett went to run his fingers through his hair and accidentally knocked off his reading glasses.

"Yeah. It's probably nothing, but neither of them was shaken up in the least by the news of Kristopher's death."

Garrett stuck the glasses back on his head and wiped coffee from the rim of the lid with his thumb. "I wouldn't put too much stock in their reactions. They didn't know for sure that Kristopher was dead, right?"

"True."

"It could be that they weren't more shaken because they think it's just a rumor."

I understood his point, but I still felt weird about how my

conversation with Heidi and Ross had gone. "Can you believe that April is the chief's top suspect?"

"No." Garrett cracked a half smile. "Now, that would be poetic justice, wouldn't it? Leavenworth's queen of the kitsch arrested. If she had done it with a stein, that would be even better."

"I hate to admit it, but that was my first thought, too. It couldn't happen to a more irritating person, but she looked really scared, Garrett."

He took a big gulp of the latte. "Yeah. I know we share the same feelings about April. She's annoying as hell, but I'm with you, Sloan. There is no way she's a killer. Can you imagine her wrestling someone like Kristopher to the ground in her petticoats and high heels?"

I shuddered at the thought. "Nope. I'm sure that Chief Meyers is following protocol. I got the sense reading between her words that she didn't want to arrest April."

"Can you blame her?"

I laughed. "I'm thinking I should walk over to the police station later and see if I can talk to April." I sighed and took a sip of my coffee. "I wouldn't say that I *want* to help April, but I feel like I should."

"You are a saint among women, Sloan." Garrett finished his coffee.

"It's not entirely selfless. I'm curious about the murder, and if I check in on April, maybe I can get some more details about what happened."

Garrett tossed the empty cup in the garbage and returned to funneling grains into the tank. "If anyone can get more details, it's you."

"What's that supposed to mean?"

"It means that thanks to your personality, people have a tendency to overshare with you. I have a theory on why that is. Do you want to hear it?"

"Is this a scientific theory?"

Garrett grinned. "Sure is. Masterminded by yours truly."

"Well, in that case, yes, please enlighten me."

"My very scientific theory goes something like this. People pour out their heart and soul to you because you do the opposite. You don't easily divulge personal details or gossip. That rattles people. They don't like the silence, so they fill it with unnecessary details about themselves."

"Intriguing."

"I prefer brilliant." Garrett winked. "I'll bill you for my services later."

"Thanks."

Kat came downstairs a few minutes later. She padded into the kitchen in a pair of sweatpants, an oversized hoodie, and a pair of fluffy slippers shaped like bunnies. "I thought I heard voices down here."

I offered her the latte, which she immediately began to guzzle. We didn't mention anything about Kristopher's murder. I had made a promise to Chief Meyers. It could wait. Kat would hear about it soon enough, and for the moment there was beer to brew.

CHAPTER

SIX

THE BREWING PROCESS WAS COMPLETELY immersive. We were using the brief reprieve from tourists to brew extra batches of our holiday line. There was a narrow window in which we would need to brew our three distinct holiday beers and then allow them ample time to ferment. At a minimum, beer takes two weeks to work through the fermentation process.

One thing that set Nitro apart from other pubs and bars in Leavenworth was Garrett's Northwest brewing style. He was committed to differentiating our offerings by using locally sourced ingredients, hops, and grains. Unlike Der Keller, which exclusively brewed traditional German beers, and the Underground, which served a rotation of German imports, at Nitro we embraced the fertile growing region in the North Cascades and drier arid deserts of eastern Washington. Our beers reflected the landscape around us.

For our holiday line, we had decided to go rogue. We

were creating three unique beers to celebrate the winter holidays and Leavenworth's famous Christmas markets. Our first holiday beer was a chocolate hazelnut imperial stout, brewed with cacao nibs, roasted hazelnuts, and vanilla beans. It would be like a holiday dessert in a pint glass. Next, we were brewing a Gose (an old German beer). Our take on the Gose was popcorn and cranberry strings used to decorate a Christmas tree. The tart beer, made from cranberries, buttered popcorn, and sea salt, would be a refreshing beer to sip while strolling through the vendor booths at the holiday market. Lastly, we were brewing a pine-infused IPA. IPAs (India pale ales) were a favorite in the Northwest. It was nearly impossible to enter a pub anywhere in Washington or Oregon without finding an IPA on the menu. Our hop-forward Christmas IPA would offer the aroma of a fresh-cut pine tree with a sweet, bright finish.

Since Nitro was classified as a nanobrewery, we had to be strategic about our brewing schedule. Our setup was tiny in comparison to Der Keller. We brewed on a ten-barrel system. Every batch we brewed on the system produced twenty kegs, which might sound like a lot, but each keg yielded approximately 124 pints. On a busy day during a festival weekend, we could go through that in a matter of hours. It was simple math. If there were twenty-five people in the bar and each of them had two pints in an hour, that was fifty pints.

Garrett and I had already brewed small batches of each holiday beer in our test kitchen, and now our task was to take the recipes and produce them on a grander scale. Once we had each beer fermenting, we would return to our smaller setup in the kitchen and test another round of beers for January debuts. Like many retail shops, the business of brewing meant planning months in advance.

We had launched our holiday line with the chocolate stout. Garrett had cranked Christmas music while we brewed a traditional stout. It had been fermenting for a week, and assuming the gravity (or sugar content) was where we wanted it, it should be ready for the next step—adding delicious cacao nibs. Tracking a beer's gravity was something that Garrett took seriously. Some of the sugar in the wort would ferment into alcohol, and the remaining sugars would add sweetness and give the beer body. We charted the beer's original gravity right before we pitched the yeast, and then would take readings regularly until the beer reached its final gravity number.

"Hey, Sloan, you gonna taste that?" Garrett asked, lugging a bucket of cleaning solution from the opposite end of the brewery.

Kat followed behind him with a spray bottle and a stack of clean rags. She didn't have a good pair of brewer's boots yet, so I had loaned her an old pair of mine. The bright yellow boots were giant on her.

"Be careful in those," I cautioned. She looked like a little girl trying on her mom's high heels.

"They're, like, thigh-high." Kat laughed. "I stuck two pairs of socks in the toes, so I'm good."

I made note of the stout's gravity and then siphoned a taste. Even without the cacao nibs, it had a dark, biscuit flavor with notes of caramel.

"Try this," I said to Garrett, handing him a plastic taster.

He set the bucket of iodine and water at the base of the fermentation tank. He closed his eyes and swished the beer around in his mouth. "Nice. I'm already getting a hint of chocolate. How's the gravity?"

"Right where we want it."

"Excellent." He finished off the taster. "You want to get the nibs ready while Kat and I give everything a good scrub?"

"I'm on it." I left them and went to the kitchen. Brewing is as much about cleaning as anything else. Cleanliness is as close as it gets to godliness in the world of craft beer. Everything in the brewery sparkled, yet before we began brewing en masse, we would do another clean-down just to ensure that no speck of dust tainted our final product. It didn't surprise me that Garrett's previous career was in the tech industry. Working in a brewery was much like working in a lab.

I tugged off my fleece and rolled up my sleeves. Thank goodness Garrett had had the foresight to keep his great-aunt Tess's industrial kitchen intact. Having the commercial space allowed us to prepare and serve pub fare in the bar and gave us a space to use for our smaller test batches.

Cacao nibs contain magnesium, a mineral known to relax anxiety. It wasn't a surprise that I often craved a piece of dark chocolate in the late afternoon. Hopefully our holiday stout would be a smooth-drinking chocolate escape. I preheated the oven to 350 degrees and then went to the built-in pantry to grab a bag of the chocolate beans. After spreading them on cookie sheets, I slid them into the oven to roast for ten to fifteen minutes.

Next, I gathered hazelnuts. The benefit of brewing was that we never needed to worry about finely chopping or deshelling nuts or any other fruits or berries used in the brew. Everything would be strained out. It made prep work easy. I tossed the nuts (shells and all) in olive oil and coarse sea salt. Then I arranged them on industrial cookie sheets. Once the cacao nibs were done, the hazelnuts would go in. The heat should bring out a nuttiness and intensify their flavor.

Before my timer dinged, the kitchen smelled like homemade chocolate cake. The ambrosial scent of the roasted cacao nibs was near perfection. Some of our pubgoers loved the smell of brewing—the steeping grains and intense hops. Others didn't enjoy it quite as much. I was sure that no one would object to the decadent chocolate flavor. I removed the trays from the oven and slid in the hazelnuts. Then I shook the nibs into an industrial mixing bowl. Per the unofficial brewers' code of taste everything, I popped one of the cacao pieces in my mouth. It had a nice crunch and the deep, rich flavor of dark chocolate chips.

Those will do beautifully, I said to myself as I took the bowl to the brewery.

"That smells so crazy good." Kat held up her hands, which were protected with rubber gloves. "I want to dive into that bowl."

Garrett agreed. "Seriously, I thought you had gone on a tangent and decided to bake a cake. If those smell that good, I'm calling it now—the stout is going to be our bestseller."

I held out the bowl. "Do you guys want to taste them? They're like a grainier dark chocolate."

"I do." Kat yanked off her gloves. "Aren't they, like, health food or something?"

"You could say that. They're packed with antioxidants, so sure, this can be our healthy beer."

"Mmmm. It's really good," Kat said through a mouthful of

the chocolate. "That would probably be amazing ground up and served on ice cream."

"Good idea." I offered her more and then turned to Garrett, who was cleaning hoses. "You want any before I dump them in?"

"I'll pass. The smell is enough for me."

"Stay tuned for roasted hazelnuts," I teased as I climbed the ladder on the fermenting tank. At the top, I lifted the hatch and dumped the cacao nibs straight in. Steam began to form. I shut the hatch and returned to the kitchen.

It didn't take long for the aroma of roasting nuts to mingle with the lingering chocolate. I returned to the pantry for popcorn and coconut and peanut oil. I planned to pop the corn on the stove. Microwaved popcorn is great for movie night or an afternoon snack, but for this signature holiday beer, I wanted to make sure that we extracted as much flavor from the popped corn as possible.

Ursula had taught me her tried-and-true technique for stovetop popcorn years ago. The result was that nearly every kernel of corn ended up popped to fluffy perfection without a hint of bitter, burnt flavor. I started by pouring the oils into the bottom of a thick-bottomed pan. They would need to come to temp. Next, I turned the burner to medium high and waited for it to begin to sizzle.

To test whether it was hot enough, I tossed in a couple of kernels. Once they popped, I added the rest of the kernels, covered the pot with the lid, and removed it from the heat for thirty seconds. This is a critical and necessary step. I remembered Ursula having Alex count down from thirty to one when she would make homemade popcorn with us on family movie nights.

"*Ja,* Alex, it is good. You must be patient with the kernels. Ziz way zey warm together and will pop at once when we put it back on ze stove."

It became like a game. Alex loved the anticipation of counting down. As soon as he would shout, "Number one," Ursula would place the popcorn back on the burner. Alex would clap at the sound of the kernels bouncing off the pan. Ursula would shake the pan and lift the lid ever so slightly to allow air to escape in the popping process. As soon as the corn finished popping, she transferred it into a large mixing bowl and tossed it with melted butter and sea salt.

I felt a pang of nostalgia as I repeated the steps she had taught me many years ago.

The timer for the hazelnuts buzzed just as I poured the last few ounces of melted butter over the popcorn.

"My God, Sloan, what are you doing? Trying to torture us?" Garrett came into the kitchen. He had swapped his reading glasses for his chemistry goggles.

"What?"

"Kat and I are dying. First the chocolate, now this. You're killing us. We've decided we should add roasted nuts and popcorn to our snack menu at the bar."

"That's a great idea." I thought about the suggestion for a second. "What if I come up with a menu that features one or more of the ingredients from our holiday line?" I had enjoyed the freedom that Garrett allowed me when it came to Nitro's small pub menu. We weren't interested in a full-scale restaurant menu like Der Keller's, but we did like to offer our customers small bites to go with their pints.

"I'm game," Garrett replied, digging his hand into the bowl of buttered popcorn. "This beer and the hazelnut stout—no problem. But I can't wait to see what in the world you come up with for our hoppy holiday pine."

I frowned. "Yeah. I'll have to think on that one." The beer featured hops and pine needles. Neither ingredient jumped out at me as something customers would rush to eat on their own. But maybe I could experiment with a pine shortbread cookie. I had made shortbread with lavender and rosemary. The hint of herbs balanced the cookie's natural sweetness. Pine might just work. I could cut the shortbread in the shape of Christmas trees and dust them with green sugar.

I didn't mention the idea to Garrett. I would do some test runs on my own and see if they were worth pursuing. "The nuts are ready," I said.

Garrett chomped on the popcorn. "Sloan, this is insanely good. What did you do?"

I told him about Ursula's stovetop method.

"Thank goodness for your mother-in-law. I don't know if I want this in the beer. I want to devour the entire bowl."

"I can pop some more. It only takes five minutes." My cheeks felt warm. I wasn't sure if it was from the heat in the kitchen or Garrett's effusive praise.

"How long does it stay fresh?" Garrett asked, taking another handful.

"Once it's buttered like this?" I asked. "Not long. If we want to serve it in the bar tonight as one of our snack items, I can pop another batch and keep it in an airtight container up at the bar. We can toss it with butter and salt right before we serve it."

"Do it." Garrett washed his hands before wiping them on a towel and then used it to pick up the tray of roasted nuts. "I'm off to add these."

I set the popcorn aside. Then I rinsed a bucketful of whole cranberries and set them to boil in a large stockpot on the stove. I covered them with water and added an assortment of holiday spices—cinnamon sticks, nutmeg, vanilla, and candied orange peel. The goal was to create a cranberry syrup or compote that we would add after steeping the grains.

Sugar is a brewer's best friend. Sugar activates the yeast and helps ignite the fermentation process. The natural sugars in the cranberries would bring the Gose's sugar content higher. We would need to adjust our sugar levels accordingly.

Brewing is a science first and an art second. Everything from the temperature of the boil to how long the grains are left to steep can dramatically change a beer's flavor profile. Garrett and I were vigilant when it came to following a beer through each step (start to finish) and documenting any tweaks we might make along the way. Adding an extra handful of popcorn or doubling the cranberry compote without noting it in the recipe would make it nearly impossible to re-create a consistent beer. Nothing was left to chance.

That didn't mean that we were opposed to experimenting. Far from it. Tinkering with a beer recipe was one of my favorite parts of the job. We left the experimenting to the kitchen, our own version of a mini test lab. But when brewing for public consumption, we wanted to be able to produce the same quality pint after pint. One advantage to being small was our ability to stay nimble. Bigger operations like Der Keller might brew one or two gorgeous IPAs in mass quantity, but we could brew dozens of different styles of IPAs in a short time span because our equipment was smaller and we had more of it. Beer takes the same amount of time to create whether brewing one gallon or ten thousand gallons. Der Keller and the other "big guys" in the craft world had distribution contracts that required them to deliver their most popular beers by the keg and caseload. We weren't tied to the same rigorous brewing schedule. Producing something new all the time kept our beer fresh and interesting and kept our customers coming in more frequently to try our latest offerings. In the last decade, there had been a growing wave of nanobreweries throughout the Pacific Northwest, and I attributed the success of the nano movement to beer lovers' insatiable desire for unique and interesting flavor combinations and mash-ups.

Regardless of the size of their operations, brewers are often fanatical when it comes to guarding their recipes, and Nitro was no exception. Garrett kept our coveted recipes under lock and key (literally). Leavenworth isn't the kind of place where most people lock their doors. Neighbors often pop into one another's houses to borrow a cup of sugar and drop off a bundle of garden roses. Garrett had come from Seattle, a large city where he would have never considered *not* locking his front door. It had taken me a while to get in the habit.

Kat breezed into the kitchen. "Garrett asked if the popcorn is ready." Her youthful cheeks were dewy with sweat.

"Yep." I handed her the bowl.

"Can I sneak a taste?" She took a big handful.

"Absolutely." I walked to the stove to stir the cranberries. "This needs to simmer. I'll come help get the boil going for the Gose."

The remainder of the morning was hard physical labor. Brewing isn't for the faint of heart. It requires stamina and plenty of arm strength. Lugging huge bags of grains and stirring the wort with a stainless-steel paddle always left my forearms aching, and yet somehow also left me energized. There's something about working up a sweat that beats any other form of therapy.

At Nitro we brewed the hard way. We didn't have silos or augers like the big guys to avoid the heavy lifting. We worked our glutes lugging heavy bags of grain. In my opinion, the extra muscle was what made all the difference in flavor. Brewing by hand allowed you intimate control of the final product, and for me, it was a labor of love. The muscle aches were a reminder of pouring my heart and soul into a beer. Maybe I was biased, but the effort expended for each pint was what made our beer so much better than the mass brewers'. It was like comparing Ursula's homemade cookies with a store-bought package.

With cookies on my mind, I turned my attention to creating a pine shortbread. A mildly sweet, buttery cookie with touches of pine should be an excellent accompaniment for our hoppy beers. I'd never been much of a forager, although many brewers I knew trekked in the woods on the hunt for wild herbs and flowers. Since this was a test batch, I decided to snag some needles from one of the evergreen trees in Waterfront Park.

Nitro was on Commercial Street, two blocks from the park.

I wasn't sure if picking pine needles from a city tree counted as foraging, but I was up for the adventure. I grabbed my scarf and swapped my boots for tennis shoes. As I headed down the hill toward the park, I passed the Underground. DO NOT ENTER and CLOSED signs had been posted in front of its stone façade entrance. Ross had said something about electrical issues.

I thought about taking a closer look, but overheard voices.

Ross stood next to a man holding a clipboard. "You're not shutting us down. This is ludicrous! I'm not in violation of anything. This is all because of Kristopher Cooper."

I didn't wait to hear the man's response. This changed everything. If the Underground was being shut down, Ross had a very solid motive for murder.

CHAPTER

SEVEN

I HURRIED TO WATERFRONT PARK and took one of the trails
that wound along the Wenatchee River. A single kayak cut
through the water. Numerous walkways and trails shot off in
every direction. One that connected to the Enchantment Trail
system was littered with bear scat. *Perhaps not that one*, I thought
to myself as I headed for a clump of evergreens nearby.

Foraging a few pine needles was easy. I rubbed them between my fingers as I took a longer route back. The slow-
moving water of the river and earthy scent of the pine needles
helped center me. When I passed the Underground again,
Ross was still pleading his case to keep the bar open. I made a
mental note to follow up with Chief Meyers about the status
of the bar.

Baking, like brewing, was a welcome escape. I started by
creaming butter, sugar, and flour together. Then I added a
touch of salt and lemon zest. I blitzed the pine needles in a
food processor until they were finely chopped into tiny pieces.

Then I worked them into the dough. To add a touch of whimsy, I rolled the dough out and cut it into Christmas tree shapes. I finished each tree by dusting it with green sugar. The shortbread would bake for ten minutes or until it turned golden brown.

As the first batch of cookies came out of the oven, Garrett came into the kitchen. "The next batch of hops in the hopper."

"In the hopper?" I scrunched my nose. "What's the hopper?"

"I was trying to be funny. Obviously, it didn't work." He made a time-out signal with his hands. "Stop the presses. Did you make pine cookies?"

"Guilty as charged. Try one."

Garrett reached for a cookie and took a bite before I could warn him that they might be hot. "Sloan, these are amazing," he mumbled through a mouthful of the buttery shortbread. "Where did you get pine needles?"

"Waterfront Park. Foraging. We can get more for the beer once it's ready for dry hopping." I broke one of the cookies in half and tasted it. The pine flavor came through nicely, without being overpowering. I was pleased with the light, buttery finish and touch of sweetness.

"You're going to have to stop me, Sloan. I might eat the entire tray."

I gave him my best mom face. "You can eat the entire tray after lunch. We have more brewing to do."

We spent the next three hours sweating in the brewery. Garrett called for surrender sometime in the early afternoon. "I'm famished."

"Me too." We'd been at it all morning. "Why don't I run over to the German deli and pick us up some lunch? Kat can open the bar."

During the interim between festivals, we had scaled back our hours. Instead of opening by eleven or noon, we opened most days around one or two o'clock in the afternoon and stayed open until eight or nine, or whenever everyone wandered home. Since there were very few breaks throughout the year when it came to events in the village, most locals hunkered down when things were quiet. They tended to opt for dinners at home and early bedtimes.

Garrett climbed off the ladder. "Great. As long as you don't mind. I'll finish cleaning up and making final notations in our tracking sheets."

"It's a plan." I brushed grain residue from my hands onto my jeans. "I could use a short walk." That was true, but I had an ulterior motive. The police station was on the way to the German deli. I could stop in and see if Chief Meyers would let me see April.

I pulled on my fleece. My skin felt damp. I went into the bathroom and splashed water on my face. My olive-toned skin was blotched with color. I tied my hair into a long, low ponytail and dabbed my cheeks with a towel. For a morning spent in the brewery, I didn't look terrible, but then again, I'd never been much into makeup or jewelry.

The one thing that I had been noticing lately was that the signs of age were beginning to show with circles under my eyes and fine lines on my brow. I blamed Mac. As I did for most things.

Unfortunately, I knew that there was no fighting it. Stress aside, I was in my mid-forties. Aging was inevitable, and one incredibly valuable lesson that I had learned in watching Ursula evolve in her later years was to accept it. She hadn't tried to run from the fact that her body was changing. She had embraced it with a happy heart and broad smile. Even though she was in her seventies, her bright eyes gave her a youthful appearance. She had taken a fall a while ago, leading to hip surgery. Ursula was feisty and had been back at Der Keller (with the help of a cane) the minute her doctor gave her permission to return to "light" activity.

I twisted a black cashmere scarf around my neck and ran some lip gloss over my lips. Then I stood back and appraised my appearance. Not bad. My walnut eyes were bright, and the ponytail accentuated my Greek bone structure.

The village was still relatively sleepy, but there were more people out and about than there had been earlier. Shop owners polished windows and worked on holiday displays. Overflowing flower baskets with fall foliage and red and yellow geraniums lined the street. I spotted Conrad, the owner of The Nutcracker Shoppe, in deep conversation with Ross. I couldn't be sure, but their body language didn't appear to be overly friendly.

Conrad held a two-foot-tall Santa Claus nutcracker in his arms. He seemed to be trying to get Ross to come into the shop. Ross wasn't budging.

Was Conrad trying to make a sale? Ross didn't strike me as the nutcracker type. Or had something happened with Kristopher last night? They had both been with him after the fight at Der Keller. What if one of them killed him and asked the other to cover it up? Or what if they had teamed up? Could there be any connection with the Underground's closure?

Slow down, Sloan. I was spiraling into random theories without having learned any more details about the case or tangible evidence.

I didn't want to be Conrad's next target, so I crossed the street and kept my head low.

The police station was at the far end of Front Street. I walked through a scattering of dried leaves and past the park. Then I continued on until I reached the small building with a wooden sign carved with the word "Polizei" flanked by two beer barrels. To call it a station was a stretch. It was more of an office, with a long front desk that blocked entry to the back area. Leavenworth's main police station was outside of the village core. This space was mainly used to deal with any minor issues like petty theft or drunk college students.

Chief Meyers stood at the outdated oak desk that had been scratched and stained. It looked as if it had been in use since the 1970s. She was on the phone and held a finger up to me when I entered.

April was seated in the very back of the office. Her head was buried in her hands, and it sounded like she was sobbing. I pretended to be very interested in an assortment of posters on the wall in order to avoid April seeing me. I studied a poster about motorcycle and biking safety with the tagline BE SAFE! BE SEEN and then turned my attention to a rack with brochures and flyers on the fines for littering in the village, encouraging pedestrians to cross the street in marked crosswalks, warnings about wildlife encounters, and information about the non-emergency contact line.

"Sloan, what can I do for you?" the chief asked when she finished her call.

"I was wondering if I could talk to April?" I kept my voice low so that April wouldn't hear us. Her head was still buried in her hands. I didn't think she had noticed me yet.

Chief Meyers glanced over her shoulder. "Two minutes." Then she stuck two fingers in her mouth and whistled. "Ablin, you've got a visitor."

April looked up. Her makeup was streaked with tears, her braids had unraveled and were a twisted mess. Large rings of smeared mascara under her eyes made her look like a rabid raccoon. She rubbed her eyes. "Sloan? Oh, thank God. Is it really you?"

I gave her a smile, trying to mask my shock at her appearance. The chief lifted the far corner of the desk, which was on a hinge. I ducked under and walked back to where April was seated.

"How are you doing?" I sat next to her.

She massaged her temples. "How do I look? No, don't answer that. I don't want to know. I'm sure I'm hideous. Chief Meyers has had me locked in here like a common criminal for hours."

I kept my face passive and decided that it was probably best not to mention her mascara.

"I'm sure it's a formality. Chief Meyers is a consummate professional."

"A consummate professional who has tossed Leavenworth's official ambassador in jail?" April wailed.

Again, I didn't mention the fact that we were miles away

70

from the county jail. "What happened, April? You were pretty wound up last night with Kristopher."

"I know. I was furious with him. He's such an ass. He was only at Der Keller to try and get everyone fuming. It worked." Her eyes were wild with fear. "Sloan, you have to help me. It was awful. I found Kris's body in my office, I showed up to find a dead body and the police at my building, and now Chief Meyers thinks that I killed him. How long have we been friends, Sloan?"

Friends? My first instinct was to answer never. That was also the second time I had heard April call him Kris. Did she know him better than she was letting on?

Luckily, April didn't wait for me to answer. "Sloan, you're my oldest and dearest friend, you have to help me. I'm begging you. Absolutely begging."

It was a challenge to keep from responding with a sarcastic comment. I twisted my scarf to keep quiet. April had never begged for anything in her life. She demanded.

"What do you want me to do?"

April laced her fingers together. "You have to help me. I didn't kill Kris, but I think I know who did."

CHAPTER
EIGHT

"YOU KNOW WHO KILLED KRISTOPHER? Why didn't you tell the chief?" I looked from April to the front, where Chief Meyers was instructing a young police officer on the proper protocol for filing reports.

April scowled. Her lipstick had smeared across her chin, making her look like a drunk college student the morning after Oktoberfest. "Give me more credit than that, Sloan. I'm not an idiot. Of course, I told the chief my theory, but she doesn't believe me. It looks bad. Really bad. Everyone saw me yelling at him last night and then he ends up dead in my office. It's not good. We need to find evidence. Hard proof. And fast."

"How am I supposed to do that? I'm a brewer, April, not a detective." I pointed to my outfit.

"Sloan!" April wailed again, which made Chief Meyers whip her head around and stare at us.

"One more minute, ladies," the chief said, tapping a black

exercise tracking watch on her wrist. Chief Meyers was old-school. I was surprised to see her wearing a fitness tracker.

"Sloan," April hissed, "you have to help me. I know that you're not a detective, but I also know that you have an in with the chief. She admires you for some reason. I've never understood why, but she seems to take you into her confidence. I suppose it's probably due to my high status in the village. You obviously don't have the same kind of demands and pressures as I do."

Ah, there was the April I knew. My "dear" friend who always found a way to turn a compliment into an insult.

"She trusts you," April continued. "And I know that you and Garrett consulted with her on the unfortunate accident that happened at Nitro." Her voice was laced with envy.

The unfortunate accident that April was referring to was actually a murder, but in true April fashion, she had reworked the story to make it more palatable for tourists. *No one wants to visit a charming village where there's been a gruesome murder, Sloan,* she had said not long after the case was closed. *For the sake of Leavenworth, if the topic comes up in casual conversation, let's just say that it was a little accident.*

Chief Meyers cleared her throat. "Okay, ladies. Let's wrap it up."

April grabbed my arm. "Sloan, please. I'm begging you. I'll do anything. I'll owe you big time. Was I pissed at him? Yes. And I told him that to his face, but I did not kill him."

"But I saw you after Mac broke up the fight. You were with him and a few other people at The Nutcracker Shoppe."

She kept her hand on my arm and nodded frantically. "Yes. I was with him outside Conrad's shop. That was the last

73

time I saw him, I swear. I told him he had to stop this madness for the sake of Leavenworth. That was it."

I noticed for the first time that April's freckled forearm was scratched and cut up. "What happened to your arm?"

She yanked her arm away and covered the scratches with her other hand. "Nothing. It's fine."

I couldn't help wondering if one of the reasons that the chief was keeping April was due to the cuts and scratches on her arm. Had she been in a fight? Maybe Kristopher had struggled when she killed him. I studied her. Her frilly barmaid's dress was torn at the seam, revealing a nasty bruise on her left leg. What wasn't she telling me?

"Look, I was supposed to meet Kris at my office early this morning," April said, using her other hand to shield the physical evidence on her arm. "When I got there, he was already dead."

"Okay." The fluorescent lighting made April's streaked makeup appear even more garish.

"No, don't look at me like that. I can tell that you don't believe me." April caught me staring at the tear in her skirt and shifted in her chair so I couldn't see the bruise.

"I didn't say that." However, I might have been thinking it. April's behavior wasn't exactly giving me confidence in her innocence.

Chief Meyers started to walk toward us.

"Sloan, please." April clasped her hands in prayer. "Go talk to Ross. He and Kris were going at it when I left them last night. Ross is convinced that Kris was trying to get the Underground shutdown. I think he killed him. That's a motive."

"All right. Time's up." Chief Meyers tapped on her watch.

74

I stood. April shot me a final, pleading glance. "Talk to Ross," she mouthed as the chief showed me to the door.

Meyers grabbed a khaki-colored police jacket from a hook by the door and walked outside with me. "Well, what do you think?"

"About April?" I shrugged. "She seems like her normal irritating self, but I did notice her arm is cut and scratched. She has a large bruise on her leg, and her dress is torn. She blew me off when I asked her about it."

The chief frowned. "I know."

I told her about April's suggestion that Ross could be involved and asked her about the Underground.

"We're looking into everything at the moment. I'm off to see Ross next, so I have no intel on what's happening with the Underground, but I have to tell you, Sloan, that there's some pretty incriminating evidence stacking up against April right now, not just the cuts and bruises."

"Do you really think she could have done it?"

Chief Meyers was noncommittal. "Stranger things have happened. Not many, but you never know."

I left feeling conflicted. It would have been smartest to leave the situation alone, and yet I felt strangely compelled to help April.

Bad idea, Sloan, I heard my inner voice respond. *April Ablin is your nemesis. Would she go out of her way to help you?*

Probably not, I answered back. But then again, I wasn't sure. April was annoying, but she had shown flashes of kindness. Usually followed up with some kind of a snarky response or underhanded comment. The most appealing reason to help April wasn't entirely selfless. If she owed me a favor, maybe I could get her off our backs once and for all about making Nitro more "in line" with Leavenworth's aesthetic, as she constantly liked to remind us.

April had been insisting—no, demanding—that we adhere to the village's guidelines on businesses in the downtown corridor. Much to her chagrin, we were well within our right to do whatever we determined with the interior of Nitro's building, while ensuring that the outside façade remained a replica of a German utopia. According to city code, every commercial building in the village had to maintain a Bavarian aesthetic, but there were no regulations about interior designs. Garrett had been extremely cautious about adhering to city code when he began renovations on his great-aunt Tess's inn. He had given the inn's chocolate brown balcony and spires a fresh coat of paint and stained the lion's head that was carved into the peak of the roof. From the outside, Nitro looked like it belonged in a pastoral village. The inside was where Garrett's vision for blending his love of science and the craft of brewing came to life. I liked the fact that we got the best of both worlds—German charm and modern designs. Nitro wasn't alone. Sure, there were a handful of businesses that went all in with the German kitsch, decking their interiors with cuckoo clocks and lederhosen, but most of our fellow business owners in the village opted for a more modern store layout inside.

I headed for the German deli. There were many unanswered questions, like how had April injured her arm if she hadn't killed Kristopher? And why was she meeting Kristopher in her office this morning? I wished that I had had more time with her.

The deli had red, yellow, and black German flags strung above the front door. It was one of the most authentic shops in town. I weaved through rows of imported German candy—licorice, marzipan, Black Forest gummy bears. I always liked to stop and browse the interesting imports in the housewares aisle like German pottery, spätzle presses, and *Feuerzangenbowle,* a terracotta fire punch cup set.

There was a short line waiting for sausages and the house special—sauerkraut made daily in huge vats. A mural depicting a scene from an outdoor German market had been painted behind the deli counter. I drooled at the sight of giant cured pickles and the scent of fresh baked bread.

"Sloan, what can I get you?" the butcher asked when it was my turn. He was a portly man with a wide smile. I'd never seen him without an apron and matching white butcher's hat.

I had been eyeing a platter of *Kartoffelkloesse,* simple but delicious German potato dumplings. The melt-in-your-mouth dumplings were stuffed with buttery croutons and best eaten with warm sausage gravy.

"I'll take a double order of the dumplings with extra gravy, and a side of the red cabbage and apples."

"Excellent choice." The butcher packaged up my lunch order. I hoped that Kat and Garrett would enjoy a classic German feast, since I had originally suggested picking up sandwiches. I didn't think that they would mind. One of the benefits of living in Leavenworth was the vast array of authentic Bavarian cuisine. The dumplings smelled so delicious that I briefly considered keeping them all for myself.

As I left the deli, I couldn't stop thinking about April. Chief Meyers was right. It didn't look good for her. If Hans hadn't held her back, she might have pummeled Kristopher last night. Had her obsessive love for Leavenworth finally gotten the best of her?

CHAPTER

NINE

ON MY WAY FROM THE deli, I made a quick stop at the pizza shop to place an order that I could pick up on the way home later.

When I arrived at Nitro, I noticed that Kat had propped the open sign on the sidewalk. She waved as I came inside. There were five or six people I recognized drinking afternoon pints at the bar and at a few of the high-top tables. I didn't stop to mingle. Instead, I stopped at the bar to check in with Kat.

"How's it going?" I rested the food on the edge of the distressed wood bar. "I got us lunch."

Kat tucked her abundant curls behind her ears and leaned over to take a whiff. "Wow. That smells awesome."

"Are you ready for a break?"

She shook her head. "No. If you don't mind, I'll take my break after you eat. I just poured a taster tray for that table by the window. I'm trying out some of what you've taught me." She reached under the bar and pulled out a notebook. "I jotted down notes on what each of them usually drink, and I made guesses on which of our beers they'll like the best. I told them that I'm training, and they thought it would be fun to put me to the test. Once they finish the taster tray, we're going to compare my guesses with the beers they actually liked best."

"I love it. Let me know how it goes." I crossed my fingers for her and picked up the food.

Garrett was in the office. I knocked on the door and held up the bag. "Lunch is delivered. I'll get it plated up in the kitchen. Come on in whenever hunger calls."

He shot me an okay sign. "Thanks. Be there in a sec."

I went to the kitchen and divided the dumplings into three portions and slathered them with gravy. I heated the first plate. Once the microwave dinged, I put in the second plate and scooped the red cabbage salad onto the warmed plate.

"What is that smell?" Garrett asked, coming into the kitchen.

I handed him the warm plate. "Give it a try. I hope you like it."

"I know I like it. I don't have to taste it, it smells amazing." He cut into one of the puffy dumplings.

I followed suit. The buttery pastry melted in my mouth, as did the spicy sausage gravy. "I saw April Ablin."

Garrett raised an eyebrow. "Yeah?"

"Yeah." I sighed. "I don't know what to think. April doesn't seem like a killer, but she wasn't acting like herself. You missed most of the action last night, but she was seriously ready to jump on Kristopher. I've never seen her that furious. Her face was as red as the cranberries." I went on to tell him about the scratches and bruises.

"I can't believe I missed it. By the time I left everyone was gone." Garrett helped himself to another bite. "Did Chief Meyers mention the cause of death?"

"No, she didn't, and I didn't ask. I should have." I kicked myself internally. Why hadn't I asked Chief Meyers when I'd had the chance?

"It's not your job, Sloan." He stabbed his fork into one of the dumplings. "I'm sure the chief is investigating every angle and lead."

"Right, but if there was a fight that led to Kristopher's murder, then it's no wonder that the chief arrested April. She alluded to the fact that there was circumstantial evidence pointing to April."

Garrett was thoughtful for a moment. "I don't see April as a killer, but I guess stranger things have happened."

"That's verbatim what Chief Meyers said." I dipped a bite of dumpling in the gravy. "The problem is now I feel like I have to help April. How did that happen?"

Garrett threw his head back and laughed. "It's the con of being a nice person, Sloan. Maybe you should try being mean for a while."

"Maybe." The conversation shifted. We discussed beer recipes while we finished our lunch, then I went to relieve Kat at the bar.

"Well, how did the tasting quiz go?" I asked, glancing toward the front table where the group was sipping pints.

"Not bad." Kat showed me her score sheet. "I got two out of three. The last one threw me because the woman said that she doesn't like hops and usually drinks ciders. I suggested our honey wheat ale, since it's not hoppy and a little sweet. Guess which her favorite was?"

"Pucker Up?"

Kat folded her arms across her chest and glared. "How did you know? I don't get it. She said she doesn't like hops, and that's the hoppiest beer we serve."

"True. And, honey wheat would definitely appeal to a non-hops lover, but Pucker Up is brewed with Citra hops. It has such an intense citrus flavor, much like a cider. I'm not surprised she liked it."

"I bow down to you." Kat gave me a half bow. "I was way off on that one. I guess I have a lot more to learn."

"You're doing great. Remember, I've been in this business for twenty years, and I'm still learning new things every day," I reassured her. "Potato dumplings and sausage are waiting for you in the kitchen. Microwave it for a minute and then serve yourself some red cabbage on the side."

"Thanks." Kat grinned. "You and Garrett are the best."

I took over the bar and sent her on break. I felt maternal toward her. She wasn't that much older than Alex. It was also no secret that I had attachment issues. Bouncing between foster homes during my early and late childhood had meant that I had developed a thick skin and a natural skepticism about people's motives. I didn't trust easily, with one exception—the Krauses. Their unconditional love for their sons and for the community of friends they had created in Leavenworth had given me a glimpse into what it meant to have a family. Under the protection of their caring arms, I had slowly let down my guard. It hadn't come easy. Otto and Ursula were persistently patient. They must have recognized that my sense of abandonment ran deep. Deeper than even I could see. I remember many evenings gathered around their family table. After dinner Ursula would brew a strong pot of coffee and bring out one of her wonderful desserts. She and Otto would regale us with stories of the old world while we sipped coffee and savored slices of cake.

In the early days of knowing them, I didn't say much. I was more comfortable listening. Ursula would ask gentle questions to draw me out. She never ventured into the territory of my past or asked anything that might trigger an emotional response. Our conversations typically drifted to food and the art of brewing. Hans and Mac would have fiery debates about Der Keller's future. Mac was always on the hunt for the newest trend. Hans wanted Der Keller to maintain its well-earned reputation for being one of the founders of craft brewing in the region. He wasn't opposed to expanding the brand, but he was cautious in his approach. Mac, on the other hand, wanted Der Keller on every tap from the northernmost corner of Washington to the southernmost corner of California. From there he had grand plans for national expansion and exporting to Germany.

Der Keller had a large distribution area throughout Washington, Oregon, Idaho, and Northern California, but none of the other Krause family members were interested in expanding brewing operations like Mac. Leavenworth was home. As Otto would say, "When you live in a place as beautiful as ziz, why would you ever want to leave?"

Ursula had a way of reining Mac in without crushing his dreams. It was a balancing act that I was always impressed with.

Her watchful eyes would follow along as he expressed his desires to conquer the beer world. She would allow him to talk, listening without interruption. When he would finish, she would clasp her hands together and nod. "*Ja,* ziz is a vonderful idea, son. It is good if you spend some time zinking and planning it. You can give us a proposal, *ja*?"

She was a master. Mac would never follow through with the level of work that any of his grand schemes required. She knew it. And so did he.

I should have been more like Ursula. The realist in me could never get past some of his most outlandish ideas—like franchising Der Keller in all fifty states. If I had gone along with his dreams, would things have eroded between us?

"Sloan. Hey, Sloan." A voice brought me back into reality.

I looked up to see Hans on the opposite side of the bar.

"I'm going to guess that the faraway look in your eyes has nothing to do with beer, am I right?" Hans propped one elbow on the top of the bar. "The counselor is in, if you pour me a pint."

Hans was joking, but he wasn't far off. He had inherited his mother's ability to size someone up in a matter of seconds.

"Pouring pints is what I do. What can I get you?" I motioned to the tap handles.

Hans didn't hesitate. "I'll take a Pucker Up IPA while you've still got it."

I reached for a cold glass, angled it under the tap handle, and slowly began to pour.

"Don't worry. This is our bestselling beer. We're going to keep it on rotation throughout the year."

Hans watched me pour.

"I'm guessing you heard about April?" I asked over my shoulder.

He rested a tan forearm on the bar. "The rumor mill has been working overtime, that's for sure. I can't picture April as a killer. She has too much to lose."

I glanced at the bar and tasting room. There were only four customers in the pub. Two older gentlemen were playing chess at a high-top table, and a younger couple was sampling one of our taster flights.

"Me too. Although I think she's hiding something. I'm just not sure what." I capped off Hans's pint with a frothy layer of foam. "Do you know much about Ross?"

"Ross?" Hans took the pint and looked thoughtful for a moment. "The owner of the Underground?"

"Yeah." I nodded and took another quick look to make sure no one was listening. "He's been in Leavenworth a long time, right? I can't remember, but I feel like the Underground opened when Alex was in preschool."

"That sounds right." Hans smelled his beer. I recognized the familiar step immediately. Any professional brewer smells and appraises a beer before drinking it. Brewing was ingrained in Hans whether he realized it or not. The irony was that Hans had a much more natural gift when it came to his palate than Mac.

"Why do you ask?"

"I went to see April at Chief Meyers's office, and she told me that Ross and Kristopher got in a fight after the meeting last night, and earlier I noticed that the bar is shut down. Ross said something about electrical issues, but he was begging whoever he was talking to when I saw him to keep the bar open."

"Really? I don't know anything about the Underground being shut down, but I can ask around." Hans closed his eyes while he took a sip of the beer. A hint of a smile passed across his face. "You and Garrett sure know how to brew, Sloan."

"Thanks." I appreciated the compliment.

He took a larger sip and then rested the pint glass on the bar. His hands were rough from years of being scuffed up from sandpaper. "I'm trying to think through how everything went down last night. It was so . . ." He searched for the right word.

"Not Leavenworth-like?" I offered.

"Yeah. Come to think of it, after the fight broke up, Kristopher came back to Der Keller about fifteen or twenty minutes later. He was still trying to rile people up and was handing out campaign brochures to anyone who would take one."

"Let me guess—no one bit?"

Hans raised his pint glass. "Not a single person." His light brown eyes met mine.

"Hmmm. I'm not sure how that plays into the timeline of his murder. I saw him with April, Ross, Conrad, and Valerie on my way to the car. April claims he and Ross were fighting when she left, but maybe she is lying." I reached under the counter for a Tupperware of popcorn and a bag of Doritos. Garrett and I had learned early on that we both shared a serious addiction to the nacho-cheese chips. "Do you want something to snack on with your beer?"

Hans started to refuse. "I'm good."

I cracked open the Tupperware and held it out for him to smell. "It's your mom's recipe."

"Sloan, you're killing me. You know I can't refuse, and I'm

trying to work on my waistline." He pinched his khaki Carhartts.

"Yeah, right." I filled a small bowl with the flavorful popcorn and handed it to him."

He took a handful. "Back to Kristopher. Nothing happened. Kristopher spouted off a bunch of statistics on how alcohol is a detriment to society and Leavenworth's youth, but no one paid attention. By that point, it was so late that everyone wanted to go home." Hans paused. "You know, come to think of it, I did see Ross heading over to talk to Kristopher when I walked my parents to their car. I didn't see them fighting, but Ross was moving toward Kristopher."

"Hold that thought." I left Hans briefly to check on one of the tables who were giving me the universal signal they were ready for another round. After refilling a couple of pint glasses, I returned to Hans. "Sorry, I didn't mean to derail the conversation. Did you need something, or are you just here for the beer?"

"Sloan, I'm always here for the beer." Hans grinned. He drank another large sip to prove his point. His physical appearance was so different from Mac's. Hans was taller and leaner, with muscular forearms from lifting heavy pieces of wood and running his table saw. "But, yeah, I am here on business. Mac wants the three of us to meet sometime this week to talk about next steps for Der Keller."

A gnawing feeling churned in my stomach. "Okay."

"Hey, I'm not thrilled about it either, but I have learned over the years that the best way to deal with my brother is head-on."

"I'm in the not-at-all camp right now." I was also in the I-don't-have-another-choice camp. For Alex's sake, I had been putting on a good front when it came to dealing with Mac. And then there was the issue of our ongoing partnership in Der Keller.

"What's tonight like?" Hans asked. "You want to get it over with?"

"Can't." I wiped down a spot on the bar. "Alex is having friends over to study, and I promised to bring them pizza."

"We can come to your place if it's easier. Have him on your turf?"

"No. I don't want to have any conversations around Alex."

"That's fair. Why don't you take a look at your week and come by my studio sometime? I'm wide open, so whatever works for you is fine with me." Hans finished his drink. "Remember, we're a team on this. I've got your back, Sloan."

"I know, and I appreciate it. I just wish there was a way I could avoid talking or seeing your brother for a while. Or forever."

Hans laughed. "You're not always alone on that."

He left, holding the door open for a regular who was entering the pub. I thought about Ross as I poured a pint of our Cherry Weizen (another Oktoberfest specialty). Maybe April had witnessed a fight. I would have to swing by the Underground and see if I could get anything out of him. As for Mac, he could wait until tomorrow or never.

CHAPTER

TEN

THE AFTERNOON WAS UNEVENTFUL. LIKE cleaning, a big part of brewing was waiting. We were in the waiting stage for our holiday line. By late afternoon, the tasting room had picked up a bit, with locals stopping by for a happy-hour pint before heading home. I enjoyed the energy of the small crowd. Garrett stayed in the back most of the day, while Kat and I tag-teamed the bar. She had an easy style with customers. I was glad to see her building rapport with some of our regulars.

"Do you want me to spend some time looking for more beer themes online tonight?" Kat asked when she came up to the bar with a tray of empty tasters. "It's been slow enough that I can make some notes while I'm working."

"That would be good." We were planning to design each room upstairs with a unique theme. Kat and I had brainstormed a list of potential themes that we presented to Garrett. After much discussion, we had narrowed it down to four ideas. Kat and I had been putting together mock-ups of each theme. Every room would represent one of the components of beer—grain, hops, yeast, water.

Hops and water had been easy to design around. We planned to use fresh dried hops to make wreaths and garlands for the hop room. We would accent it with photographs of Washington's world-famous hop fields and decorate the room in hop-inspired pale green paint. For the water room we would showcase Leavenworth's snowcapped mountains, Icicle Creek, and the Wenatchee River. Kat came up with the idea of adding a small indoor water fountain so that guests could drift off to sleep with the relaxing sounds of trickling water.

The grain and yeast rooms had been more challenging. We were considering painting the grain room in sepia tones and covering one wall with a mural of golden Yakima Valley wheat. Yeast on its own wasn't particularly compelling. Yes, it was the magic ingredient in beer, but it was hardly photogenic. We'd been going back and forth about keeping it as a theme or swapping to something else when Kat stumbled upon a quote online: "Every loaf of bread is a tragic story of grains that could have become beer but didn't."

We decided to paint one wall in the yeast room with chalkboard paint and cover it with funny quotes about beer. We'd decorate the other walls with chemistry posters and beer charts to play up the science behind Nitro. Kat had been amassing quotes and anything else that might work in our soon-to-be-spruced-up guest rooms.

Kat's enthusiasm for scouring the Web to find the coolest products and accessories was refreshing. She wasn't the slightest bit jaded. Her earnest spirit brought a lightness to the pub.

And I had to admit that I had a newfound excitement about the project. Garrett had given us complete autonomy. After so many years of living in Mac's shadow and constantly second-guessing myself, something as simple as redecorating a guest room felt almost monumental. The worst part was that at least half of the blame was mine. I had allowed myself to be consumed by Mac's larger-than-life personality. I was determined not to let that happen again.

"Let's go over the final sketches tomorrow morning," I said to Kat, doing a last scan of the bar before I left.

"I'll poll everyone who comes in tonight. Get opinions on what else they might want for an immersive beer experience." Kat pointed to her sketchbook. "I'll show them our ideas and see what they think—cool?"

"Cool." I smiled. "See you tomorrow." I left Kat and went to the office to say good-bye to Garrett. He was flipping through a pile of beer supply catalogues.

"How many trees do you think were killed to produce this stack?" Garrett didn't look up. "I have to give them credit for creativity. Listen to this. 'It's beginning to look a lot like Craftsmas' or 'I'm knocking back some Rein Beer this year.'"

I chuckled. "Brewers never pass up a good pun."

"How did that trend get started?" Garrett licked his index finger and turned the page on the catalogue.

"Good question. We should stick Kat on researching that. She's in her element looking up beerish stuff for the guest rooms."

"You should take these away from me," Garrett replied, holding up the catalogue. "I've suddenly decided that we should be selling beer-themed ugly Christmas sweaters and red and green growler koozies."

"Why not?"

"No. Sloan, you're supposed to be the voice of reason around here. Stop me." He pretended that his hands were shaking as he tried to force the catalogue shut.

I laughed. "Is that all I'm good for? Being the adult?"

"Hardly. You're the backbone of this operation. I literally have no idea what I would do without you. How did I ever think I was going to launch Nitro on my own?" Garrett's voice had a raspy quality.

"Glad to be of service." I kept my tone carefree.

Garrett tossed the catalogue in the pile on his desk. "Are you out of here?"

"Yep. Mom duty calls. I'm on pizza delivery tonight. Alex and his friends are having a study session for midterms at our—" I stopped myself. "At my place."

"My mom could have learned a lesson or two from you. She failed to deliver pizza for me and my friends. When I had friends over to study, she'd tell us to grab whatever was in the fridge. I should have reported her to the authorities for neglect." The minute the words escaped Garrett's mouth, a look of horror flashed across his face. "Oh, crap. Sorry, Sloan. I was being glib. I shouldn't have said that."

"It's no big deal." I tried to shift the conversation. "The big dilemma is whether to grab salads to go with their pizzas or cookie dough."

"Duh. Cookie dough." Garrett stood. "Really, Sloan, I didn't mean to be insensitive. I'm so sorry."

"Stop. It's fine. I'm a grown woman, I can handle a joke."

Garrett sighed and looked at his feet. "I know, but—"

"Seriously. It's fine." I glanced at the atomic clock above the door. "Look, I've got to jet and get these dudes carbo-loaded on pizza. I'll see you tomorrow."

I bolted before he tried to apologize again. Garrett was far from insensitive. I knew he was making a joke. I didn't care. What I cared about was the look of pity he had given me when he realized his oversight. I had never been able to stand the thought of anyone pitying me. My entire childhood had been a rotation of teachers, social workers, and medical professionals who had given me the same look of sympathy. I hated it.

I shook off the familiar feeling of anger welling in my stomach as I walked to Kuchen, the pizza shop. Translated, *Kuchen* means pie. Another clever pun. I supposed Leavenworth and breweries had that in common. Of course I knew from Otto and Ursula that our Americanized version of a German village sometimes left gaping holes in translation. Like the fact that Ursula would refer to *Kuchen* as a sweet pie, not a pizza. It was one of the many quirks that made me appreciate our little town even more.

A breeze sent leaves swirling from the trees. I could see my breath in front of my face as I rounded the corner onto Front Street. It was almost time to break out my winter parka and snow boots.

The pizza shop's sign always brought a smile to my face. It was designed with a Bavarian scroll and German Alps, only the Alps were slices of pizza lined up to look like a mountain range.

A small crowd of thirty to forty people had gathered in front of the shop. As I got closer, I noticed Valerie Hedy in the center of the action. She held a megaphone to her lips.

"Thank you all for your support," she said as I joined the circle of people. "I've been in contact with the police as well as the current city council, and there has been no decision made as of yet."

"What's she talking about?" I asked the woman standing next to me.

"Valerie is trying to petition to keep the ballot as is. It's so close to the election. The ballots have already been printed. There's not time to try to recruit another candidate. I heard someone say that it's too bad Kristopher wasn't married. His wife could have stepped in."

"Really?"

The woman nodded. "Yeah, I guess it happened in a senate race in Missouri a few years ago. One of the candidates died in a plane crash. His name remained on the ballot, and he actually won, so his widow agreed to fill his seat."

"That's crazy." I inched to the left to get a better view. Valerie was dressed in campaign gear from head to toe. The megaphone seemed like overkill. It wasn't as if she was speaking to a crowd of hundreds, but then again, maybe it was due to her diminutive presence in front of crowds. Gone was the forceful personality I had witnessed during her confrontation with Kristopher last night.

Valerie continued speaking into the megaphone. "The council is reviewing electoral procedures. They think there's a very likely chance that the election will go on as is. The ballots have already been printed. That means that Kristopher's name will still be on it."

"Does that mean you could lose to a dead guy?" someone behind me asked.

Valerie gave a small laugh and then tried to make her face look serious. It didn't exactly work. She looked like she'd just tasted a bad batch of beer. "Obviously, we are all mourning the loss of Kristopher. Yes, we were opponents, but he served this community well for many years, and I respect him for that."

"You didn't answer the question," the person repeated.

I turned around and realized it was Conrad, the owner of The Nutcracker Shoppe. He waited with his arms folded across his chest for Valerie's reply.

"Well, technically, yes. Assuming the council grants approval for next Tuesday's election to proceed as planned, then yes, Kristopher's name will still be on the ballot."

"So, you could lose to a dead guy," Conrad said again. He was bundled up in a nutcracker stocking cap and matching scarf. I had to give him credit for embracing the vibe.

Valerie flashed him a forced smile. "Technically speaking, yes."

"Wait. Hold on a second." Conrad pushed closer to Valerie. "What would happen if he wins?"

"I'm confident that, thanks to you wonderful voters, we won't have to worry about that." Valerie's smiled was plastered on. It made my cheeks hurt.

Conrad wasn't satisfied. "But what if you don't?" His tone was almost threatening.

Valerie's lips pursed and her smile tightened further. "I don't foresee that being an issue. As many of you who were at last night's event at Der Keller know, I've been so fortunate

to have the support of Leavenworth's small business community, teachers' association, as well as law enforcement—"

"We get it," Conrad interrupted. "What I want to know
is what happens on the off chance that Kristopher wins? Does
that mean his insane prohibition plan wins too? We're going
to take Leavenworth back to the 1920s? How did that work
out back then?"

The energy in the crowd began to shift. People murmured
under their breath. Valerie was starting to lose control.

"No. Definitely not." Valerie shifted her weight from one
side to the other. I got the feeling she was ready to be done
with Conrad's questions. "The council is, as we speak, reviewing other instances here in Washington State where a de-
ceased citizen has been elected into office. Believe it or not,
it has happened before. But the odds of Kristopher winning
were slim to none already, and now that he's dead, the odds
are even more astronomical. The council will have a contingency plan in place in the event he should win."

"What's the contingency?" Conrad refused to back down.
The woman next to me rolled her eyes.

Valerie shrugged. She looked around desperately as if hoping that someone—anyone—would ask another question. No
one did. "I can't tell you for sure, but they mentioned potentially appointing someone to the council for the first year of
his term, and then his seat would be reopened for election the
following year. Whoever they appoint would have to run if
they wanted to remain in office."

"Who would they appoint?" Conrad asked. He unwrapped
and wrapped the wool nutcracker scarf as he spoke.

"I have no idea." Valerie turned away from him and shifted

focus in the opposite direction. "That does bring us to tonight. Thank you so much for being willing to go door-to-door with me. Our efforts tonight are about reminding people to get out and vote on Tuesday." She motioned to a woman standing next to her, who handed her a box. Valerie opened it and held up a door tag. "These vote reminders need to be hung on every door in town. You don't need to knock or engage in discussion with anyone. All that we're asking you to do is leave one of these door tags on the handle. If you happen to meet anyone while you're volunteering, simply remind them that the election is on Tuesday and to be sure to cast their vote. Now more than ever, we need to get people out to the polls. We don't want voters to be complacent just because Kristopher is dead. Every vote counts."

She passed around the box.

"I'd like you to go in teams of two. We'll meet back here for drinks and pizza as soon you're done. Any questions?" She intentionally kept her gaze away from Conrad.

I ducked behind the group and headed into Kuchen while they divided into teams. The scent of wood-fired pies immediately warmed my senses.

"Hi, Sloan, I've got a bunch of piping-hot pizzas with your name on them," the pizza shop owner said to me.

"That's good, because I've got a bunch of hungry teenage boys at home, and I fear for my safety if I show up empty-handed."

He handed me the boxes of pizza.

"Any chance you have some of your world-famous cookie dough pizzas left?"

"I do, indeed. How many can I get you?"

"Better go with three," I said. The cookie dough pizza was an ingenious build-your-own dessert. It was a sweetened pizza dough liberally buttered and sprinkled with cinnamon and sugar. It came with containers of chocolate chip cookie dough, chunks of chocolate, caramel sauce, marshmallows, and nuts. The boys could sprinkle the sweet pizza with pieces of dough, marshmallows, and nuts. Then the desserts would be baked until the cookie dough and marshmallows melted into the crust. It was one of Alex's favorite weekend desserts. Mac used to bring home pizzas on Fridays, and the three of us would curl up on the couch together for a movie marathon.

Those days are over, Sloan, I said to myself as I waited for the owner to assemble the cookie dough pizzas. When he returned with more boxes, I had to take two trips to the car. I thanked him, paid for the pizzas, and headed for home. A slice of pizza and cold beer sounded like just what the doctor ordered after this insane day.

CHAPTER

ELEVEN

"WHO'S HUNGRY?" I ASKED WHEN I returned home to find a group of famished boys in my kitchen.

Alex and his friends inhaled the pizzas. It never ceased to amaze me how much food teenage boys could consume. I snuck a slice of sausage, tomato, and olive onto a plate for myself and poured a pint of Der Keller's winter ale. Mac had installed a beer fridge with four taps in the garage. We kept small kegs of Der Keller's beer on tap for parties, family dinners, or unexpected guests.

"You guys need anything else?" I asked Alex and his friends, who had taken over the dining room table. Backpacks and soccer gear were piled in front of the fireplace. Textbooks, notebooks, and smartphones lined the table. The kitchen had always been my favorite, a sacred space in the house, with its high-beamed ceilings, wood-burning fireplace, and clapboard walls. Lately, it had lost some of its charm. Hearing the sound of the boys' laughter helped remind me of what a happy place this used to be.

"Thanks, Mrs. Krause," they called in unison.

They were a good group of kids. Most of them had known each other since they were in diapers. I was glad that Alex had a solid support system.

I left them to study and polish off the few remaining pieces of pizza. I went to my bedroom and made myself comfy on the couch. Our master bedroom was the size of a small house. It had a large bathroom with a claw-foot tub and a seating area with two plush chairs, a love seat, bookshelves, and a television. The seating area was arranged near the oversized windows that looked out onto the backyard. I rested my plate on my lap and turned on the TV. I wasn't much of television person. More than anything because I'd never had time. Between my work at Der Keller, raising Alex, and always being ready to entertain last-minute guests Mac would bring home, I rarely had time to myself. That had changed. Now I had too much time on my hands.

I flipped the channel until I landed on the local news. The lead story was about Kristopher's murder.

"Scandal rocks the beloved Bavarian village of Leaven-worth, Washington," a young reporter said with the intonation of a soap opera star. "I'm here live in the beer capital of the Pacific Northwest with Police Chief Meyers." She thrust a microphone in Chief Meyers's face and began bombarding her with questions.

Chief Meyers answered nearly every question with "I can't talk about any details in an open investigation." Her stern face was impassive, as was her body language. I could tell the young reporter was getting frustrated with the chief's canned responses.

The journalist was from a Seattle news station. They had pulled old stock footage of Kristopher from ribbon-cutting ceremonies and more recent clips of him campaigning against beer and its many evils. I sat up and scooted closer to the screen when a grainy picture from the early nineties appeared. I paused the TV and replayed it three times.

I couldn't believe what I was seeing. In the old footage, April Ablin was standing next to Kristopher. According to the reporter, the picture was from Kristopher's first election. April must have been in her early twenties. She looked younger, but otherwise much the same. With one glaring difference. April wasn't wearing a dirndl or a single piece of German clothing. In its place, she wore a T-shirt that read KRIS FOR COUNCIL.

April had not only known Kristopher for decades, but had supported his campaign? Had my initial reaction to her arrest been correct? She had obviously had some kind of relationship (either professional as a supporter of his campaign or maybe a friendship) with Kristopher. Why hadn't she mentioned anything about it to me?

I watched for a few more minutes while the reporter shifted her focus to Leavenworth's response to Kristopher's controversial plan to ban alcohol. She cut to footage of the huge Oktoberfest crowds.

Forget it. Why am I getting involved in this? I thought, changing the channel. I didn't owe April anything, and if she was withholding important details like the fact that she had campaigned for Kristopher, how could I trust her?

I landed on old reruns of *The Brady Brunch*—the perfect complement to eating my pizza and drinking my beer in peace. If only my concerns could be like those of the Brady family, who were entangled in a dispute over who had dibs on the attic bedroom. *The Brady Bunch* epitomized the idea of family when I was a kid. During stays at particularly challenging foster homes, I would imagine myself as one of the Brady clan.

When I finished my dinner, I went to check on the boys. Not surprisingly, there wasn't a single crumb left in any of the pizza boxes.

"Anyone up for a dessert break?" I brought out the dessert pizzas and toppings.

The boys wasted no time making space for the dessert pies. They slathered sweet toppings on the crust. I baked the pizzas for ten minutes until the marshmallows, chocolate chunks, cookie dough, and caramel melted together in an oozing, bubbling, gooey lather.

"Careful, it's hot," I cautioned as I delivered the sugar bombs to the table.

Alex caught my eye. "Thanks, Mom, you're the best."

"Mrs. Krause is the best," one of his friends echoed.

I made my exit. I wasn't fishing for compliments. Knowing that my son had a stable childhood and that he felt protected and loved was my only mission in life.

I tried not to let angry thoughts at Mac creep in. When I had first caught him shagging the beer wench, I had been almost stoic. Fuming, yes. But I had been able to keep my emotions in check. As the weeks had worn on, however, I was finding it more difficult to maintain any level of calm, even at the thought of him. Hans had told me that what I was experiencing was normal. That I was moving through the stages of grief. He was probably right, but it didn't make it any easier.

At some point, I must have fallen asleep because I woke to the sound of the front door shutting.

"Mom, you still awake?" I heard Alex call.

"Yeah. One sec." I rubbed my eyes and walked down to the kitchen.

"You weren't awake, Mom." Alex knew me too well.

"I might have drifted off," I admitted. "But I heard the guys leave."

"Sorry. I told them to be quiet."

"They were. Don't worry." In truth, I hadn't slept soundly since the day Alex was born. I remembered many nights spent listening to his breathing pattern on the baby monitor and racing in to check on him at the slightest cough or sniffle. Some of my girlfriends used to complain about the sleepless nights with young babies. I never minded. My connection to Alex was the deepest form of love I had ever experienced. I welcomed the sleepless nights. They confirmed our bond.

"Go back to bed, Mom." Alex loaded dishes in the dishwasher.

"How did studying go?"

"Good." He rinsed a plate in the sink. "I feel good about it."

His quick response alerted me that there was something he wasn't telling me. I went around to the opposite side of the counter and pulled out a barstool. "Is there something else going on?" I asked, sitting down.

Alex kept his back to me. I had learned that it was easier for him if we didn't maintain eye contact while having difficult conversations. "Dad asked me about my plans earlier."

A chill ran down my spine. I pinched the top of my thigh to force my voice to remain neutral. "Oh yeah? Your plans for what?"

"For moving in with him." Alex barely spoke above a whisper.

"Did you say 'moving in with him'? Where? He's staying at a hotel." I felt like my insides were being ripped out.

Alex turned to me. "I know. He said he's starting to look for a place. He wants me to come with him to give him feedback on which places I like, and then he asked what I wanted to do long term. Whether I want to stay and live with you or move in with him."

Rage pulsed through my body. Why would Mac put Alex in the middle? We had already discussed this and decided that we were going to proceed slowly so as not to disrupt Alex's school and social life. Alex had been staying with Mac at his hotel every few nights, and I had made it clear that Mac was welcome to see Alex as much as he wanted.

I'd been reading every book I could get my hands on about divorce and best practices for making the transition as painless as possible for teenagers. Everything I had read talked about the importance of not throwing the other parent under the bus. As much as I wanted to rail on Mac, I inhaled deeply and pinched my thigh harder.

"I hadn't heard that Dad's looking for a place. He and I were supposed to have dinner with Uncle Hans, but I postponed it so that I could be here tonight."

"You didn't have to do that."

"No, I wanted to. I love getting to see your friends, and honestly, I was wiped out from the day." I realized we hadn't talked about Kristopher's murder. Odds were good that news had hit the high school. The gossip mill didn't miss much, not even schools in Leavenworth. I changed the subject momentarily to buy myself time before diving into the subject of Mac. "Did you hear about what happened to Kristopher Cooper?"

"Yeah, our poli sci teacher told us about it. That's so crazy. He was killed, right?" Alex loaded dessert plates into the dishwasher.

I gave him a very condensed version.

"They think April killed him?" Alex scrunched his nose. Then he ripped a hunk off one last slice of the dessert pizza. "I mean, she's kind of over the top, but you don't think she could have done it, do you?"

"No," I responded honestly. April wasn't telling the truth about something, but I still didn't think she could be the killer.

"Carly's mom said that the newspapers and TV stations from Seattle are going to turn this into a circus."

"I was watching the news earlier. They're already in the village and reporting live from the scene of the crime."

Alex shook his head. "Great. The one time it's slow around here."

"Exactly." I had composed myself enough to continue the conversation about Mac. "Back to Dad, I support you in anything you want to do. If he's looking for a more permanent place, you should definitely go check it out with him—if that's what you want to do."

"Yeah." He didn't meet my eyes.

"He and I will figure out the rest. You don't need to worry about it."

"I know."

"No, really. I don't want you to worry about it, okay?" I tried to make eye contact with him, but suddenly he appeared to be fixated with his slice of dessert pizza.

"Mom, I know. I know. I get that you don't want me to worry or that you don't want me to feel like I'm in the middle, but the thing is, I am in the middle."

"But—" I started to respond.

He cut me off. "Mom, look. It's just the way it is. Half my friends' parents are already divorced. I've seen how it goes, and I appreciate that you and Dad aren't being awful to each other, but I'm going to be in the middle." This time he met my gaze. His eyes held a depth that nearly took my breath away. From a young age, Alex had been an old soul, wise, kind, with a deep inner knowing. My job as a parent was to give him the tools he needed to navigate adulthood and a soft shoulder to rest his head on.

I massaged my jaw. "You're right, but my point is that we can follow your lead. You're old enough to make your own decisions, and we will both respect that. By putting you in the middle, I mean neither of us are going to say it's him or me."

"Duh, I know." Alex stuck out his tongue in an attempt to be funny.

I didn't feel like laughing. I had known this issue was going to arise sooner or later, but I had put faith in the fact that it would be later. I couldn't believe that Mac was looking at houses, but in his defense, he'd been at the hotel for weeks now. His move was going to force the issue.

Alex wrapped the half of a slice of dessert pizza in tin foil. "Dessert for my lunch tomorrow."

"Too bad there aren't any other leftovers."

"It's cool. Tomorrow is taco bar."

I could tell that Alex was done with the conversation. I kissed him good night and dropped the subject. Now the odds of falling asleep again were definitely against me. Mac and I might not be on the best of terms, but there was no way I was letting him rope Alex into our problems.

CHAPTER

TWELVE

THE NEXT MORNING, I TEXTED Mac first thing telling him we needed to talk ASAP. He responded with a heart-shaped emoji and "Miss you too, baby."

He was trying to rattle me. I had told him at least a million times *never* to call me baby.

We agreed to meet at Der Keller for lunch. I wasn't looking forward to sitting down with him, but it had to be done. After getting Alex off to school and myself organized for the day, I wanted to get to Nitro early. We had days of work ahead of us to get the upstairs transformed for guests. If I could get an early start while things were quiet, all the better.

However, as I steered my Mercedes (an old birthday present from Mac) onto Front Street, I quickly realized that there was going to be nothing quiet about the morning. News media vans lined the street. Reporters were camped out in Front Street Park near the gazebo and set up on the steps of the police station. I counted at least five vans and dozens of reporters and camera crew. Obviously, Kristopher's murder had made headline news. Great.

I parked in front of Nitro. The air felt oppressive and strangely still after the past few days of breezy mornings. I wondered if it was the calm before the storm—literally and figuratively.

As I was getting my things out of the back of the car, I heard a harsh whisper behind me. It made me startle.

"Sloan! Sloan, over here."

I looked around and spotted April limping toward me. She wore a baseball hat, dark sunglasses, and a black trench coat. If she was trying to look inconspicuous, she was just the opposite.

For the first time ever, she didn't have a spot of makeup on. I could make out every freckle on her face. Instead of aging her, her clean skin gave her a more youthful appearance. She must have been in bad shape, because April without layer upon layer of makeup and sans a frilly German dress with an apron was almost unrecognizable.

"You're free?" I tried to make a joke.

"Not funny, Sloan." April glared at me as she limped closer.

"Sometimes humor is the best medicine."

April clasped the bridge of her nose with her thumb and index finger. "Sloan, I don't have time for humor. I have a splitting headache, and I'm only out because Chief Meyers has me on village arrest."

"Village arrest?" I wrapped my scarf tighter around my neck.

"Yes, I'm not allowed to leave the village. I can't even go as far as Safeway. Chief Meyers wants me within walking distance of her office." She pushed her sunglasses down and darted her head from the left to the right. "You weren't followed, were you?"

"Followed? I work here." I pointed behind me to the Nitro sign hanging above the patio. "At least you're not in jail, right? Can we talk inside? I'm freezing."

She did another survey of the area. "Fine."

I unlocked the front, set my things down on one of the high-top tables, and turned on the lights and heat.

"Why is it so cold in here?" April asked. Her lips had a bluish tint that matched the nasty bruise on her thigh.

"Good question." We kept the brewery at a steady sixty-eight degrees. If the temperature got too low, it would stop the yeast from fermenting. With temps starting to drop into the thirties, it was time to adjust our heat settings.

"What's going on, April? You asked for my help, but you're not telling me everything. I know it. You're limping, you're bruised and scratched and acting like you're in the Witness Protection Program."

"It's the press. I can't let them see me like this. My reputation is at stake." April removed her sunglasses. "I told you everything yesterday. I was supposed to meet Kristopher at my office. When I got there, he was already dead, and Chief Meyers thinks I did it."

"I'm beginning to agree with her, April. You're a mess. You're obviously injured, and you refuse to tell me why. Unless you come clean, the only logical explanation I can come up with is that *you* killed Kristopher."

"NO!" April responded in a shrill tone that was so loud it probably had woken Garrett and Kat. "I fell mountain biking. I've been trying to use extra makeup to cover up all of the bruises and scratches, but it came off. That's all. I've been bruised for a couple of days. There was a tour group in town from San Francisco, and when their biking guide canceled because he had the flu, I stepped in. That's what I do. I would do anything for this town, you know that, Sloan. It's my duty as Leavenworth's ambassador."

I narrowed my eyes. "Like kill off the one person threatening to change our way of life."

"No! How many times do I have to say it? I did not kill Kris." Her voice wavered, like she was about to cry.

I moved toward the bar and flipped on more lights. April followed me.

"Why are you being so weird about falling on your mountain bike? Why didn't you just say that from the beginning?"

April sat on a barstool. "Because it's embarrassing."

"More embarrassing than being arrested for murder?"

She rested her chin on her hands. "No, I told Chief Meyers what happened on the bike. She had to do her 'due diligence,' as she called it, and track down the tour group to confirm my story. I didn't say anything because I bruised my body and my pride."

I walked behind the bar and opened a canister of coffee beans. If I was going to deal with April this early, I needed more coffee. We kept a stash of coffee, teas, and assorted fancy sodas for designated drivers and anyone who didn't imbibe. "April, I was watching the news last night and they showed old footage from Kristopher's first campaign."

Any color that was in her face evaporated.

"I saw you," I said as I scooped coffee into the industrial pot and added water. "You were standing next to him—

wearing one of his campaign T-shirts, and you're the only person in town who calls him Kris. If you want my help, you have to start being honest with me."

"It's not what it looks like." She gnawed on her fingernails, which were still painted with mini Oktoberfest flags.

"What is it, then? You either have to tell me everything or go find someone else to help you."

"No, no, please. I can explain."

Seeing April beg was poetic justice.

"You're right. I did campaign for Kris, but that was many, many years ago. I was just starting my career. I was working as an administrative assistant for the real estate office, and the owner, who I eventually bought the business from, was a good friend of Kris's. He was a backer of Kris's campaign, and I volunteered. I went door-to-door. It was great exposure for me. Working on his campaign launched my career. It cemented me in Leavenworth. I owed him for that."

"I don't understand." The coffee started to percolate, filling the cavernous bar with a wonderful aroma.

"When I first met Kris, I was impressed with his values and his vision for growing our community. Over time, our visions of Leavenworth's future veered in very different directions. I sympathized with his frustrations, don't get me wrong. I know that the festivals bring in a certain level of unwanted outcomes—like extra garbage and excessive drinking. But without them, we would be bankrupt. Kris and I met on more than one occasion, and I tried to negotiate with him to find a middle ground and some viable solutions for better crowd management, but he wouldn't budge."

"Is that why you were meeting with him yesterday?"

April lifted one hand, then the other as if weighing the question. "I suppose in part. Kris was getting ready to run a last-ditch advertising campaign. He knew he was trailing Valerie, but he thought that he had a secret weapon." April paused and pointed to her chest. "Me. He found that old footage that you saw in the news, and he wanted to rerun it with an updated slogan about how Leavenworth's welcome wagon has endorsed him for over twenty years."

"Let me guess, you didn't give him permission to use your endorsement?" I removed two ceramic coffee cups from the open shelves next to the taps and then found a carton of cream in the mini fridge.

"No way." April looked aghast. "Can you imagine? He wouldn't listen. He was going to run the ads without my consent. I told him that if he did, I would take him to court." She pressed her hand lightly on the bruise.

"Did he back off?"

April shook her head. "No. That's why we were going to meet yesterday. I had consulted an attorney. I planned to give Kris a cease-and-desist order. That's why Chief Meyers has focused her attention on me."

"Motive," I replied. Without asking, I poured her a cup of coffee and added a splash of cream. I set it in front of her and then poured a cup for myself.

"Thanks." April wrapped her hands around the cup. "Yes, but I've explained that he didn't have a legal leg to stand on. Why would I kill him when the only thing I needed to do was hand him a piece of paper?"

Fact-check that later, I thought to myself. To April, I said, "Or why wouldn't you just come out and say what you said to me if Kristopher had gone forward with the ad campaign? Everyone in town would have understood that your views had changed."

April frowned. "I guess, but I wasn't about to let Kris take advantage of my celebrity status like that."

Celebrity status? I choked back a snicker. *Don't go there, Sloan.*

"As you can see, it's all circumstantial evidence," April continued. "Chief Meyers doesn't have anything on me, which is why she had to release me."

"That's good news, then. You don't have anything to worry about." I leaned against the back of the bar and sipped my coffee.

"Oh, go slow, Sloan. You're not getting off that easy. You made a promise to help me."

Had I promised? Or was April trying to get me on a technicality?

"You have to help figure out who the real killer is. I won't let my stunning reputation as Leavenworth's ambassador be tarnished by this terrible affair. Have you spoken to Ross yet?"

"Not yet."

"What have you been doing while I've been stuck in jail this entire time?" Her hands remained glued to the coffee cup. She hadn't taken a sip.

"This *'entire* time' is only a single day, April. And for your information, I've been working."

She scoffed. "Working? You mean brewing beer? That's hardly a top priority. There's been a murder in town and your best friend is accused of doing it, and instead of pouring every ounce of energy into solving the case, you've been pouring pints?"

April, my best friend? Oh, good lord, help me.

"I can't have anything to do with this. In fact, I think it would be wise if we weren't seen around the village together for the next few days. That way no one will suspect that we're working together. Start with Ross. I'm telling you he had it out for Kris and he was strong enough to do it."

"What do you mean strong enough?" My curiosity was piqued.

She finally took a sip of the coffee. I recognized the strategy all too well. She was trying to buy time to formulate her words. "I mean in terms of killing him."

I frowned. "Yeah, thanks."

"Okay, here's the thing. I had two—no three—strikes against me. That's why the chief arrested me. Kris was killed in my office, I had a nasty fall and look like I've been in a fight."

"And number three?" I refilled my cup.

She cracked her knuckles. "They think he was killed with something that belongs to me. They haven't found the murder weapon yet, but they're convinced they know what it was."

"What is it?"

April's shoulders heaved. "My ceremonial ribbon cutting scissors. I overheard the chief on the phone. They think that there was an argument that turned violent, and that Kris's killer grabbed whatever was nearby. That happened to be my ribbon cutting scissors. They can't find my scissors. They're missing. The chief has asked me a million times when I saw them last. I can't remember." She looked to me for moral support.

"Those giant scissors?" I flashed to a memory of a picture of

April at the grand opening of The Nutcracker Shoppe, holding a pair of silver scissors that must have been two feet long.

"Yes, I loved those scissors. They symbolize our wonderful business community here in the village. When I got to my office that morning, I noticed that there was a sun-bleached outline on the wall where the scissors usually hang, but I didn't take them down. The killer must have yanked them off the wall." She pressed her nearly full cup of coffee back to me and stood up. "I have to go. See what you can learn from Ross and let's meet in my office later. Use the back entrance." With that she left.

It might have been a mistake, but I believed her. Her story made sense, and no one in Leavenworth had a bigger ego than April. Plus, I had learned something very valuable—how Kristopher had been killed.

I dumped April's coffee into the sink. What had I gotten myself into? April wasn't going to let this go. I was committed now. The only good thing was that she wanted to keep a low profile. That was fine by me. The less we saw of one another, the better for me. And the faster I figured out who killed Kristopher, the sooner April would be out of my hair.

THIRTEEN

I WATCHED APRIL SLINK DOWN the sidewalk. She kept her head low and glanced behind her every so often as if she was worried that she was being followed. She wasn't.

Once April was out of sight, I went to top off my coffee and brew a fresh pot. The scent must have roused Garrett and Kat, who both shuffled into the kitchen not long after the aroma wafted upstairs.

"How did it go last night?" I asked Kat, handing her a mug. "Did it ever pick up?"

"Not really." She rubbed her eyes. "I got a bunch done on the room designs, though, so that's good."

Garrett removed a carton of heavy cream from the fridge. "She wouldn't let me see her ideas until you two go over them, but I could tell from everyone's reaction in the bar that I'm going to like them."

Kat gave me a sheepish smile. "I hope you guys love them. There is one thing. We're going to need to find someone with some artistic talent to design or draw some of the funny beer sayings for the yeast room."

"I know just the person," I said. "My son, Alex, wants to be a graphic designer. He helped us with the bar menus. I'm sure he'd love to help with the room renovations."

"Do you think he would do it?" Kat asked.

"I'm sure. It's great for his portfolio. He's already starting to think about college and design programs. Most of them require a portfolio of sample work."

"Awesome. When can he come by?"

"Maybe after school. I'll text him and ask. He has midterms this week, so I know his class schedule is swapped around, which means he might have some extra time."

"Cool." Kat added enough cream to turn her coffee as pale as wheat. "Do you want to take a look at what I found and then we can show Garrett our sketches?"

Garrett grabbed a bagel. "I know when I'm not wanted. I'll be in the office if you need me, but you probably won't."

"Nah, we won't, will we, Kat?" I teased.

"My own pub, and I'm not even needed." Garrett pretended to be hurt. I enjoyed his playful banter. Garrett was serious about brewing. I appreciated his calculated approach to the process, but I also appreciated that he had a lightness about him too.

"That's what happens when the women are in charge."

"Hey, more power to you." Garrett said, balancing his coffee and bagel. "I was raised by two strong women—my mom and Aunt Tess—so I'm all for letting you two take control. I'm not an idiot. You'll get no pushback from me."

We chuckled.

Then Kat clicked on her phone and scrolled through a dozen images she had saved. We picked our favorites, printed them out, and added them to the ever-growing design file that was overflowing with clippings from magazines, paint swatches, and our notes. "Hopefully, Garrett will like the ideas." Kat tucked her phone into her pocket.

"Garrett would be happy if we covered every wall with old grain sacks," I said.

Kat was about to shut the file, when she remembered something, and started flipping through the piles of assorted papers. "I almost forgot. Someone called here for you last night. I wrote down her name and number on the back of one of these pages."

My stomach dropped. I knew who had called. I didn't need to see the paper. It had to be Sally, my former social worker.

Sally had been responsible for placing me in foster care and checking in periodically over the years. Most foster families I was placed with didn't work out. That meant that I spent more time than usual in Sally's office. She had been my one touch of stability in a rotation of constant change. Sally had introduced me to classical music and sparked my interest in baking and food. She had been the one to suggest that I attend culinary classes at the local community college and had even helped me get scholarship money.

She and I had lost touch once I married Mac, but recently she had resurfaced. We had met at Nitro a few weeks ago, when she showed up with my original case file. Everything in the file had been wiped clean. It was as if my early years in state care didn't exist. Sally was concerned. She had confessed that she had often wondered about my situation. Orders to move me from house to house didn't come from Sally, but rather from her supervisors. She had explained to me that this wasn't typical protocol. She had also told me that she had once tried to adopt me. That news had stung in the most wonderful way. As a child I had dreamed of venturing into Sally's office for a monthly check-in appointment and her leaning over her messy desk and telling me that I had a permanent home with her.

Sally had become convinced that her boss didn't want her or anyone else to find my birth parents. When I had started asking about my past, she went searching for her old files only to find that her notes had vanished. She was sure that someone had intentionally destroyed her notes to make sure I wouldn't have a sliver of information to go on in my search for my birth parents.

I had lived for years under the assumption that my parents didn't want me, that they had abandoned me on the steps of a hospital because they didn't care. Sally's revelation changed that. She thought that the reason they left me was the opposite—because they loved me too much and they were in some kind of trouble that would put me in danger.

Part of me had wondered if Sally might have been a bit paranoid. But then she showed me the file and explained that she made one inquiry for me and suddenly every note in my file vanished. That couldn't be a coincidence. Sally had driven to Leavenworth and refused to discuss anything at length over the phone for fear that someone might be listening. She had been on her way to meet her sister for an Alaskan cruise right after our meeting. We had agreed to be back in touch upon her return. She had made it clear that, in the interim, I should leave the subject alone. We were going to have to figure out a calculated approach.

Kat found the note. "Um, Sally. She said you'll know what it's about."

"Yeah. Thanks."

"Here's the number," Kat said, starting to rip off the top half of a glossy magazine page.

"I have it."

"No. She was very clear. She told me to give you this number and said to tell you it's new."

"Okay."

Kat ripped the rest of the page and handed it to me. I folded it into a square and tucked it into my jeans pocket. I had the sense that Kat wanted to know more. I changed the subject. "Let me text Alex about stopping by after practice and then we can go bombard Garrett with our ideas."

I tried to keep my fingers steady as I texted Alex to ask him if he'd be interested in working on the design project. I already knew the answer but wanted to shoot him a text while it was fresh in my mind. The keypad felt even smaller than normal as I attempted to type a coherent message.

Had Sally found something new? Or was she just calling to check in? I hadn't spoken to her since she had left for the cruise. We had agreed to reconvene once she had returned and had a chance to do some covert digging into what happened to my case files. I wasn't about to risk calling her from here. I would have to wait until later and return her call from the privacy of home.

To get my mind off Sally and Kristopher, Kat and I pitched our plans to Garrett over more coffee.

"When can I start ripping down wallpaper?" Garrett flexed his muscles.

"Have you ever tried taking down wallpaper?" I asked.

He shook his head.

"It's the worst. It's not an easy process." I explained how removing wallpaper involved steaming and hours of scraping.

"That doesn't sound fun." Garrett frowned.

"No, but we have the time now, so if we're going to do it, we might as well take the plunge."

"It sounds like we need supplies," Garrett said.

"We need to start by taking everything out of each room and then assessing what we might be able to repurpose and what we need to donate. I was thinking that since we're in the fermenting process, we can use the brewery as temporary storage."

"That works for me. What's first?"

"First I'll swing by the hardware store and get wallpaper stripper, scrapers, and rubber gloves. Do you two want to start bringing the furniture down and stacking it in the brewery? Kat already knows some of what we think might be worth keeping, right?"

Kat nodded. "There are some real treasures up there. We'll try to salvage as much as we can. My generation loves anything that's been upcycled, so Sloan and I decided not to throw anything away until we've gutted, cleaned, and painted each room."

Garrett looked a bit like a deer in headlights. "Just tell me what to do and how much this is going to cost me."

I laughed. "That's the other goal with reusing some of your aunt's original furniture. It will cut our costs in half."

"Now, that is music to my ears." His smile made his entire face light up.

They went to start moving loads of furniture. I grabbed my wallet and jacket. The hardware store was on the opposite end of the village from Der Keller. I kept a quick pace. I didn't want to risk a run-in with April or Mac. At the moment I couldn't decide which would be worse.

Downtown was humming with press activity and preparations for the light festival. April might not have been paranoid after all. I avoided three reporters, all of whom thrust microphones in my face, asking for a comment on the recent murder. "No thanks," I replied, hurrying across the street. The hardware store was nearly empty. I found the supplies we needed, along with some new paint samples to try.

"Good morning to you, Sloan," the owner replied. "We've had a regular rush for a Friday."

"Oh, really?" I thought he was kidding as I glanced around the vacant store. "Have people been hiding out from the barrage of press?"

"Uh-huh. And Ross, the owner of the Underground, was just here. I guess he's painting the outdoor walkway. It's that time of year. Everyone wants to get projects done before winter sinks in and the tourists come back to look at the pretty lights strung up in trees."

"Right." I paid for my things. I should have gone straight back to Nitro, but knowing that Ross was working on an outside project was the perfect excuse to take the long route. Thankfully, that would keep me away from the eager reporters as well.

I headed toward Blackbird Island. Sunlight filtered through the trees and glistened on the Wenatchee River like falling confetti. The mountains rose like sturdy towers. I paused and took a cleansing breath. *This is why you live here, Sloan.*

Then I continued on to the bar. The Underground's stone façade and intricate stained-glass windows always reminded me of a castle. In order to enter the Underground, guests descended down a pressed-stone ramp into the basement of the property.

When I arrived at the bar, there was painter's tape stretched between two chairs to block the entrance. The closed signs were still posted. Ross stood on the sidewalk. He was dressed for painting in a pair of old holey jeans and a sweatshirt. His bald head reflected the sunlight.

"Hey, Sloan." He stopped stirring a bucket of forest green paint. "What's going on?"

"Projects." I held up a bottle of wallpaper stripper. "Great minds think alike, huh?"

"I guess it's that time of year." He didn't sound very enthusiastic.

"What are you painting?"

Ross pointed to the entrance that led to the tunnel underground. The old green paint was chipped and cracking. "Touch-up. Nothing special, but they're saying it might snow by the first of next week, so I figured I better get a jump on the outside."

"Are you doing interior projects too? Didn't you say something about an electrical issue?"

A strange look crossed over his face. "Yeah, that's right. Electrical and some other stuff. We had to shut down for a couple days to get it all done."

Was it possible that I had misinterpreted what I had seen yesterday? Maybe Ross had been arguing with a contractor about needing to stay open during repairs.

He stabbed the stir stick in the paint bucket. "That's the plan, if I can get the state liquor board off my back."

"Why?"

"Kristopher." He sighed. "I don't have proof that he's the person who called in a complaint with the state, but I mean— come on—he's the guy."

"What happened?" I couldn't believe that Ross was willingly telling me about Kristopher.

"He called in a complaint on every business with a liquor license in town." He wiped green paint on his sweatshirt. "Have you had a nice visit from the state yet?"

I shook my head.

"Don't worry. You will."

"Kristopher was trying to shut you down?"

"He was trying to shut everyone down. I think he realized that his shot at election wasn't looking good, so he decided to try for an alternative—to personally call in violations to the state liquor board."

"What were you violating?"

"Nothing. Kristopher knew that. He didn't care. He was on a singular mission. I'm not sure he was thinking rationally." Ross picked the stir stick up again and began to circle it through the thick paint. "Keep an eye out. I would expect a nice visit from the state any day now if I were you."

"Thanks for the heads-up."

"No problem. We have to stick together."

I decided this was the best opening I might have to ask Ross about what April had seen. "Since we're on the subject, can I ask you something?"

"Shoot."

"Well, I was there when everything blew up at Der Keller after the community meeting. I know that everyone was pretty heated, but I heard from someone that they saw you and Kristopher arguing again much later, after things had calmed down."

Ross dropped the stir stick. Green paint splattered on the sidewalk. "Crap." He reached for a rag and started dabbing the green paint. "Yeah. He and I had a talk. He had some nerve. Did you know he went back over to Der Keller and tried handing out campaign posters? The guy had no shame. Mr. Pious campaigning at the biggest brewery in town while trying to shut us all down. That's rich."

Paint smeared on his fingers as he spoke, but Ross took no notice.

"I confronted him about why the hell he felt like he needed to tattle to the state about me. I've never served a minor in my life. He claimed that we were the bar that overserved the frat guy who threw up on his shoe. He couldn't let it go. I told him that my bartender refused to serve the guy the minute he stumbled into the Underground, but Kristopher didn't believe it. He called the state and said we 'have a practice of routinely serving minors.' My ass. We have a policy of upholding the law. That's what I told Kristopher."

Ross's speech sped up as he recalled the exchange.

"I told him if he didn't call off his dogs, I would throw up on his shoes every time I saw him in the village—while I was stone cold sober."

"It sounds like you were pretty upset."

"Pretty upset?" Ross yelled. "I was pissed, Sloan. You should be too. The man was shady. He tried to pretend like he was this wonderful member of the community who had spent his career 'serving' Leavenworth. He wasn't. He was a prick."

I wondered if April had been on to something. Ross was getting more and more agitated the longer we spoke.

Ross finished dabbing the paint splatters with the rag, then he jabbed the stir stick into the bucket. "Wait a minute— why all the questions? Are you working undercover for Chief Meyers or something? I can tell by the look on your face that you're not asking out of curiosity. You think I'm a suspect or something?"

"I never said that." That wasn't a lie.

"Well, don't worry, I didn't kill him. I didn't need to. I have video footage in the bar to back up my statement. I've already turned that over to the liquor board. What would be my motivation to kill him? I was excited to watch him go down in flames on election day next week."

His response wasn't what I had expected.

"If you want to know who killed the troll, I would talk to Valerie Hedy. She and Kristopher had a wicked fight. I overheard her. She told him she was going to kill him."

"What?"

"Yeah. I already told this to Chief Meyers. I don't know exactly what they were fighting about, but her exact words were 'I will kill you, Kristopher. You're not going to get away with this.'"

"You're sure?"

"Positive." Ross dipped a paintbrush in the paint. "I don't know why the chief is dragging her feet. I'm surprised Valerie isn't already in jail."

I left him to his painting project. Ross seemed adamant that he hadn't killed Kristopher, and his motive was nonexistent if he really had proof that no one had been overserved at the Underground. Valerie had threatened to kill Kristopher. Was there anyone in Leavenworth who didn't want the man dead?

FOURTEEN

STRIPPING LAYERS OF WALLPAPER DISTRACTED me for the remainder of the morning. The thick, sticky wallpaper remover felt like working with slime. Garrett, Kat, and I were splattered with the milky substance. My arms ached from scraping section by section.

"This is going to take an eternity," Garrett complained, stepping back from a two-foot square area he had been scraping for at least an hour. "I had no idea there would be three layers of different wallpaper."

"I think they used to slap another layer over the top of the old paper when they got tired of the design, because it was much easier than doing this."

Kat massaged her shoulder. "At least I might get some new muscles out of it."

"Why didn't we think of that?" Garrett asked.

"Think of what? Muscles?"

He stared at me. "Sloan, you're not firing on all cylinders, are you? I meant why didn't we think of putting new wall-paper up instead of endless scraping?"

"Right." It was true my head felt slightly fuzzy. Some of that could be due to Kristopher's death and the fumes from the wallpaper remover, but most of it was because I had to meet Mac for lunch soon. "We're making progress."

"At a snail's pace." Garrett stood back to survey the bed-room. "This is only one room. We might need to rethink our plan if we're going to try and get everything done and the guest rooms listed before the holiday festivities."

He was right. This was going to take forever. "You know, let me call Ursula. I remember her renting a steam machine to strip wallpaper years ago when they did the first round of expansions at Der Keller. I'll ask her whether that was more efficient."

There had to be a better way. "I have a lunch appointment," I said, wiping the sticky paste on a towel. "I'll check in with Ursula and let you know what she has to say." I didn't mention that my lunch meeting was at Der Keller. Not that Garrett would mind that I was fraternizing with the enemy. There was no such sentiment in the beer world. Maybe for a rare brewer, but the craft beer community was known for embracing col-laborations and promoting one another's products.

Kat held up her hands that looked as if she'd dipped them in the thick paste. "I'm going to take a shower and get ready to open the bar, as long as that's cool?"

Garrett nodded. "Yeah. I think we could all use some fresh air. The fumes are starting to make me see stars." We had cracked the window in the bedroom, but it was true that there was an overwhelming chemical smell. To me he said,

"Let's reconvene after lunch and see if we even want to continue with this slop."

I didn't spend an extra second changing or checking my appearance before my meeting with Mac. The worse I looked, the better.

I strolled along Front Street past the huge construction lifts where city workers were concentrating on hanging lights from the highest points of each building's roof peak. The media circus continued near the gazebo. I spotted Chief Meyers in the center of the action. Was she hosting a press conference because there'd been new developments in the investigation?

Mac was notoriously late for everything. It wouldn't hurt if I listened in for a few minutes. I stood at the edge of the crowd. A reporter asked the chief about potential suspects.

Chief Meyers took command. "As I've repeated, we have a number of persons of interest in this case, and my team is pursuing every lead." She narrowed her intelligent eyes toward the reporter's camera. "We are asking the public that if anyone has any information pertinent to the investigation, you come to the station immediately."

I was impressed by how deftly she ignored the dozens of hands that flew in the air and the following assault of questions:

"Would you call this a crime of passion?"

"Is Beervaria as we know it dead?"

"How safe are the charming streets of Leavenworth?"

"Will you cancel the light festival if the killer isn't caught?"

For a second I lost track of the chief's responses, because about twenty feet away I spotted someone crouched behind an oak tree. At first I thought it was one of the workers on a lunch break, but at closer glance, the person appeared to be eavesdropping on the press conference. That didn't make sense. There was no need to hide. The press conference was taking place in the middle of the public park.

I shielded my eyes from the sun and squinted to try and get a better look. Could that be right? It was Valerie Hedy. Why would she be spying on the press conference?

Chief Meyers cleared her throat, turning my attention away from Valerie. "I can assure you that Leavenworth is one of the safest places to live and visit. There is no talk of canceling the festival. As to your other questions, as I have explained, this is an open investigation and I cannot comment at this time. Thank you." She ambled off the gazebo stage toward me, as a few reporters tried unsuccessfully to get further comment.

I looked back to the oak tree. Valerie had vanished.

"Afternoon, Sloan." Chief Meyers gave me a curt nod in way of a greeting.

"You handled that well." I glanced to the throng of reporters summarizing the chief's statement. "I've never seen this many press in town."

"Slow news cycle." She adjusted the walkie-talkie that was clipped to her waist. "Which way are you going?"

"To Der Keller." I motioned across the street.

"I'll walk with you."

"April stopped by the pub this morning," I said as we crossed the street. "She said that you think the murder weapon is her ceremonial ribbon cutting scissors."

Chief Meyers made sure the press were out of earshot.

"That's right. My guys are trying to track down the murder weapon, but the coroner's report confirmed my suspicions. Kristopher was killed with a large, sharp object. The stab wounds in his stomach are consistent with something like the scissors."

I shuddered at the thought. "How gruesome."

"Murder is always gruesome, Sloan. Doesn't matter how it's done."

She had a point.

"April also mentioned that there might have been a struggle."

"Did she now? Can't imagine April sharing sensitive information."

I had to smile. This was as close as the chief got to joking. "Is it safe to assume that this wasn't a premeditated murder?"

She stopped and waited for two elderly women carrying stacks of paper lantern supplies to pass. Volunteers were already beginning to stage activities, like lantern making, at the Festhalle. "It's never safe to assume anything, but my best guess at the moment is that our killer was in a rage and got hold of whatever was convenient."

"If that's the case, you might need to arrest everyone in the village."

"Kristopher didn't do himself any favors. Which, if you think of it, is a strange campaign strategy." Her walkie-talkie crackled. We arrived at Der Keller. "This is your stop. Let me know if you hear anything new."

"Will do." I was glad that she had confirmed what April had told me. If the killer had acted in a moment of intensity, then that kept Valerie and Ross high on my list.

Der Keller was buzzing with a lunch crowd. The patio doors had been opened, allowing natural light and the crisp fall air in. I thought about how many lunches I had spent here throughout the years, pouring pints, chatting with customers, sitting on the patio nibbling on pretzels dipped in cheesy beer sauce, and laughing with the Krause family. It was a struggle not to feel like an outsider now.

I spotted Mac at the bar. He was chatting with one of the young beertenders behind the bar. Shocker. The young woman wore the traditional Der Keller barmaid's red-and-white-checkered dress with a short, ruffled skirt and plunging neckline.

Not surprisingly, my *husband* was flirting as if his life depended on it. *It might,* I thought as I walked to the bar. I wanted to throttle him, but instead I cleared my throat and waited for him to come out of his barmaid trance.

"Oh, hey, Sloan, you snuck up on me." He gave the slightest shudder as if trying to force himself to stop staring at the pretty young thing pouring his pint. "What happened to you? You're a mess."

"Nice to see you, too." I pointed to the patio. "Shall we?"

The barmaid handed him two pints. "I ordered for you," he said, handing me a Der Keller glass stein.

I could tell from the color of the beer that it was a Doppelbock. A strong choice for a lunchtime pint. I wondered if Mac was hoping that the beer's high ABV content would help ease my response to him putting our son in the middle of our battle.

Little did he know that I was already in the loop. I was sure he had hoped to take me by surprise.

"Seriously, what are you brewing at Nitro?" Mac asked, letting his eyes travel from my head to my waist. "You're covered in—what is that? Glue?"

"Wallpaper stripper."

"Wallpaper stripper? What are you guys doing over there?"

I didn't intend to give Mac any insider information about our plans to open beer-themed guest rooms. "A little sprucing up."

He narrowed his eyes as he sat at a hand-carved picnic table next to a trellis. In the spring and summer, hop vines snaked up the trellis, but they had been cut back for the winter. "What do you need to spruce up? You just opened."

"I'm not here to talk about Nitro." I sat across from him.

"Is this how it's going to go with us, Sloan? We're going to snap at each other and be bitter?"

It took every ounce of self-control not to reach across the table and punch him. "I'm not snapping at you. I'm simply telling you that my work life is off-limits. As for being bitter, I think you lost any right to comment on my feelings after I caught you with the beer wench." I paused and took a long sip of the Doppelbock. "I'm here to talk about our son."

Mac's ruddy cheeks lost some of their color. "Listen, Sloan, I don't want to fight. I've told you a thousand times that I made a mistake. A stupid mistake. But you won't let me make it right."

"You don't need to make it right. What's done is done. It's time for us to figure out how we move forward from here."

"You mean apart." His face reminded me of when Alex was younger and would come inside for a Band-Aid after scraping his knee.

"Yes, I mean apart." I didn't try to sugarcoat it for him.

There was no chance of our reconciling. As angry as I was at him, there was no point in giving him false hope. It would just make things harder for me in the long run.

"You won't even consider counseling?"

Was it just the lighting, or had he bleached his hair? It looked blonder.

After I had caught Mac with the beer wench, he had given his full attention to trying to make amends. From overflowing flower arrangements at my doorstep to handwritten notes expressing his love and sincere regret, he had made a concerted effort to apologize. His latest kick was couples' counseling. *Sloan, we've hit a rough patch,* he had said, offering me a brochure for an intensive couples' therapy retreat. *Lots of people go through what we're experiencing. We just need to get our groove back.*

I had wondered if he was reading Terry McMillan novels. *How many couples attending this retreat caught their partner fooling around with a twentysomething?* I had retorted at the time. That had shut him up. He had dropped the subject of any potential reconciliation. Until now.

"Mac, we've already been through this."

"But, Sloan, you can't throw away years of good times— wonderful times—because of one mistake."

"One pretty huge mistake, Mac."

He fiddled with a bar napkin. "I know."

The problem with Mac was that I got very little satisfaction in making him feel bad for cheating on me. He was doing a fine job of self-loathing without any help from me.

"Mac, listen, we've talked about this at length. I can't overlook the fact that you cheated on me, but I also know that wasn't our only problem. That was one of many."

"That's why I don't understand why you aren't willing to give counseling a shot. We can work through our problems, Sloan. I know we can. You're the strongest person I've ever met in my life. We can get through this." He reached for my hand. I didn't pull away. Not because I wanted to be comforted by Mac, but because I could see how much pain he was in.

His cheating had been a catalyst of self-reflection for me. I had been unhappy for years, but I had stayed for what I was now coming to understand were all the wrong reasons. I had been convinced that Alex needed a stable nuclear family. But now I realized that my happiness mattered too. I didn't want to model suffering through an unhappy marriage for Alex. Or send a message that putting my own dreams on hold was the right way to live. Mac was right about one thing. I was strong. I was strong enough to know that our "marriage" had ended many, many years ago, and once I had understood that, there was no going back. There was no getting our groove back or coming through a rocky patch. We were done. The sooner he realized it too, the sooner we could maybe even become friends.

CHAPTER

FIFTEEN

MAC SHIFTED UNCOMFORTABLY. "SLOAN, YOU are the most maddening woman I've ever known."

"I can live with that." I set my beer on the table. "Should we talk about Alex?"

"What about Alex?" He leaned against the hop fence.

"Mac, don't do this. Let's try and talk like adults."

"Do what?' He yanked a wilted hop from the vine and crushed it in his hand.

"I know you already talked to Alex about moving in with you."

His fist squeezed the hop tighter. "I don't know what you mean."

This was not going to be easy. I had hoped that Mac would be mature for once, but I should have known it would go like this. "Alex told me that you asked him to go look at a couple of places."

"So?"

"So, what are you planning?"

"I'm planning to get out of that stupid hotel room. Do you know what it's like being cooped up in a hell hole for weeks on end?"

His spacious hotel suite was hardly a "hell hole."

"April is going to show me a condo that overlooks the Wenatchee River near Blackbird Island and a penthouse apartment in a new development over by the high school. I asked Alex to come to help me decide and so that he can pick out his room."

"That's it right there." I stopped him. "His room. We haven't even begun to discuss arrangements for where he's going to live once the divorce is final, and you're already dragging him into this."

"Why do you always think the worst of me, Sloan?" Mac sounded genuinely injured. "You're jumping to conclusions without even giving me a chance to explain."

I was quiet.

"I'm not going to fight you for custody, Sloan. Alex loves you more than anything in this world. I assumed that he would live with you but come stay with me a night or two a week and every other weekend, like we've been doing since you kicked me out."

Technically he had left by choice when I asked him to, but I didn't bring that up.

"I want him to come with me, so he can feel like he's a part of the decision. I know it's going to suck for him to go back and forth between our places. I think it already does for him. He asked me the other day about whether he could have a couple of drawers in the dresser, so he could leave some stuff at the hotel. I know that I screwed up with you and with Alex, and I'm just trying to do the best I can to make it up to him."

Mac kicked a leaf on the rustic tiled patio floor. "Sloan, give me a little more credit, okay?"

"Okay." I felt bad. Mac and I had struggled for years, but he was a good dad. I couldn't take that away from him. He had been involved and active in Alex's life since the day he was born. It wasn't just for show. Mac and Alex were exceptionally close. They used to spend hours building elaborate LEGO cities on the living room floor, camping out in the backyard, and going for long weekend rafting trips on the Wenatchee River. Mac was a hands-on dad. He adored Alex as much as I did. Alex had been our one point of connection as things became cool between us over the last few years.

"Sloan, you can't really think I'm going to try and pull Alex into a battle with us, can you?"

"No. I guess not. I hadn't expected Alex to say anything about you moving into a permanent place. It took me by surprise."

"Temporary."

"What?"

"I never said the place I'm getting is going to be permanent. I've talked to my folks, and I know it might take you some time to really forgive me, but I'm not giving up on us."

"Mac, you should." I took another sip of beer. Nearby I saw one of the lifts raise a worker fifty feet in the air so that he could reach the top of the tree. "I apologize for jumping to conclusions and thinking the worst, but I don't want to give you false hope. I'm proceeding with the divorce."

He tossed the crushed hop on the ground. "That's fine, but that doesn't mean that I can't keep trying to win you back."

There was no point in responding. We were destined to continue to circle in a never-ending loop. I was glad that he was moving on—at least to the point of finding an apartment—and I was relieved to hear that he wasn't intending to go to war over custody of Alex. That was enough for the moment.

"Hey, is your mom around?" I asked.

He nodded across the street. "She was over in the bottling plant earlier. Why?"

"I have a wallpaper question for her."

"I'm sure she'd love to see you, if she's still around." Mac paused. He looked like he was going to say more, but he shook his head and stood up. "Come on, I'll walk over with you." He extended his hand to help me off the bench.

I took it. It was hard to remember that there had once been a time when his touch had sent shivers up my spine. Now it felt like holding the hand of an old friend. As soon as I was on my feet, I dropped his hand.

Der Keller's brewing operation was the biggest industry in the village. We exited the patio and crossed Front Street to the bottling plant, where dozens of workers bottled, packaged, and shipped Der Keller's award-winning German beers. Otto stood near the conveyor belt. He wore a pair of safety goggles over his reading glasses and peered at a sheet of labels.

"Ah, Mac and Sloan! I didn't see you come in," he said when he noticed us. He handed Mac the sheet of labels and kissed my cheek. "Look at ziz. It does not seem centered, does it?"

Mac studied the labels briefly. Then he held the sheet up

to the light and tilted it about twenty degrees. "No, these are totally off."

"*Ja.* Ziz is what I tink." Otto scratched his head. "I do not know how dis happened. We have been using the same printer for years." He motioned to a crew member to shut off the system. Once the conveyor belt had stopped, he picked up a bottle and showed it to us. The crooked label was immediately evident.

"We're going to have to sell these at a discounted rate in dock sales," Mac said to his father. "Good thing you caught it now."

"*Ja.* We will have to see how many bottles are in ziz batch."

Dock sales were a way for larger breweries like Der Keller to offload extra products or flops, like a beer with a wonky label. Twice a week, Der Keller opened its loading dock to the public where they could purchase cases of beer at a discounted rate.

"Did you need something, Sloan?" Otto asked, after explaining to the waiting staff that they would need to check every bottle that had gone down the line in the past hour.

"Is Ursula here?" I asked.

Otto took off his safety glasses. "*Ja,* she is maybe in with delivery?"

"I'll check." I left him and Mac trying to figure out if any of the mislabeled bottles could be salvaged and went to see if Ursula was in the back. In addition to bottling, Der Keller had a fleet of delivery vans that distributed their beer throughout the Pacific Northwest. I found her double checking the drivers' delivery schedules. Ursula walked with the support of a cane due to her recent surgery, but aside from that, there was nothing slight or meek about her stature. She commanded a serene, yet forceful presence.

"Sloan!" Her face lit up when she saw me. She shuffled toward me.

"Ursula, how are you?" I greeted her with a long hug.

"I am vonderful. Ziz cane, it is making me angry, but otherwise I am good. How are you, my dear?"

"Good." It was a half-truth. "I was hoping that you might be able to give me some suggestions on taking down wallpaper."

Ursula made a gagging face. "Oh, ziz is the vorst project. Do you remember when we took down the old wallpaper here?"

"Yeah. Didn't you use some kind of a steam machine?"

"*Ja.* It was no fun, but ze steamer, it was better."

"Where did you get one?"

"I still have it. It is in ze closet at home. Would you like to borrow it?"

"You still have it? Yes, I'd love to borrow it."

"I hope zat it still works. It has been many, many years of sitting in ze closet, but you are velcome to use it."

"That would be great. I can swing by after work and pick it up, if that's okay."

"*Ja.* Sure. I made ze bee sting cake last night. You and Alex should come to dinner. We can catch up and zen I will give you ze steamer."

I hesitated. As much as I wanted to have dinner with Otto and Ursula, it felt weird to invade their family time, especially given the awkward state of things between me and Mac.

"Sloan, you come. It will be just us and you and Alex, *ja?*" Ursula must have sensed my resistance.

"If you're sure?"

"*Ja,* I am sure. We would love to see you, and I made your favorite cake. Do you remember ze first time you tasted it?"

I thought back to the memory of Ursula's delicious cake. She called it a bee sting cake for me, but the traditional German name was a *Bienenstich*. A yeast cake, almost like a sweet bread with pastry cream and almonds toasted in honey, butter, and heavy cream. Ursula had made the cake on one of my first family dinners. I'm not much of a fan of sugary cakes, but the *Bienenstich* was beautifully balanced, and Ursula's homemade pastry cream was a thing of legend. I had eaten two generous slices and would have gone back for thirds if I hadn't been worried that my stomach might revolt.

Ursula remembered that I enjoyed the cake and had made it for my birthday every year since.

"Yes, it's the best thing I've ever eaten. You made one last night? It's not even my birthday."

"*Ja.* I know, but I had a feeling zat maybe you might be coming to dinner." Ursula gave me a knowing grin. "Come by anytime. I will cook some stew."

My mouth watered at the thought of an Ursula meal. I knew that Alex wouldn't turn down his grandmother's cooking either. We agreed upon a time. Before I left Der Keller, I shot Alex a text, asking him to come by Nitro after practice and informing him of our dinner plans.

I should have felt relieved as I returned to Nitro, but instead I felt nostalgic. Otto and Ursula had done everything they possibly could to make me feel like I was still a member of the Krause family, and yet I knew in my heart that as soon as the divorce was final, I was technically on my own again.

CHAPTER

SIXTEEN

AS PLANNED, GARRETT, KAT, AND I regrouped after lunch. Kat had opened the bar and was filling small wooden bowls with peanuts. Garrett was testing the taps.

"I vote that we give that a try tomorrow morning," he said. He had swapped his wallpaper-scraping attire for a pair of jeans and a gray Nitro hoodie with our atomic logo of the beer elements. "I don't know about you two, but I'm happy to spend the rest of the afternoon pouring pints and chatting with customers."

"Alex agreed to stop by after school. Maybe we can start brainstorming some ideas for the posters with him," I said to Kat.

"Oh yeah, totally. I've been pinning stuff like crazy on my Pinterest boards. He's going to think I'm nuts."

"He's fifteen. I think he'll be thrilled to be part of this."

Garrett went to check on the gravity of our holiday beers.

Brewers use different techniques when it comes to checking the gravity. Some check two or three times near the end of the fermentation process but otherwise leave their beer alone to do its thing. Garrett was slightly more obsessive. He measured the decline of sugar every day (or even multiple times a day) to get a sense of how the beer was progressing.

I went to help Kat in the tasting room, which had a decent post-lunch crowd, including a table of retirees who had decided to take the train from Seattle for a quick midweek getaway. I spent a good thirty minutes chatting with them and giving them a rundown of our beer selection. One woman asked if it would be possible to see our brewing operations, and I happily obliged. Beer education was one of my favorite parts of the job. I loved getting to share my knowledge. It never failed that tour groups would leave slightly awestruck about the many steps and variables involved in brewing. I hoped that they also left with a new appreciation of beer's many nuanced flavors and with some tips on how to expand their tasting repertoire.

After the tour, I poured the group a tasting tray and had them put their newfound beer education to the test. I smiled as they took turns holding each tasting glass to their nose before sipping. They were quick studies. I was impressed with how easily they identified the citrus tones in our Pucker Up IPA and the earthy chocolate notes in our stout.

I left them to their expert tasting and went outside to check on the patio tables. Nitro's small patio didn't rival Der Keller's, but we had created an intimate, cozy outside seating area in the enclosed space with a collection of small wrought-iron bistro tables and potted plants. Once the snow began to fall, we'd have to bring everything inside, but for the moment, locals were soaking up the lingering late-afternoon sun.

A group of city light installers took up one of the tables and a small crowd wearing Valerie Hedy T-shirts had pushed together a collection of two-person tables. I took their orders and when I returned with a tray of drinks, Valerie Hedy had joined her campaign team. I delivered the contractors' drinks and took a minute to think about how I might approach Valerie. As it turned out, I didn't need a reason. She gave me a friendly wave.

"Sloan, good to see you," she said as I passed around drinks to her campaign volunteers. "Did you get a sign for the window? We'd absolutely love to have your support." She pointed to the young man sitting next to her, who produced a poster from his saddlebags. "Please take a couple. As you know, the election is next week, and we're counting on your support."

I took two of the posters with Valerie's face plastered on them along with the slogan LET THE BEER FLOW. VOTE FOR VALERIE HEDY, PROUD CITIZEN OF BEERVARIA.

"Is it even an issue now that you're the only one running?" I asked.

Valerie glanced at her team. "It's even more important now than ever before. Who knows what Kristopher's campaign might have up their sleeve? I wouldn't put it past them to try something sneaky."

"Like what?"

"A special election, asking the council to appoint someone rather than have the election go on as planned. There are several possibilities, and my team and I are reviewing every single one of them. Isn't that right?" She waited for her volunteer crew to nod in agreement. "Do you happen to have a minute to chat in private?"

I couldn't believe the stars had aligned. I wanted nothing more than a chance to speak to Valerie alone and see if there was any merit to what Ross had told me. "Sure, would you like to come inside?"

Valerie stood. She advised the volunteers not to imbibe too much. "Remember we still have dozens of doors to knock upon this afternoon."

I took her inside and back to the office. "Have a seat," I said, gathering up some of our notes and sketches for the upstairs remodel.

"What's all this?" Valerie asked. "It looks like fun."

I explained our plans to open up the inn to beer tourism.

"Brilliant. Absolutely brilliant idea. Yet another reason to hang those in the front window," she said, pointing to her campaign posters, which I had set on the desk. "We absolutely cannot run the risk of Kristopher getting elected postmortem."

"Are you sure that can happen? I heard part of your speech at Kuchen last night, and it sounded like the city council was going to make a decision about how the election would proceed."

Valerie took one of the posters and rolled it up into a tube. "Unfortunately, I'm sure. More than sure. I confirmed everything with the mayor this morning. I make it my job to be sure of everything. You can't be too careful in politics, especially in small-town politics, you know?"

I nodded. Although I wasn't entirely certain I did know. Valerie was obsessed with the idea of losing to a dead man.

"The numbers looked good on paper, but believe it or not, Kristopher has a rabid following. I wouldn't put it past them to try something underhanded next week."

"Like what?"

Valerie shrugged. "I don't have any solid details, but there are some rumors swirling that are pretty nasty and not in line with Leavenworth's family values."

"I don't understand."

She glanced at the door. "Do you mind if we close that?"

"Sure." I got up and shut the door.

"Sloan, I know that we don't know each other very well, but I have respected and admired your work for many years. You're a pillar of this community, and I feel like I can trust you to be discreet. If I share something with you, can I count on you to keep this between us?" She unrolled her campaign poster and then scrunched it up into a tube again.

A pillar of the community? That was an exaggeration, to say the very least.

"Of course." I was surprised that Valerie wanted to share a secret with me. We had known each other as acquaintances since I'd first moved to Leavenworth. With only two thousand people in town, it was impossible not to know everyone, but Valerie and I had never spent time alone together or connected socially. I knew her from community meetings and town events, and had served her a number of times at Der Keller.

She let out a long sigh. "I'm telling you this because I know that you've recently been through a bit of drama with Mac, and you handled it so well—so professionally. You never seemed to let the gossip mill here in the village rattle you. I'd really appreciate your input on a touchy issue."

"Okay." I had no idea where Valerie was going with this.

"Many, many years ago in college, I made a stupid mistake." She stabbed the top of her thigh with the tubular poster.

"You're not alone in that."

She tried to smile. "Yes, but when you run for public office, your past mistakes have a way of haunting you."

I waited for her to continue.

"You know what Oktoberfest is like for college students, right?" She squeezed the poster so tight that the tube folded in half.

"Yeah. Having lived here for decades, I think I've seen it all." I chuckled.

Valerie frowned. "I came to Leavenworth for the first time with a group of my sorority sisters my junior year of college. I fell in love with the town and surrounding mountains immediately. In fact, as soon as I graduated, I moved here."

"That's a recurring theme in the village."

"Yes, but let's just say that I wasn't on my best behavior while I was here for Oktoberfest that first year. I drank way too much, as college students tend to do."

I nodded.

"I got really plastered, and I made a stupid, stupid mistake."

"Okay." I couldn't imagine what Valerie was referencing. Most college students who came to Leavenworth for Oktoberfest came to imbibe.

"My sorority sisters and I rented a guesthouse at the end of town, and one night after we were kicked out of the tents, we stumbled home and decided that it would be fun to give everyone on the sidewalk below us a show." She laid the poster on the desk and tried to smooth it out. The attempt was futile. The poster was wrinkled and crumpled. There was no chance of rescuing it.

"A show?"

She buried her face in hands. "Yes. We went topless and flashed everyone from the upstairs balcony of the villa. It was stupid, Sloan. A drunken mistake. I was a straight-A student in college. I came to blow off some steam and ended up making a poor choice that I've regretted for years."

"I don't get it, Valerie. I mean, of course, I understand that it's an embarrassing memory, but you were young and drunk. We've all done stupid things that we regret."

"I wish it was just that." She sighed again. "Someone recorded video of our drunken escapades. I never knew that a video existed until last week when I received a threatening note from Kristopher telling me to drop out of the race or else he would release the video."

"What?" Add blackmail to the ever-growing list of Kristopher's seedy campaign tactics.

"I have no idea how he found the video. He must have done some serious digging to come up with it." She twisted a piece of hair around her finger and then yanked it from her head.

I winced in response.

"The man was insane. I tried to talk to him, to reason with him, but he wouldn't hear it. He knew that I was in the lead, and he was desperate. Why would he do something so terrible? If that video gets out, it will kill my chances of getting elected and ruin my career."

I hated to admit it, but Ross's theory that Valerie could have killed Kristopher was looking more likely. She obviously had a major motive. Not only did killing him basically guarantee her a win, but it also ensured that he couldn't release the embarrassing video.

I wasn't sure how to respond.

Valerie stood and paced in front of the whiteboard. "I'm sorry to burden you with this, Sloan, but like I said, you held yourself with such strength and grace in the face of town gossip about your husband." She gave me an awkward, apologetic smile. "Sorry—I mean about Mac. I know he's soon to be your ex."

"Yep." I tried to steer the conversation away from me. "Was there anything you needed?"

"No, I should let you go, but I would love to have your official support for my campaign, and personally, I'd love any advice you might be able to offer about what I should do if the video somehow surfaces in the days before the election."

Maybe I should have been flattered that Valerie had been impressed by how I had handled Mac's infidelity, but her praise made me cringe internally. "I don't understand. Kristopher is dead. How would the video get out?"

"That's the thing. I have no idea how many people he shared it with. For all I know, he and his campaign planned to release it this weekend—right before the election, to sink my chances. I've been walking around on eggshells, waiting for my phone to blow up. The worst part is that the village is swarming with press. Every time I see someone with a camera, I hide or run away. I'm waiting for it all to come crashing down any moment."

Ah, so that might explain why I had seen Valerie hiding behind the oak tree in Front Street Park. Or it could be a convenient excuse. Maybe she had seen me staring and had crafted this story to distract me.

I thought for a moment before responding. "My advice, if the video does get released, is to stay calm and own up to your mistake. People in Leavenworth are reasonable. There might be a few gossips who will get a good laugh at your expense, but most people won't even give it a second thought."

"You don't understand the magnitude of this, though. I have long-term hopes for higher office. City council is a stepping-stone to running for state government, and maybe more after that. If this video gets released, my political career is dead." She shook her head. "I could have killed Kristopher myself. I'm not surprised someone beat me to it. For all of Kristopher's pious talk of the evils of alcohol, the man didn't have an ethical bone in his body."

CHAPTER

SEVENTEEN

VALERIE'S PITCH GREW SHARPER AS she continued to speak.
"Righteous Kristopher had to turn a city council election into
a slanderous campaign. Part of me wants to call a press conference and tell everyone that he was basically blackmailing
me. Either I dropped out of the election, or he would release
the topless video of me. Can you believe it?"

I shook my head. "It's too bad that it turned ugly."

"It didn't turn ugly. He made it ugly."

Her polished exterior was showing signs of cracking. "Can I
get you a drink? A beer maybe? Hops are a known relaxant,"
I offered.

"No. I'm fine. Sorry, was I just yelling? I guess I'm worked
up about the situation and on edge because I'm waiting to get
a phone call any minute informing me that my picture is plastered on the news from here to Florida. This will make national headlines if it gets out. I guarantee it will go viral."

"Are you sure? I don't think you need to worry about that. Leavenworth's city council seat isn't exactly headline news."

"Have you seen the crews around? I've been avoiding the Seattle reporters like the plague. You know the old saying 'All politics is local'?"

I nodded.

"This is a prime example of local political drama. One of the candidates is murdered, and his opponent has a viral video. I can see the headlines now. It's complete and utter disaster. I'm sure the minute the video is leaked, I'll become the prime suspect. I wouldn't be surprised to see national news outlets begin to descend on the village."

"Since you mentioned it, I have a question about Kristopher's death."

"What?"

"I heard from someone in town that they saw you arguing with him after the incident at Der Keller the other night and that you went so far as to threaten to kill him."

Valerie's jaw hung open. "Who told you that?" Then under her breath she muttered, "I was so careful."

"Careful about what?" I wasn't about to pretend like I hadn't heard that comment.

She pounded her forehead with the palm of her hand. "It's not what you think. I can tell from your reaction that now you're wondering if I did kill him."

"I didn't say that."

"You didn't have to." She looked to the ceiling. "It's true. Kristopher and I got in a fight the night he was killed, and I did say something like, 'If you share that video publicly, it will be the last thing you do.' But I didn't mean the last thing as in murdering him. I meant it in terms of his political career. I was trying to warn him that releasing the video would have unwanted effects on him, too. Digging up old dirt on me certainly wasn't going to strengthen his righteous image. I was pissed at him, but I didn't kill him. I have an alibi. I was with my campaign team all night. We had an emergency meeting back at my house to map out a damage-control strategy in case the video did get leaked."

"So your campaign team knows about the video?"

Valerie gave me an incredulous stare. "Yes, they know about the video. They know about everything. You can never be too prepared when it comes to running a political campaign. We've left nothing to chance. We've dotted every 'i' and crossed every 't.' I refused to play dirty, like Kristopher, but that didn't mean that we were going to lie down and die— we were intending to fight."

It was hard to get a read on Valerie. She seemed to be contradicting herself. "Your campaign team was at your house the night that Kristopher was killed?"

"Yes. We pulled an all-nighter. Three of my team ended up sleeping on the floor and couch. We never left."

She was either telling the truth or trying to establish an alibi. Her answer sounded slightly rehearsed.

"Have you spoken with Chief Meyers?"

"Only about twenty times. The chief has interviewed every member of my campaign team. Each of them has confirmed that they were with me the entire night. It would have been impossible for me to kill Kristopher."

The fact that her loyal campaign volunteers were vouching for her wasn't exactly a solid alibi in my opinion. They could be lying for her, or she could have snuck out when they fell asleep, killed Kristopher, and returned home unnoticed. That happened in the movies. Why couldn't it happen in Leavenworth?

"I know that Chief Meyers is doing her job, but I'm getting tired of her recurring questions about my whereabouts when Kristopher was killed. She must have asked me a dozen times exactly what time I fell asleep and who was at my house. We were in crisis mode. I don't remember when I finally fell asleep, but I know for sure that I didn't kill him."

It felt like we were stuck in an endless loop. Valerie continued to insist on her innocence, and I had no idea whether I should believe her or not. At least Chief Meyers was already in the loop. The fact that she had questioned Valerie more than once must have meant she had some suspicions about her story, too.

She glanced at her watch. "Is that the time? I need to go. Thanks for listening and for the advice, Sloan. I'm sorry I'm such a mess at the moment, but I'm sure you can understand how much stress I'm under."

"Yeah."

"And you'll keep this conversation between us?"

"Absolutely." I opened the door.

Valerie gave me an awkward hug before returning to the bar. I wasn't sure what to think. She had been insistent that she hadn't killed Kristopher and gone out of her way to make sure that I knew she had an alibi, yet it seemed like she had the most to gain by killing him. She had basically guaranteed herself a win. Then there was the issue of the video. Was she lying? What if she had killed Kristopher to get the tape? That would have been one way of ensuring the old footage was never released.

I was more confused than ever. Valerie didn't strike me as a killer, but I had been wrong in the past. And I had learned that people can and will do unexpected and out-of-character things—like murder—when they feel like they don't have any choices. Had that happened to Valerie? Was she desperate enough for a win and to maintain her reputation?

"Mom?" Alex's voice made me startle.

"Hey, I didn't hear you come in," I said, standing to give him a hug.

"I said Mom, like, three times. You were spacing."

"Probably true." I ruffled his hair. "How was the test?"

"Fine." He tossed his backpack and soccer gear on the floor. "I think I did well."

"I'm sure you did."

He looked around the tidy office. "Do you have any snacks? I'm starving."

"Shocker." I laughed. "Is there ever a time that you're not starving?"

"No. But cut me some slack. Coach made us run five miles at practice."

"I'll grab something for you in the kitchen and go see if Garrett can take over for Kat in the bar, so we can go over our ideas with you. Remember we're doing dinner at Oma and Opa's tonight. Pace yourself on the snacks, rumor has it that Oma is making her Bienenstich cake."

Alex pretended to wipe drool from the corner of his mouth. "Forget the snack. I'll save myself for cake."

"I'll find you something light." I left to put a plate of apples, crackers, and cheese together for Alex and see if Kat was free to chat.

Garrett was already at the bar.

"Mind if I steal Kat for a few?" I asked, balancing the plate of snacks for Alex and a bowl of popcorn for the bar.

Garrett reached for the popcorn. "I think it's a fair trade. Kat for a bowl of your delicious fresh popped corn."

"Thanks a lot." Kat curled her lip.

"No, that's high praise," Garrett replied. "Sloan's popcorn is the stuff of legends. I guarantee this entire bowl will be gone by the time you two come back."

The popcorn had been a hit. I made a mental reminder to order some red-and-white-striped bags to serve it in. We'd been putting it in our wooden pub bowls, but bagging it would allow our customers to take it to go as well.

Kat and I returned to the office, where Alex had turned on my laptop and opened his design program.

"Alex, you remember Kat, right?"

He stood and wiped his palms on his warm-up pants. "Hey, how's it going?"

Was it my imagination, or had he intentionally tried to make his voice sound deeper?

Kat grinned, revealing her dimples. "Thanks for agreeing to help with this. I'm pretty good at taking photos, but design isn't really my thing."

Alex cleared his throat. He squared his shoulders as he spoke. "It's cool. I'm trying to build my portfolio for college."

"Do you know where you want to go yet?"

I almost interjected something about the fact that Alex was only a sophomore, but I didn't want to mortify him. It was apparent from the way he was fidgeting that he had a crush. I couldn't blame him. Kat was attractive and radiated a natural energy. She was also seven years older than him. The odds of her reciprocating his feelings were nonexistent.

Alex had had a girlfriend, but they had been on-again, off-again for the past few months. Whenever I asked him about how things were going with Carly, he would mumble something noncommittal.

Kat pulled a chair next to the desk and sat down. Alex pointed to the open seat in front of the laptop. "Do you want to sit, Mom?"

"Oh, my gosh, what a gentleman." Kat's jaw dropped open as she turned to me. "He's going to be a heartbreaker, isn't he?"

Alex's face flamed with color.

I handed him snacks and ignored Kat's comment. "No, I'd like to stand. I've been sitting too much today."

He sat and reached for an apple slice. "Do you guys want to show me what you're thinking so I have some ideas on how to get started?"

Kat pulled out her phone and began scrolling through the photos she had bookmarked. Alex took notes on the laptop. "That's cool. I like the clean lines on that image. I know that my mom is drawn to a more minimalistic design, and that's sort of Nitro's vibe. Is that what you're thinking for the guest rooms, too?"

"Yeah, for sure." Kat pointed out another photo on her phone screen. "Kind of like this? I like the rounded corners of this poster, instead of the standard rectangle."

"That's easy to do."

We spent about an hour looking through examples. Alex asked questions about font, branding, and color palettes. I was impressed with his maturity and professionalism. Not many fifteen-year-old boys were as articulate as Alex. I felt a swell of pride watching him in action. At least I had done one thing right.

CHAPTER

EIGHTEEN

ONCE ALEX HAD A GRASP of our vision, it was time to leave for dinner at Otto and Ursula's. Kat gave us each a quick hug, which made Alex's cheeks blaze again. He told her that he would have some preliminary designs for her to look at by the end of the weekend. I was sure that our project was going to take top priority, given the fact that he kept glancing at Kat and then looking at his feet as we walked out together.

My only concern (aside from not wanting his heart to get broken) was that his crush might interfere with studying for midterms.

"Remember, this a side project," I cautioned as we got into the car. "I know that you still have to study for midterms."

"It's fine, Mom. I have one more test tomorrow and then a three-day weekend. Since I don't have a midterm Monday, I'm off. I can sketch out some ideas this weekend and then make any changes on Monday. It will be fun."

"I'm glad you're willing to be part of it." I didn't want

to embarrass him, so I changed the subject. "Dad and I had lunch today."

Alex tried to sound nonchalant, but I could hear a tightness in his response. "Oh yeah. About what?"

"Lots of stuff. Like Der Keller. I think Uncle Hans is ready to hire the first person who walks through the doors. He's been there a lot."

"Yeah, every time I've been there, he's been working."

"Right. Our goal is to hire a general manager to take the pressure off of him and Dad." I navigated out of the village and onto the highway. Otto and Ursula lived on the opposite side of town. "We also talked about Dad finding a new place, and we're in complete agreement that we want to keep things as normal for you as possible. Our plan, assuming you're okay with it, is to keep the schedule the same. You'll be with me on school nights and stay with Dad every other weekend and whenever else you want. Maybe nights like Sunday, when you don't have school the next day? That way you won't have to worry about having school things at two places."

"That's cool." Alex stared out the window. I knew that he was holding something back.

"Unless you would rather stay at Dad's more. We can do alternating days, if that feels better."

"Mom, it's cool."

Alex had shut down. I wasn't going to get more out of him by forcing the issue. At some point I would have to push him out of his comfort zone, but that wasn't tonight.

We arrived at Otto and Ursula's, and to my delight, Hans's beat-up pickup truck was parked in the driveway. The Krauses' three-story Victorian sat on two acres with a woodshop and views of the rugged Enchantments. The alpine lake wilderness area known as the Enchantments boasted some of the most spectacular views and hiking in the region. When Alex was young, Mac used to strap him to a baby backpack and we would venture for miles through glacial lakes, past tundra meadows where mountain goats would gather to munch on the wild grasses. The grueling hike could be treacherous, with steep crevasses and slippery, craggy terrain. Mac would always ignore my warnings to watch his footing as he scrambled up the side of a cliff in order to get a better view of a frigid lake.

"You didn't say that Uncle Hans was coming," Alex said, practically jumping out of the car.

"I didn't know he was."

"Is Dad coming too?" Alex already had one foot out of the door.

"Oma didn't say," I lied.

Otto came out onto the wraparound front porch to greet us. A hummingbird buzzed by my ear en route to refuel at one of the many glass feeders hanging from the porch.

"Sloan, Alex, come in," Otto said, rubbing his arms. He wore a white wool sweater that I guessed had been hand knitted by Ursula. "Ze air, it is cold tonight, *ja*?"

"My math teacher told us it might snow, Opa," Alex said, greeting Otto with a hug.

Alex towered over his grandfather. I loved watching the two of them together. Otto, like Hans, had always had an affinity for woodworking. He had created a woodshop in the backyard where he, Hans, and Alex had spent countless hours whittling toy trains and building hand-carved furniture. It hadn't come as much of a surprise that Hans decided to make a career out of his childhood hobby. I think that Otto and Ursula had been disappointed at first that Hans didn't follow in their footsteps and opt to manage Der Keller, but at the same time, they were supportive of whatever led their boys to happiness. Hans was obviously happiest when he was coated in sawdust and running a fragrant sheet of cedar through his saw.

"Can I take Alex for a moment, Sloan?" Otto asked, inviting us inside. "Hans has something to show him, *ja*?"

Hans appeared in the doorway. He waved to me and then nodded and winked at Alex.

"Of course. He's all yours." I greeted Hans with a kiss on the cheek. "I'll go see if Ursula needs help."

The three of them hurried off to the workshop. I wondered what Hans wanted to show Alex.

"Ursula, are you in the kitchen?" I called.

"*Ja.* Come in, come in."

The vintage kitchen paid homage to the Krauses' roots with a blue-and-white-tile backsplash, butcher-block countertops, and a hanging pot rack above the island with dangling copper pots and pans. A collection of German china was displayed above the sink. Ursula stood at the stove, a traditional alpine-style apron with creamy white lace tied around her waist. Her cane was propped against the cupboards.

"Shouldn't you be using that?" I asked.

"*Ja,* but it is too hard when I am making ze dinner. I will use it when I am walking, I promise." Her eyes twinkled with mischief.

"Isn't the idea to use it all the time so your hip can heal?"

Ursula swatted the air. "No. It is fine, Sloan. I will take it easy. You can set ze table, okay?"

I gave her a stare that I usually reserved for Alex. "I'll gladly set the table, but I'm keeping an eye on you, young lady. If you overdo it, I'm going to force you to sit."

She laughed. "You are as bad as my doctor."

I knew Ursula's kitchen as well as my own. I removed a stack of white china plates with a blue filigree design that had originally belonged to her grandmother and placed them on the large oval dining table.

"Dinner smells amazing. Is that your famous sauerbraten stew I smell?"

"Ja."

Ursula's stew was perfect fall comfort food, simmered for hours with pork, cabbage, onions, potatoes, carrots, celery, spices, and her magic secret ingredient—crushed gingersnap cookies.

"Did you peek in at ze cake?" Ursula pointed to the fridge, where photos of Alex in his soccer uniform and all of us at a variety of family picnics and holidays covered every square inch of the double doors.

"No, don't tempt me. I might skip dinner and dive right into the cake."

"Take a look and see what you zink." Ursula rolled up the sleeves of her red sweater.

I opened the fridge. The bee sting cake sat on a porcelain cake plate. Ursula had cut the golden, doughy cake into two layers that were sandwiched together with luscious pastry cream. The top of the cake had been baked with the buttery almonds, toasted with honey. They had crystallized into a crunchy crust.

"It looks better than I remember it."

Ursula smiled. She wiped her hands on a dish towel and removed her apron. I almost jumped to her rescue when she reached for her cane and nearly missed. Fortunately, she caught herself on the counter.

"It is okay. I'm fine. Come sit." She motioned to the table.

I pulled out a chair for her.

"Will you get some of ze beer? I have bottles chilling in ze fridge. We can share one while we wait for ze men to return from ze workshop."

"What would you like?" I returned to the fridge. It was difficult to resist the cake. Would anyone notice if I took a swipe of the oozing pastry cream?

"You choose. You are ze guest."

"That's so much pressure," I teased. Then I removed a bottle of Der Keller's signature German pale ale. It was brewed with imported hops from the village where Otto and Ursula had first met. The beer poured the color of a copper penny.

I gave a glass to Ursula and sat next to her.

"Good choice." She raised her glass to mine. "Prost."

"Prost."

The beer had a bready aroma and a hint of grapefruit. The first sip brought out the flavor of caramelized toast and candied lemon.

"It is good, *ja*?" Ursula sipped her beer.

"One of the best." Since we were alone, I wanted to ask her about my parents, but before I could think of a way to start the conversation, she asked about how the wallpaper project was progressing.

"Would you like to borrow ze steamer?" she asked.

"We would love to. I told Garrett about it, and he's ecstatic about trying anything that doesn't involve sloppy glue remover and scraping."

She smiled. "*Ja*, you will still have to scrape, but it will be easier, I zink."

"Thanks again for letting us borrow it."

"It is nothing. Do you want me to show it to you?" She started to get up.

"No. Sit, relax. It can wait until after dinner. You should just enjoy your beer."

"Sloan, you know ziz is never a problem for me." Smile lines creased her face. Her thick white hair made her look almost angelic.

We laughed for a minute. I shifted in my chair. "Ursula, I've been wanting to ask you something, but haven't been able to figure out a way to start, so I guess I'm just going to come out and ask."

"*Ja*, anything for you, Sloan." She placed her hand over mine. Her fingers were warm to the touch. "Is it about Mac?"

"No." I shook my head. "Mac and I are doing the best we can. I would never put you in the middle of it. Mac is your son."

She held my gaze with her commanding eyes. "And you are my daughter."

I fought back tears. "Actually, that's what I want to ask you about."

She removed her hand from mine. "*Ja?*"

"It's about my parents."

A strange look flashed across her face. Was I imagining things? Or did Ursula know something that she wasn't telling me?

"What about zem?" She clasped her hands around her pint glass. When she raised it to her lips, I noticed that it trembled ever so slightly.

It was the same reaction that I had witnessed when she had seen the photo of the woman who bore an uncanny resemblance to me. I had created a gallery wall at Nitro with old photos from Garrett's aunt's collection. On opening night, Ursula had stared at the photo in disbelief. Anytime I asked her about it, she denied that she'd had a strange response. Strangely, she had cautioned me not to go searching for answers about my parents. I hadn't told her about my meeting with Sally. I had needed some time to figure out what our next move was going to be.

"I met with my social worker a few weeks ago."

Ursula's face went ashen. "*Ja?*"

"Yes, Sally. She came to Nitro to share my old case file with me."

I waited. Ursula took a large gulp of her beer.

"Sally, as I'm sure I've told you dozens of times, saved my life. If it hadn't been for her, who knows where I would have ended up."

"Sloan, do not say ziz. You have always been strong." Ursula patted my wrist.

"Maybe, but Sally was my constant, my one steady point person in a tumultuous sea of changing families. I'm sad that she and I lost contact after I moved here, but we picked right back up where we left as if no time had passed."

"*Ja,* I can see ziz." She tried to steady her hands by firming her grip on the pint glass. "What does ziz have to do with me?"

"Sally is helping me look for my parents." I didn't share any details about the missing therapy notes and Sally's suspicion that someone higher up in the organization had ensured that I would never find my parents. Nor did I mention Sally's concern that hunting down my history could be dangerous.

Ursula took another long drink from her beer. She traced the rim of the glass with a shaky finger. "And you want to try to do ziz, Sloan? What if finding your parents leads to unhappiness? I do not want for you to be unhappy. You have a vonderful family with us, *ja*? Why do you need to do ziz?"

"I know. I can't thank you enough for opening your arms to me and making me part of this family, but I have to do this. I have to know what happened. In part because of what's happened between me and Mac. As hard as it's been, the past few months have shed so much light on my choices. I don't want to repeat the past, and in order not to do that, I have to understand my past."

A sad smile spread across her face. "*Ja*. I understand."

"Ursula." I reached for her arm. "Is there something that you know? That you're not telling me?"

She set down her beer. I watched as her breath quickened and she blinked rapidly. A tear slid down her cheek. "*Ja*, Sloan. *Ja*."

My stomach flopped. Maybe I shouldn't have pressed her. What if whatever she was about to tell me would change our relationship forever?

CHAPTER

NINETEEN

I HELD MY BREATH WHILE I waited for Ursula to reply. She knew something about my parents. Why hadn't she told me?

Deep creases formed in her brow. "Sloan, I do not know ze best way to tell you ziz. It happened a long, long time ago, you must understand. And zen, ze men, zey came and zey told me I must not ever speak of it again. I have held on to ziz story for so long I am not sure my memory of it is even correct."

"Okay."

"So many years have passed. I have zought many times about what to tell you zat I know, and zen I have stopped myself. Can you ever forgive me?" Her hands shook violently.

I placed my hands on top of hers to try and calm her. "Ursula, you don't need to ask for forgiveness. I love you, and nothing can change that." I wasn't sure that was true. Until Ursula divulged what she knew about my parents, there was no way to know whether she had withheld the truth for good reasons.

Still, I wanted to encourage her to continue. The suspense and knowledge that Ursula was involved in any small way was making my head spin.

"I love you, too, Sloan. Ziz is why I have never told you." She squeezed my hands and then released her grip.

"Please, Ursula. I have to know," I pleaded. My skin felt cold and clammy despite the fact that the kitchen was warm from bread baking in the oven and Ursula's stew simmering on the stove.

"*Ja*. I know. It is time." She clasped her hands together as they trembled. "You see, ziz was very early on, when we had only been in Leavenworth a short while. Der Keller had only been open for a few years. Otto and I, we worked around ze clock. We were at ze brewery day and night. Hans and Mac too. Zey grew up in ze pub. It was good, and it was bad. We never had a break. Der Keller, it was our life."

I had heard versions of this story many times.

"Otto, he was very worried it was too much for ze boys. We came to America to give zem a good life, but if we were working all ze time, was zat good? We got a late start on our family. We were older zan many of ze parents of ze boys' friends, and we were running a pub and trying to grow a business. Mac was going to start school, and we were worried zat we wouldn't have enough time to help him with his schoolwork and care for Hans. Hans was very young, just in preschool. It was hard to manage ze brewery and care for ze boys."

My beer had begun to go flat, but I sipped it anyway.

"Otto received a call from a man who wanted to buy Der Keller. He was from ze East Coast and looking to invest in ze very early craft beer craze zat was just beginning to happen here. He asked if he could come and spend a week here to see ze brewery, meet us, and discuss a deal."

"You were going to sell Der Keller?" This was part of the story I had never heard.

"*Ja.* We came very, very close to selling." She hung her head for a moment as if the memory was too painful to bear.

"I can't believe it. I can't imagine Leavenworth without you and Otto. Why didn't you ever say anything?"

Her shoulders hunched. "I will get to ziz. But first, I must tell you about ze visit. Ze man arrived vith his beautiful young sister and her daughter." She raised her eyebrow and looked at me.

"You mean me?"

"*Ja,* I zink so. You are ze girl in ze picture you found. At least, I zink. I cannot be sure, but it must be you."

"I don't understand."

She nodded. "I know, I vill continue. Ze man, his name was Forest. Ziz is what he told us, but we would come to learn zat he lied about many things."

"He was my uncle?"

Ursula frowned. "He says zat ze woman, Marianne, was his sister, but Otto and I were not sure. Zey did not act like brother and sister."

"What do you mean? Do you think they were together?"

"I do not know. Marianne, she was always timid around Forest. I wondered if she was scared of him, maybe."

I tried to stay in the moment, but it was hard not to jump to conclusions. Was Forest my father? Why were they pretending to be brother and sister? And why was she afraid of him?

Ursula continued. "At first, we were excited. It seemed like Forest was impressed with Der Keller. He told us of his plans to expand ze brewery, hire more workers, distribute ze beer far away. At ziz time, we couldn't have even imagined zat our beers could be sold in Spokane or Seattle, but Forest was sure zat we would become a national brand."

"When was this?"

She looked to the ceiling for a moment. It was decorated with tin tiles. "Ziz would have been in ze 1970s, or maybe it was very early 1980s."

That math worked. I would have been six in 1979.

"Otto and I could not believe our good fortune. We had never imagined zat someone might want to buy Der Keller. At ziz time, we only had three part-time staff to help with ze brewery and tend bar. It was much like ze size of Nitro."

That wasn't a surprise. When I used to give tours at Der Keller, my talk would always include a brief history on the brewery's evolution. I would show beer enthusiasts photos of Der Keller's first primitive equipment and tiny tasting room. Then I would take them through the bottling plant and finish each tour in the restaurant. Inevitably people would be awed by the brewery's humble beginning compared with today.

"Forest made us an offer zat we couldn't believe. Zat is when ze problems began. If it seems too good to be true, zen it probably is, *ja*?"

I nodded.

"*Ja*." She shifted in her chair. I wondered if her hip was bothering her or if the memories were painful. "Otto did not trust Forest. He said from ze start zat he had a funny feeling about ze man, but we were new business owners and we were flattered zat he was interested in Der Keller and we had never seen ze kind of dollar signs on ze contract."

I had no idea where she was going with this. How long had Alex, Hans, and Otto been in the workshop? I said a silent prayer, begging them not to interrupt the moment.

"We took ze paperwork to a lawyer, who said immediately it was no good."

"No good how?"

"Forest was not who he claimed to be. He said zat he had many, many business investments, but our lawyer told us ziz was not true. Forest was trying to scam us. His contract was a fake. It would have signed Der Keller over to him for nothing. Our lawyer was sure zat he was trying to take advantage of ze fact zat we were immigrants. He reported Forest to ze authorities and told us not to say anything. Two days later, some FBI agents came to Leavenworth and arrested Forest. He had done ze same thing many times. He would take control of ze business, drain ze bank accounts, and disappear."

"Ursula, I'm so sorry. That's terrible."

"*Ja*. It was embarrassing. Otto and I felt so stupid. How could we have trusted such a criminal, and why did we not trust our first instinct?"

"You can't blame yourself."

"No, no, I do not blame myself any longer. I did for some years after, but zen I came to realize it was an important lesson for us. It made us stronger. It made us realize zat it was worth putting in ze long hours and work to make Der Keller ze best brewery it could be. I vonder if Forest had never come what might have happened. In some ways I must be grateful to him."

Not many people would have shared Ursula's perspective on narrowly missing being scammed out of a business and thousands of dollars. It was just like her to shift from anger to gratitude.

"How does this relate to me? What happened to Marianne?"

Ursula stared at her beer, which hadn't been touched. "We did not spend very much time with Marianne and her daughter. Zey were very private, but we did have zem to dinner one night before we learned of Forest's true colors. Ze girl—you—were very astute. You would watch everyone with such intensity. You were a quiet child, but so polite and so smart. Otto and I both commented on ziz. But when Forest was arrested, Marianne disappeared along vith you. Ze FBI men said it would be better if we never spoke of what had happened. It was strange, but at ze time, we were embarrassed, as I said, so we set it aside and didn't worry about it. Zen, we met you at ze farmers' market. You remember?"

I nodded. "Of course."

"I recognized you immediately. Vell, I was not sure, but your eyes, zey were ze same. Otto too. We did not know what to do or say, and zen when we learned your story and how you had been abandoned, we wondered if maybe it was because of us. Did Marianne need to disappear because Forest was arrested? Is zat why she left you? We felt so terrible, but zen we were not sure. It was so long ago. Maybe we were wrong. Maybe it was our imagination. How could we know? We had only met ze girl for a few days, and she was so young, but yet you looked like Marianne. Could it be you?"

I wasn't sure how to respond.

"We did not know, but we decided we would adopt you.

We would make you our own. We had always longed for a daughter, and we fell in love vith you instantly. So did Mac. But even if Mac had not, we still would have made you part of ziz family."

My stomach swirled with anxiety. Otto and Ursula had known about my family the entire time I had known them? My God. How had they kept that from me?

Ursula must have sensed my discomfort. "We did not say anything because you were so clear about not wanting to look into your past when we met you. I asked you a number of times, do you remember?"

I nodded. That was true. Ursula had tried to get me to open up about my childhood and had often asked in the early years of knowing them whether I had any interest in trying to track down my birth parents.

"Otto and I agreed we would not say anything unless you were ze one who made ze choice to begin to search for ze truth."

"But I did, just a few weeks ago, and you told me not to."

"I know. I am sorry, Sloan. Please forgive me. I beg ziz of you. I did not know for sure if it was you until zat night at Nitro. When I saw ze picture on ze wall, I knew right away. I almost collapsed. I could not tell you. Not now, after all of ziz time has gone by. What would you do? What would you say? You are my daughter, and now you would hate me." She buried her head in her hands as huge tears poured from her eyes.

I couldn't breathe. I couldn't swallow. This wasn't possible.

Her entire body shook with emotion. "I can never forgive myself. I should have said more long, long ago, but I did not. At first it was because I was not sure why ze FBI asked us never to mention Marianne to anyone. Could Marianne have been in some kind of trouble? Were zey protecting her? Would we put her in more danger? But, zen it became about you. I couldn't let you go. I did not want to risk zat you would be so angry at me I might lose you forever. Can you understand?"

I tried to nod, but nothing felt real. My body had gone numb. I had loved Ursula more deeply than maybe anyone in my life. She was the only mother I had ever known. How could she have kept this from me? Her words were a blow. Maybe worse than when I'd caught Mac with a young woman not that much older than Kat. Ursula had known critical information about my past and had failed to share it with me. I couldn't respond to her question because I wasn't sure I could forgive her.

CHAPTER

TWENTY

"MOM!" ALEX'S VOICE CUT THROUGH the tension in the kitchen. "Mom, where are you?"

I forced myself to swallow. "In the kitchen."

Ursula started to say something, but I held up my index finger. "Not now. Say nothing."

"*Ja,* okay."

"Mom." Alex burst through the kitchen door. "You have to come see this. You won't believe it." His boyish face beamed with excitement. Fortunately, his enthusiasm made him oblivious to the thick layer of emotion in the room.

"Great." I forced a smile.

"*Ja,* go see." Ursula pretended to wipe something from her eyes. I hoped Alex wouldn't notice the fact that her eyes were bloodshot and puffy from her tears.

I stood to shield him from Ursula. "Let's go see this mystery object."

Alex rubbed his hands together. "Uncle Hans and Opa have been working on a surprise."

"What is it?"

"You have to wait and see." Alex grabbed my wrist and dragged me out the back door. The blast of cold air outside felt like an assault. I wanted to pinch myself. Maybe I would wake up and my conversation with Ursula would be nothing more than a bad dream. "Cover your eyes, Mom," he said.

The woodshop was a few hundred feet from the house. Alex led me through dewy grass. "Your hand is sweaty, Mom. You're not getting sick, are you?"

"No. No. It was hot in the kitchen. That's all."

"It's always hot at Oma and Opa's house. I don't know how they can wear wool sweaters inside." He stopped. "We're heading inside the shop. Keep your eyes closed."

The smell of fresh cut wood and resin hit my nose. It made me think about the pine-infused beer we were trying to master at Nitro.

"Okay, go ahead and open your eyes," Alex commanded after positioning me.

I opened my eyes. There were four beautiful hand-carved canoes lined up on sawhorses. "Wow, did you make these?" I asked Hans.

"With the help of this old man." He nudged his father's arm.

Otto shook his index finger at Hans. "Is zat any way to talk to me?"

Hans laughed and wrapped his arm around Otto. "You know I like to tease. This man is the master, Sloan. I couldn't have done it without him."

I hoped the smile on my face looked real. I was tapping into every self-preservation trick I'd learned during my years in foster care to keep from freaking out.

"They made them for us," Alex interjected. "You know how I've been wanting a canoe to float the river? It was Uncle Hans's suggestion. He and Opa have been building them in secret for weeks. Now I get to help carve a custom design into mine. Isn't that cool?"

"Very cool." I ruffled his hair, which made him duck away. "You know, you might have something here," I said to Hans with a chuckle. "Have you considered woodworking as a trade?"

"Thanks a lot, Sloan." He pretended to be injured by my joke. "I know we should have probably asked you if it was okay, but we got so into the project that we kind of got carried away. I told Alex that you had to give him permission to take it out on the water. The one thing that I can guarantee is that they float. I already took them out for a test."

"Of course you can take it out," I said to Alex. "With a life jacket, and you need to take the free course that the city offers on boating safety."

"Yeah, Mom. I will. I'll sign up tomorrow."

"Ze boy will be a pro in no time," Otto said with a smile. I was sure that Ursula would inform him of our conversation later.

Otto, sweet Otto, one of the kindest men I'd ever known, had lied to me too? I couldn't look at him. What about Hans? Did he know? Did Mac? Had the entire Krause family taken pity on me? Or worse?

I forced myself to stay in the moment. If I allowed my

thoughts to drift to my mother and whoever Forest was, I would never be able to make it through dinner.

Otto placed one finger on the side of his nose. "What is ziz? I smell Ursula's cooking. We should probably go in for dinner, before she comes out and yells at us."

We left the wooden works of art and headed inside for dinner. My feet felt as if they weren't making contact with ground. Hans caught my arm as I almost slipped on the grass. I couldn't see his eyes in the dark, but I could hear the concern in his voice. "You okay, Sloan?"

"Yeah. Just klutzy," I lied.

"You're not klutzy." Hans held my arm all the way back to the house.

I did my best to laugh at Hans's jokes and taste Ursula's food. Even the Bienenstich cake couldn't wake up my senses. Fortunately, Alex was distracted by his new canoe and didn't seem to pick up on my quiet, contemplative mood. I caught Ursula's eye a few times across the table, and each time she offered an apologetic smile.

"We should get you home," I said to Alex as we cleared the dinner table. I was nearing my breaking point. I didn't think I could hold myself together much longer. "You have another midterm tomorrow, right?"

"Yeah, but it's just health, Mom. I don't need to study for health."

Hans laughed. "I think I remember saying something similar back in the day and ended up bombing my test because I had no idea what the difference between the circulatory and regulatory system was."

"See? Listen to your uncle." I swatted Alex on the hip. "It's time to get you home and have you hit the books."

"Okay." He sounded disappointed. "But can I come over tomorrow after my test and work on the design for my canoe?"

Otto nodded. "*Ja,* come over anytime. We love to have you here."

Ursula gave us both hugs. I wondered if anyone noticed that she held on to me extra long. When she finally released me, she pointed to a Tupperware on the counter. "You and Alex must take some cake, *ja*? And I will have Hans bring ze wallpaper stripper by tomorrow, okay?"

"Sure." I clutched the Tupperware and waved good-bye to Otto and Hans.

On the drive home, Alex gushed about the canoes. "Can you believe that Opa and Uncle Hans built those? They are nicer than some of the canoes I've been eyeing in *Water Magazine.* I hope that they'll teach me how to build like that."

"I know without a doubt that Hans would love to teach you the trade."

Alex was thoughtful for a moment. "Hey, is there something wrong with Oma? Is her hip bothering her?"

"Why do you ask?"

"I don't know. She seemed kind of sad at dinner. She didn't say very much. You know Oma, usually she won't stop asking me like a million questions about school and my friends. She didn't ask me anything tonight."

"Hmmm. I'm not sure. It could be that she was tired. She's still recovering from the surgery." I wasn't ready to burden Alex with what I had learned from Ursula.

"Maybe. But she seemed sad." He stared out the window. "Do you think it's because Dad wasn't there?"

"That could be. I know she and Opa are trying very hard to make sure that we're all okay. They love you more than anything. You know that, right?"

"Yeah, Mom. Duh."

I felt guilty for letting Alex think that Ursula's sadness had to do with Mac, but it wasn't fair to involve him in this. Not yet anyway.

We arrived at the farmhouse, and Alex went straight to his room to study for his health test. I made myself a steaming cup of jasmine tea. Then I put on my pajamas and cracked the bedroom window. There was something calming about the cool evening fall air and the sound of the wind rustling through the trees. I closed my eyes, trying to will any memory of my early childhood into the forefront of my brain.

Marianne. Did the name have any meaning?

I centered my breathing. Marianne. I said it aloud. Over and over again.

Who was Marianne? Was she really my mother? What had brought her to Leavenworth with Forest? Was she his sister? Or were they something more, as Ursula had wondered? Could he have threatened her? Abused her?

Sloan, you have to stop.

I sighed and reached for my tea.

Tomorrow I would call Sally. This was the biggest clue we'd had to date. There must be a record of Forest's arrest. Maybe that could be our starting point. If we could figure out who he was and his connection to me, maybe that would lead us to Marianne.

Was she still alive? Had she gone into hiding? Or worse? What if he had harmed her? Maybe that was why she had abandoned me.

My memories of being left at the hospital were fuzzy at best. The only thing that stuck in my mind was a woman's warm hand, grasping mine so tightly that it hurt. Had that been Marianne? Or someone else?

I felt completely overwhelmed and weighted down by Ursula's confession. So much time had passed. What if the trail had gone cold? What if I couldn't find her?

"Mom," Alex called from down the hallway.

The sound of his voice immediately grounded me in reality. "What's up, bud?"

"Want to come tuck me in?"

I smiled. Alex might have been closer to a man than the baby I used to rock to sleep in my arms, but he still wanted me to kiss him good night. "Coming." I set my tea on my nightstand and went into his room. "How did the studying go?"

He was already in bed. His backpack was packed and ready for the morning. "Not too bad. I think I've got a handle on this whole health thing."

I kissed his forehead. "I'm sure you do."

"Mom, there was a chapter about depression."

"Oh yeah?" I tried to keep my voice as calm as possible. Was Alex depressed?

"It went through all of the signs and symptoms, and I think that maybe Dad is depressed."

Of course Mac was depressed. He had ruined a long-term marriage, disappointed his family, and was about to have to start over in his forties. Who wouldn't be depressed?

To Alex, I said, "What makes you think that?"

I couldn't see his facial expression in the dark but could hear the concern in his voice. "It's just that he has a lot of the symptoms that my health book lists as red flags for depression. Maybe that's why Oma was upset tonight. Maybe she knows and is worried about him."

"That could be." I sat on the edge of his bed. "Honey, listen, this is a tough time for all of us. I know that Dad is hurting, and he might have some symptoms of depression. But that's normal. If he wasn't depressed—if all of us weren't feeling a range of emotions right now—I would be worried."

"Okay. But do you think I should check in with him about it?"

"I think he would appreciate that." I kissed his forehead again. "There's one thing I want you to know, though, and that is that it is not your responsibility to take care of us, okay? That's our job. Even though we aren't together, I will always love Dad, and I will check in with him too. Got it?"

"Got it."

"Get some sleep. Love you." I left with a final parting kiss.

Why hadn't anyone ever warned me that parenting just got harder? Maybe the teen years weren't as physically exhausting as when Alex was a toddler. I remembered chasing him around the park for hours, wondering if he would ever wear out. Those years left me with tired arms from scooping up a toddler and a collection of clothes that were stained with grape juice and chocolate pudding. But the teen years were mentally taxing. Alex was able to make his own lunch or do a load of laundry, but it was my responsibility to make sure that he was emotionally strong and stable. Between the breakup between me and Mac and what I had learned from Ursula tonight, I was worried that I was going to fail my son.

CHAPTER

TWENTY-ONE

THE NEXT MORNING, I WOKE up in a fog. It felt like I had a hangover. My head throbbed. I was nauseous and in a daze. My only saving grace was that Alex had to be at school early to meet his study group before their health exam. I barely registered the drive to school or dropping him off. I probably shouldn't have been behind the wheel.

When I arrived in the village, I found myself parking in front of the bakery and wondering how I had gotten there.

It was hours before Garrett would be up. I might as well stop in at Strudel for a coffee and pastry. The only way I was going to survive the day was by keeping myself distracted and as busy as possible. There was one obvious way to do that— focus on Kristopher's murder. It had absolutely nothing to do with my personal life, thank God.

Once I had a latte and two apple strudels in hand, I walked down to Chief Meyers's office. I wasn't sure if she would be in the village yet, but it was worth a shot. I could fill her in on what I had learned from Ross and Valerie and see if she had any other news on Kristopher's murder that she might be able to share. Plus, I needed to kill time before I called Sally. It was only 7 a.m. As much as I wanted to pick up the phone, I decided the civilized thing to do was to wait at least until eight before placing a call to my former case worker.

The police station lights were on. I took that as a good sign that the chief might be in. I knew that Chief Meyers had a weak spot for strudel, so I hoped that my sweet bribe might make her more willing to fill me in on the latest with the investigation.

I knocked softly on the door.

Chief Meyers's deep voice bellowed, "It's open."

"Morning, Chief." I stepped inside. "I was at the bakery and picked up an extra apple strudel. Can I interest you in a breakfast treat?"

"I never turn down a strudel." She motioned for me to come behind the counter to her desk.

"Neither do I," I said as I handed her a paper bag with the German delicacy. "It's un-American. Or, actually, un-Leavenworthian? Is that a thing?"

Chief Meyers unwrapped the pastry. The flaky strudel was layered with apples sautéed in cinnamon and sugar and chopped walnuts. The top had been brushed with an egg wash and dusted with thick chunks of crystallized sugar. "What are you doing out and about this early?"

I explained how Alex had midterms.

She ripped off a piece of the strudel. "That's why I've seen so many teens hanging around the gazebo at lunchtime. I was about to send one of my guys to make sure we didn't have a bunch of delinquents running around the village."

"That's only during Oktoberfest," I joked.

"Got any news for me?" She reached for a yellow legal pad and a pencil.

"How did you know?"

She gave me a skeptical stare. "Out with it."

I proceeded to tell her what I had learned from Ross and Valerie. Chief Meyers scribbled a few notes as I spoke. When I finished, she set down the pencil and took another bite of the strudel.

"Have you learned any more information that you can share?" I asked, knowing it was unlikely that Chief could tell me much.

"Your intel on Ross matches what we've learned about the state liquor board reviewing his license. Apparently, Kristopher was not the first person to report the Underground for serving minors. Ross could be in some serious trouble, depending on what we learn from our contacts at the board."

"Really?" I was shocked by this news. "What kind of trouble?"

"According to one of my sources, Ross has been on a watch list for a while. He's in danger of having his license permanently revoked. There have been dozens of reports of misconduct, overserving, serving minors. I don't know what's been going on at the Underground, but it's given the bar's name new meaning. I've got one of my officers keeping an eye out there while we wait for copies of the reports from the state liquor board."

"I saw Ross arguing with someone about keeping the bar open. Was that one of your officers?"

The chief scowled. "Nope. Not my guy."

I took a bite of my strudel, but like last night, stress had deadened my taste buds. "I can't believe that. Ross has always been so professional."

Chief Meyers shrugged. "Sloan, if I've learned anything in this line of work, it's that people show you what they want to show you and nothing more. There's no gray area when it comes to serving minors. If Ross has been breaking the law, he deserves to lose everything, and I'll be the first one to tell him so."

"I agree." We took state regulations seriously at Nitro, as did every pub and brewery owner I knew. I couldn't believe that Ross had knowingly been serving minors. It made me wonder if I had written him off as a potential suspect too soon. Maybe since Kristopher had been so vocal about the issue, Ross had decided to silence him permanently.

"So it wasn't just Kristopher leading the charge against him?"

The chief finished her strudel. "Kristopher was leading the charge, that's for sure. He filed a number of reports with us. We didn't take them very seriously because of the other trouble that he'd been stirring up. I figured he was trying to make an example of Ross in order to lend support to his cause, but we're going to go back through the old reports and compare them with what we learn from the state."

"Wow, I'm really surprised by that. Like I said, Ross has always struck me as being very professional." Who was I kidding? After having my world turned upside down by Ursula last night, my judgment should not be trusted.

"You want this?" I passed my strudel to Chief Meyers. "I'm not hungry."

She glanced at her fitness watch and then to the flaky pastry. "Aw, why not?"

"What about April?" I asked as she helped herself to a bite.

"She's still on my list." The chief gave me a funny look.

"For real?"

"All I can say is that she is still officially on my list." She didn't elaborate, but from the emphasis she put on "officially," I had a feeling she was speaking in code.

One of her deputies arrived for his shift. The chief clammed up. I told her I would continue to stay on alert and let her know if I learned anything new. I left the office and wandered aimlessly. Had Ross really been overserving and serving minors? If Kristopher had found proof, that could give Ross a strong motive for murder. To be honest, I hadn't spent much time at the Underground. It was popular amongst tourists because of its atmosphere. Maybe I'd stop by for lunch later and see if I could learn anything from his bartending staff.

The light crews were already at work a few blocks away. I wondered if the thousands of tourists who would come to see our village illuminated for the holidays had any idea how much preparation went into the event. There wasn't any sign of the press. They were either getting a slow start or a bigger and better story had broken elsewhere.

I made my way to the gazebo. I had to call Sally. We had something tangible to work with—names, a potential arrest record, and the fact that it was highly likely I was in Leaven-worth in the 1970s.

The bench was cool to the touch. I closed my eyes and took a long, slow breath before calling Sally. My heart pounded in my chest as the phone rang. I wanted to tell Sally everything Ursula had told me last night, but we had agreed to keep our phone conversations to surface topics. Sally had suggested that until we found out how deep the cover-up of my parents' identity ran, it would be better to discuss important details and our plans in person.

She didn't answer. I hesitated. Should I leave a message?

At the last minute, I decided to leave a very upbeat message about Alex's soccer game, midterms, and preparing for the light festival. I invited her to come out for a weekend to see the display in person. If anyone was tapping her phone (and it was more likely that we were both being overly paranoid), they wouldn't be able to get anything from my message.

Now what? I wasn't ready to head to Nitro yet, but there wasn't much open in the village short of the pastry and coffee shops. I thought about taking a morning walk to Blackbird Island, but I noticed Heidi pull into a parking spot across the street in front of her hotel, the Hamburg Hostel. I decided to go say good morning. The Hamburg reminded me of Hansel and Gretel's cottage, with intentionally weathered stucco and storybook architecture where none of the rooflines are straight or plumb.

I got up and crossed the street. "Hi, Heidi," I called.

Her arms were loaded with bags. "Good morning, Sloan."

"Can I help with that?" I asked, pointing to the back of

Heidi's truck, where a dozen more paper bags had been stacked on top of each other.

"Would you mind?" She shifted one of the bags in her arms. "They're not heavy. There's just a ton of them. It's a fun holiday project I've been working on at home for our guests coming for the winter light festival. Take a look."

I opened one bag and was immediately engulfed in the scent of holiday spices.

"Aren't they cute?" Heidi asked. "I made individual packets of mulling spice. We'll leave them in each guest room as a little holiday gift. Guests can either add them to their tea while they stay or take them home as a memento."

"They smell amazing," I said, reaching for a handful of bags.

"You should smell my dining room. I was up until midnight assembling the last of them." Heidi looped the bag over her arm.

The Hamburg was one of the smaller, boutique properties in town. Heidi had owned it for as long as I had known her. She went beyond the call of duty for her guests, offering them personalized service and add-ons like her handmade mulling packets. It was one of the many reasons that the hotel was booked year-round. That and its whimsical, unique design. The front of the property had a picket fence, moat, and small pond. At Halloween time, Heidi played upon the hotel's fairy-tale theme and decorated the grounds with oversized spiders and cobwebs draped from the dark wooden shutters.

"Go ahead and put those on the front welcome counter," Heidi directed me as we entered the hotel. Inside the hotel, the fanciful theme continued with garlands of ceramic sweets intertwined along the wood-beamed ceiling, a gothic chandelier, and gleaming hardwood floors.

I set the fragrant spice packets on the welcome desk carved in a baroque style. Then we returned to her car to get the rest of them.

"Now I'm craving mulled wine," I said. The scent reminded me of the village during the winter light festival, where I would stroll through vendor booths in Front Street Park, sampling sugar doughnuts, fried potato pancakes, and steaming mugs of what Otto and Ursula called *Glühwein*—which, literally translated, meant "glow wine." It was made with citrus fruits, spices, and sugar and served at traditional Christmas markets.

Heidi reached into one of the bags and tossed me a few packets. "Take some. They're great in wine, and actually I tried one in my morning coffee with a splash of cream and a couple tablespoons of dark chocolate syrup. It was amazing."

"That does sound good." I took a whiff of the spices. Heidi had included whole cloves, cinnamon sticks, star anise, and dried orange peels. "We've been playing around with making a beer inspired by mulled spiced wine."

"You should do that. I bet it would be a huge hit, especially at the Christmas markets." She pointed down a hallway that was adorned with travel style posters from the German Alps, more of the hand-painted candy garland, and prints of German cottages. "Do you want to come to my office for a minute?"

"Sure. As long as I'm not keeping you. Are you headed for a workout?" I noted her yoga pants and warm-up jacket.

"No. I've already worked out. I'm up at the crack of dawn. Once I got serious about exercise and weight loss last year, I made a commitment to exercise daily. Since I'm so swamped with the hotel, the only time I have is in the early morning. I've gotten used to it. The good thing about being up at the crack of dawn is that the gym is never packed. Usually it's just me, Ross, and—well, it used to be Kristopher."

"Got it." I followed after her, tucking the spices into my purse. I filed that piece of information into my head for later.

Heidi's office was upstairs at the end of another long hallway. She expertly weaved past guests, greeting everyone by name and encouraging them to partake of breakfast, which was being served in the charming dining room. I almost considered inviting myself to breakfast. The buffet looked tempting, with platters of pastries, sausages, and fruits. Guests savored coffee and tea in front of a roaring stone fireplace.

When we arrived at her office, she opened the door and waited for me go in.

There were more ski travel posters, along with the sketches from the original architectural plans for the Hamburg Hostel on the walls. International magazine articles, touting the property for its incredible German hospitality, location, and comfortable beds had been framed on the bookcase behind Heidi's desk.

"Have a seat. Can I get you anything—tea, coffee?" Heidi pointed to an expensive coffee maker near her desk.

"No, thank you. I'm fine." I took a seat.

She made herself a cup of tea.

"The hotel looks amazing. I haven't been inside since the renovations." I had watched progress on the Hamburg over the last few months. The hotel had undergone major updates including electrical, plumbing, and a new roof.

"We're pleased with the end result, but the remodel process was not fun." Heidi sat down and cleared a space for her tea. She pushed aside a stack of papers, which I realized were Kristopher's campaign posters.

Without thinking, I pointed at the stack. "Were you campaigning for Kristopher?"

She looked shocked for a second. Then she picked up the stack and dumped it into a recycling bin next to her desk. "God, no. He wanted me to, but I refused. Can you imagine what would have happened to our bookings if he had managed to win the election? As of right now, we are booked every weekend through the end of the winter light festival in March. If Kristopher's ridiculous plan had been approved, I guarantee nearly every guest on the upcoming calendar would have canceled their stay."

We had been over this before, but I nodded anyway.

"I told him that he was going to single-handedly ruin everything we had worked so hard to build in Leavenworth when he was here the other night," Heidi continued.

I didn't react, but I wondered if Heidi had slipped up. What did she mean, that he was here the other night? Kristopher had been at the Hamburg Hostel? Why?

If she had slipped, she didn't notice. "He and I went round and round for ages. It was so maddening. He refused to listen to any reasonable argument. He was dead set on banning alcohol. And it doesn't make sense, because Kristopher loved Leavenworth. That much I truly believe. But why did a man who loved this village so much want to destroy it? That's what I can't get past. I was fuming. He didn't have a good response. He just kept repeating over and over again that he had his reasons."

Since she had mentioned twice now that Kristopher had been in her office, I figured it was fair game to ask a few follow-up questions.

"When was Kristopher here?"

Heidi's eyes bulged. "Um, uh. He stopped by after the town meeting."

"Why?"

She picked up a pen with the Hamburg Hostel's logo etched on the side and clicked it open and shut. "Uh, well, he . . ." She paused for a minute as if trying to think of an excuse why Kristopher would have been in her office on the night that he was killed. "He dropped off that stack of campaign flyers." She pointed the pen toward the recycling bin. "It was pretty forward of him, if you ask me. He had to have known that everyone was at the town meeting, and I guess he decided that he would make a last-ditch effort with the business owners here in the village to try and sway us. It didn't work. I told him I wasn't budging. Unless he changed his stance on alcohol, I wasn't about to vote for him."

"He was campaigning after the meeting?" Something about her story didn't add up.

Heidi nodded. "Yeah, ballsy, isn't it? I came back after leaving Der Keller to grab more supplies for the mulling spices, and Kristopher happened to be here. He was trying to convince my front desk staff to hang up the flyers. He told them that I had approved it and I was a huge campaign contributor."

"Was that true?"

"All lies. I called Kristopher out in front of my staff. I told him that if he ever pulled a dirty, sneaky stunt like that again, I would call Chief Meyers and have him arrested." She twisted the zipper on her warm-up jacket.

"And how did he respond?"

"He shrugged it off. It was bizarre, Sloan. I swear that he thought he was actually going to win."

"Really?" No one I had spoken to about Kristopher thus far had mentioned anything about him thinking he had a shot at the election.

"I assumed he was delusional, but now I've started to re-think that. What if he had something on Valerie? I wouldn't put it past him to have tried something ugly at the end. I don't know, maybe I'm just imagining things, but our conversation was weird. He didn't act like a man about to lose."

Heidi's phone rang. I took that as my excuse to duck out. I wasn't sure what to believe. She had met with him in private the night he died. I got the sense there had been more to their conversation that she had withheld. Her perspective on Valerie lined up with what I already knew, but then again maybe she was trying to shift the focus from herself.

I sighed and left for Nitro. Maybe brewing would clear my head and give me a fresh perspective on who in this quaint, calm village could have murdered Kristopher.

CHAPTER

TWENTY-TWO

HANS DELIVERED URSULA'S STEAM MACHINE as promised. He peered into the front window while Kat and I were taking inventory of our barware over a leisurely cup of coffee. One issue with running a successful pub is keeping pint glasses in stock. Glasses tend to break and have a way of wandering off—either by accident or not. Craft beer fans collect pint glasses, which was one of the reasons we sold our logoed barware and T-shirts, but even so there were a handful of people who snuck out with a free souvenir of their visit to Nitro. It didn't make Garrett angry. He had said, "Hey, if they loved our beer that much, I'm flattered. Not to mention that it's ongoing branding to have our pint glasses in circulation, right?"

Kat pointed to the window. "Uh, I think you're wanted outside."

Hans tilted his head to the side and stuck out his tongue when I looked up from my inventory sheet.

My heart skipped a beat. I wasn't sure I was ready to face Hans. "That's our steam cleaner." I dug my fingernails into my thigh. *You can do this, Sloan.*

"Morning, sis." Hans greeted me with a kiss on the cheek. I tried not to stiffen. "I have a special delivery for you."

I propped open the door for Hans to bring the machine inside. "Thanks. I can't wait to give it a try."

He scowled. "Can't wait, huh?"

I forced myself to chuckle. "You know what I mean. And, trust me, if you had tried scraping layers of old wallpaper all day, you would be excited about steaming, too." I hoped my voice sounded normal. "Have you talked to your mom?"

Hans wrinkled his brow. "This morning? No, why? Is something wrong?"

"No." I couldn't think of anything else to say.

He stared at me as if he was worried that I was experiencing short-term memory loss. "We just saw her last night, remember?"

"Yeah." Heat warmed my cheeks. "I had a question about how to use the steamer."

Hans wasn't buying it. "You? Sloan, you're the first person everyone calls when they don't have the manual or to troubleshoot brewing equipment. I'm pretty confident that you can figure out how to use a wallpaper stripper." He gave me a strange look but dropped it as we walked to the bar.

Kat clapped. "The stripper. Yay!" She tried to lift her left arm and then let it land on the bar top with a heavy thud. "Honestly, I'm so sore I can't even lift my arm over my head. That thing is going to be a lifesaver."

"Too bad I have a client order to finish, otherwise I'd be almost compelled to join you." Hans's eyes twinkled.

"I'm done with you." I tried to banter with Hans like usual, but my heart wasn't in it.

He stabbed himself in the chest with his index finger. "Some thanks I get for your special delivery."

Kat reached for a pint glass. "I could pour you a beer."

"That's more like it, but no thanks," he said with a wink. I had a feeling he had picked up on my unease. His tone was almost too jovial. "Good luck wrestling wallpaper. I'll stop by later to see how it works."

"Cross your fingers." Kat crossed several of hers.

Hans left with a wave, but not before giving me one last look of concern. Kat and I finished the inventory sheets before Garrett came downstairs.

"You got the machine?" he asked, pouring himself a cup of lukewarm coffee.

"That's been sitting in the pot for an hour. You might want to warm it up."

"Nah. The caffeine is the same cold or hot." He held up his mug, then pointed to the steam machine. "You guys want to go fire this thing up and see how it does?"

Kat nodded. "Yes, I want to get the wallpaper off, so we can get on to the fun stuff."

Ursula had not oversold the machine's capabilities. We were still hot from the steam and damp with sweat by lunchtime, but the wallpaper peeled off in long strips.

"At this rate, we're going to be done by end of day," Garrett announced, stepping back to survey our progress. We had removed all the wallpaper from the first two guest rooms and were a quarter of the way through the third room. Our teamwork was paying off. We had a system that appeared to be working. Kat and I would score and spray the walls and then Garrett would run the steamer over them. Next, we would take turns using oversized putty knives to pull back the paper.

"What do you say we break for lunch and see how much we can get done this afternoon?" Garrett asked, wiping his brow with his shirtsleeve.

"You'll get no argument from me." Even with my morning latte and apple strudel, I had worked up an appetite. "I can go grab us sausages from the Wursthouse."

"And I can pour us some pints." Garrett smiled.

Kat continued to use her putty knife on the wallpaper. "I'll keep working until you get back. I love the feeling when you can tell that you're close to pulling off a huge piece."

"Any sausage requests?" I asked them.

"No, but I'll take like two of anything you want to bring us." Garrett rubbed his stomach. "I'm starving."

"Be back in a flash." I stopped at the bathroom to splash some cold water on my face and then headed for the Wursthouse. It was a popular spot with locals and a tourist favorite. The outdoor grill had a walk-up counter where you could order sausages to go. Inside there was a dining room and a covered outdoor deck for any customers who wanted to linger over a brat and beer.

The choices and smells at the Wursthouse made my stomach growl so loud I thought it might disturb the customers waiting in line in front of me. I studied the choices, including charbroiled Bavarian-style sausages, bratwurst, chicken and apple sausages, curry wurst, and kelbassi. Since both Garrett and Kat had said that they were famished, I decided to order an assortment of everything along with sauerkraut, cold German potato salad, and kettle chips. It only took a couple of minutes for the Wursthouse staff to box up my order. I was about to return to Nitro, loaded with a huge box of spicy sausages, when April snuck up behind me. She was in the same incognito outfit I'd seen her in yesterday.

"Sloan, I've been looking everywhere for you. Have you been avoiding me?" She peered at me from beneath her oversized black sunglasses.

"What are you talking about? I've been at Nitro all morning. If you were looking *everywhere* for me, you should have come by."

"I did. I knocked five times. No one answered. I even went around the back. I swear I heard music and talking. You're trying to ditch me, aren't you?" Her eyes bugged out.

"If I was trying to ditch you, April, you wouldn't be talking to me now, would you?"

She raised her hands in surrender. "Listen, Sloan, we don't have time to play around with semantics. We have a much more pressing issue that needs our attention immediately."

I shifted the heavy box. "As you can see, I have my hands full at the moment."

"Sloan, I learned something monumental this morning. Huge. Massive."

"Okay, tell me, what is it?"

She glanced around us. "Not here. Come with me."

I protested. "I just ordered lunch. These sausages are steaming."

"It will only take a minute for me to fill you in, then you can go drop off lunch at Nitro." She yanked me across the street. When we were out of earshot of the people congregated at the grill for lunch, she leaned in close and whispered, "I heard a very interesting rumor this morning about Kris, and I desperately need your help to investigate."

"Go on." I realized that in every interaction I'd had with April the past few days that she had not once uttered a single German phrase nor made any attempt at a thick, fake accent. It was a refreshing break from her nauseating need to constantly be Leavenworth's expert on all things Bavarian. It also made me consider that she might be innocent. If April had abandoned her dirndls and braids, and spoke in complete sentences without slipping in a *guten Morgen* or *schönen Tag noch* (have a nice day), she was in bad shape.

"It turns out that he invested a large chunk of cash in a local business. A business that would be directly impacted if his plan to make Leavenworth dry came to fruition."

"Okay. Why are you telling me?"

"Because I need your help sleuthing out whether or not it's true."

"Why don't you do that yourself? Or, better idea. Go to Chief Meyers."

"I already did. The person who I think Kris was involved in a secret deal with isn't exactly a close friend of mine. Let's just say that we haven't been on good terms for a while."

Not a shocker. April had managed to irritate nearly every business owner in Leavenworth over the years.

"Chief Meyers gave me the usual canned response about 'looking into it,' but that's not enough, Sloan. My reputation is at stake. The village is swarming with press. I can't risk letting anyone think that I'm a suspect in Kris's murder a second longer." She glanced around.

"What am I supposed to do?"

"Go talk to this person. See what you can find out. Everyone trusts you, Sloan. Why, I still haven't a clue, but I know she'll talk to you."

"Who?"

"Heidi."

I almost dropped the box of sausages. "Heidi?"

April nodded frantically. "Yes, yes. I have heard from a very credible source that Kris invested in the Hamburg last year. Do you remember the major remodel the hotel did?"

I nodded.

"Apparently, that was thanks in large part to Kris's wallet. Heidi went out in search of venture capital to update the hotel, which was a wise move. I had kindly offered her a number of suggestions on how to bring the Hamburg in line with our village aesthetic. I pointed out to her on many occasions that it was turning into an unsightly eyesore."

I'm sure you did, I thought to myself.

"She didn't get any bites, probably because it was in such bad shape, but then Kris swept in and offered to be a silent partner."

"That doesn't make any sense. You told this to Chief Meyers?"

"Yes, we've already been over that. The chief is looking into it, but I want intel—now. Heidi and I had a falling-out earlier this year when I simply suggested that she might attract more guests and a husband if she cut down on her apple strudel habit. For some reason, she took that as an insult." April looked flabbergasted. "I would talk to her myself, but she's given me the cold—rather icy—shoulder ever since. My advice to lay off the German pastries paid off, because she's recently dropped quite a bit of her pudge. She should be thrilled with my input, but some people are so sensitive to constructive feedback."

I didn't comment on that. "Who did you hear this from?"

April folded her arms across her chest. "I'm not at liberty to say, but as I mentioned, my source is reputable. An upstanding member of the Leavenworth business community with a serious commitment to preserving our German heritage." She shot me a knowing look.

"Why don't they tell Chief Meyers this?"

"It's complicated. Heidi swore this person to secrecy, and they don't want to break that trust."

"But this is a murder investigation."

"I know. Which is exactly why I need your help. Promise me that you'll talk to Heidi. See what you can get out of her. Maybe there's evidence. A contract, something."

"Are you asking me to snoop around her office?"

"I didn't say that. I simply said maybe there's evidence lying around, and if there is, what harm would there be in delivering that evidence to the police?"

"April, I am most definitely not going to snoop around Heidi's office."

"Fine, but you'll talk to her, won't you? Please, Sloan. I can't stand being treated like a common criminal. You should see the looks that I'm getting when I'm out in the village. Especially from the press. I'm sure they're working on an exposé about me as we speak."

I suspected that the reason April was receiving strange looks from the press had to do with her outlandish outfit. If she was trying to look inconspicuous the trench coat and black attire had the opposite effect.

"What exactly are you asking me to do?" I repeated. My arms were beginning to quiver under the weight of the box.

"Just go talk to Heidi. She likes you. See if she'll confess that Kris was a silent partner. According to my source, they had a huge fight. Heidi was livid that he had taken such a shift in policy. She tried to reason with him about what a ban on alcohol would do to the village and to his investment in the Hamburg, but he didn't care. He was set on his mission. I know she killed him. She did it, Sloan. Think about it. They say that money is a huge motivator for murder."

I wasn't sure what to think. Given my conversation with Heidi earlier this morning, I was leaning toward believing what April was telling me.

"I'll see what I can do."

"Thank you. Thank you, Sloan. You are a true friend and a saint. Call me the second you finish your conversation with her. Then we can go to Chief Meyers together. She'll believe it if it's coming from you and if you can get Heidi to confess."

"I'll call you later." With that, I turned and made a beeline for Nitro before April could say anything more.

This was really a matter for Chief Meyers. I was sure the chief was likely pulling Heidi's and the Hamburg's financial records and looking into April's theory. However, I hated to admit it, but I was feeling more and more convinced that Heidi might be a killer.

CHAPTER

TWENTY-THREE

"WOW, THAT WAS FAST," GARRETT commented when I returned with lunch.

"It would have been even faster, had I not had the good fortune to bump into April Ablin."

He let out a low whistle. "Oh, sorry."

I set the box from the Wursthouse on one of the high-top tables and walked behind the bar to grab napkins and plates. "Can I use you as a sounding board?"

"Hit me." Garrett poured us beers. "Actually, I'm glad you asked because it seems like you've kind of been in your head this morning. I was going to ask you if everything was okay."

"It's the murder investigation. I can't get it out of my head." That was half true. I told him about my one-sided conversation with April. Then I filled him in on my talk with Heidi and what I had learned about Ross.

"You've been busy, Sloan. How have you managed to find

this all out while still working? Are you running a secret detective agency in the back alley?"

"It feels like it." I unloaded the sausages and sides. "What do you think I should do?"

"First, you should definitely fill in Chief Meyers, but April might be on to something about having you reach out to Heidi again. One thing I've learned since moving to Leavenworth is that people in a small town talk to their neighbors in a way that never happened in Seattle." He paused and brought over the first beer. "You know, I think in all of the years that I lived in my condo, I maybe spoke to my neighbors twice. Can you imagine that here?"

"It sounds dreamy."

"Maybe. There's something to be said for connection, though."

"That's why I'm wondering if I should leave this to the chief."

He poured another pint. "You definitely need to share this with her, but I think April's right about Heidi potentially confiding in you versus an authority figure."

"Don't say that to Alex. He is under the impression that I am the authority figure."

Garrett laughed. "You are. Trust me. That's why I think there's a possibility Heidi will spill whatever she's hiding—or not—to you. You don't do drama, Sloan. Everyone around here knows and appreciates that. You aren't prone to hysterics or one to spread gossip. People understand that they can come to you in confidence."

"Thanks." I was touched by his words, but unsure about

how to proceed. If only he knew the range of emotions swirling inside me.

Kat came downstairs drenched in sweat and wearing a big grin. "I got that last section done. Only one room to go."

"Cheers to that." Garrett set another pint glass on the table. "Can I pour you a beer?"

"No thanks." Kat pulled up a barstool. "I don't know how you guys can drink a pint at lunch and go back to work no problem."

"It's brewer's code," Garrett said.

"Yeah, and years of required drinking on the job," I agreed.

We dove into the sausages. I was glad I had opted to go with an assortment and ordered extra sides, because a half hour later, there wasn't a crumb left on the table.

"All right, how do we want to divide up the afternoon?" Garrett asked, tossing his napkin in the garbage.

"If you don't mind, I'm kind of into this project," Kat said. "I'd like to see it through, but if you want me to open the tasting room, that's totally cool too."

"You won't get any argument from me," I said with a wink.

"I'll come help you with the rest of the heavy lifting," Garrett said to Kat and then turned to me. "As long as you don't mind being on bar duty this afternoon?"

"Mind? Never."

They went upstairs. I cleared our lunch dishes, readied the tasting room, propped the chalkboard sign on the sidewalk, and opened the front door. The early November sun filtered through the windows.

It was a slow start. Only a few customers trickled in for the first two hours. Normally I wouldn't have minded, but without being busy, thoughts of my conversation with Ursula kept intruding. I focused on organizing the bar, not that it needed it, but I had to give my hands something to do.

Conrad, the owner of Leavenworth's second nutcracker shop, came in around three. He walked up to the bar with purpose. "I need a beer, the hardest beer you have."

"Hardest?" Beer wasn't categorized in the same way as hard alcohol. There were beers that had a higher ABV content. A double IPA or even a triple IPA might have 10 percent alcohol versus a light session ale that might only contain 4 percent.

"Whatever is the strongest. It's been a rough day."

"We don't have anything with a high ABV on tap at the moment."

"Fine. Then give me a pint of the Pucker Up."

I poured Conrad his pint. "Is there anything I can help with?"

He chugged the beer. "No. I don't think so; it's just been a bad day. I'm sure a few pints of this will take off the edge."

I wanted to caution him that chugging our hop-forward IPA was likely going to make him feel worse. Our craft beers were meant for sipping.

Conrad tapped his fingers on the rim of the pint glass. "Have you heard anything more about Kristopher's murder?"

"Not really." I wasn't going to share what I knew with Conrad, especially in his semi-erratic state.

"Me neither." He took two huge swigs of the beer. "Although I did hear a rumor that it had something to do with money."

"You did?" I kept my face passive.

He barely made eye contact. "Did you know that he was investing in a bunch of Leavenworth businesses on the side? He kept it on the down-low, because can you say 'conflict of interest'? He was an elected official. He couldn't go around secretly dumping money into local businesses without disclosing that publicly. That's unethical and against city council by-laws."

"Who told you this?"

Conrad shook his head. "I don't know. It's all over town."

Was April floating the rumor, or was there real merit to it?

"Do you know what businesses he had invested in?"

Conrad finished his pint and handed me his empty glass. "Can I get another?"

I turned to pour him a fresh pint. When I handed it back to him, I couldn't resist a word of caution. "Be careful. Our IPAs have a tendency to sneak up on you."

"I can handle it." He took a huge drink to prove his point.

Maybe he could, but if he guzzled this second pint in the same time he had polished off the first, I could refuse to serve him.

"Did you happen to hear what businesses he was financially involved with?" I asked again.

"No. It's all rumor and speculation, I guess. It sounds like he had interest in more than one business in town. Someone told me in dozens."

"That doesn't make any sense," I said under my breath.

"What?"

"Nothing." I picked up a towel. "I need to go wipe down a couple tables." I left him with his pint and went to clear a table that had been vacated. Why would Kristopher have invested in Leavenworth businesses only to then propose legislation to prohibit alcohol? The two seemed to be in conflict with each other. Every business in the village (regardless if they sold or distributed alcohol) would be impacted by such a drastic change. What was Kristopher's endgame? It didn't add up.

I cleared the table and wiped it down. When I returned to the bar, Conrad had chugged the rest of his second pint. He slapped a twenty-dollar bill on the bar. "I need to get back to the store. Thanks for the drink."

At least he had cut himself off. I watched him power-walk toward the door. Why was he so upset about Kristopher investing in local businesses? Not that I blamed him. He was right about it being a conflict of interest, and if that information had gotten out before the election, that likely would have sealed the deal for his imminent loss.

I couldn't figure out why Kristopher would have put money into businesses only to jeopardize their livelihoods. I had to be missing something. If what Conrad had told me was true, it was looking much more plausible that Heidi could be the killer.

Could she have killed Kristopher to save the Hamburg? I tried to reason through what might have happened to come up with some kind of a theory—even if it was far-fetched. If I assumed that Kristopher had secretly invested in the hotel as a silent partner and then Heidi learned of his intention to make Leavenworth dry, that gave her two potential motives. Kristopher's death would ensure that tourists kept pouring into town, and it also silenced his voice in her business decisions. I wondered what the terms of her contract with him had been.

There was another possibility. It was outlandish, but I couldn't dismiss it. What if Kristopher had a bigger plan and Heidi figured it out? What his plan could have been, I had no idea, but if he was scheming to ruin Leavenworth as we knew it and Heidi realized it, she could have decided to kill him.

I let out a long sigh. My theories were becoming wilder with every passing minute. The other thing I had to take into consideration was that, in the unlikely circumstance that Kristopher's secret investments spoke to something more sinister for the village, it put April back on the top of my suspect list. No one would protect Leavenworth like April. If Kristopher was plotting a total town revamp, then April had a clear motive.

I picked up Conrad's empty glass. There was only one way to find out. I was going to have to speak with Heidi again. I didn't know if she would tell me anything, but I had to give it a shot.

CHAPTER

TWENTY-FOUR

ALEX SHOWED UP AFTER SCHOOL. He had showered and changed into a pair of jeans and a University of Washington sweatshirt. I could smell a hint of cologne on him but didn't comment, as I was confident that his appearance had something to do with Kat.

"You're a Husky fan?" she asked, noting his purple hoodie.

"Yeah. I'm thinking about going to school there. It's on my short list."

"That's so cool. Where else are you going to apply?"

"Maybe Stanford. Cal. I want to go to a Pac-12 school and one with a good design program." Alex squared his shoulders as he spoke.

"Amazing. You must be one smart kid." Kat tapped her index finger to the side of her head. "You get your brains from your smart mom, right?"

She was oblivious to Alex's dejected look when she called him kid.

"You want to come upstairs and see the progress?"

He cleared his throat (I suspected in an attempt to make his voice sound deeper). "Sure."

Poor Alex.

"Someone has a crush, huh?" Garrett came up from behind me. He held an iPad that he used to track our beers in one hand. We watched as Alex tagged after Kat.

"Is it that obvious?"

"Nah. I just remember being his age. You can't blame the kid. He has good taste. My first crush on an older woman was Ms. Flyer. She was my French teacher, a subject I had no interest in learning before her. My mom was shocked when I asked if I could get after-school tutoring from Ms. Flyer. She thought I actually wanted to learn French."

"And?"

"She set up a conference with Ms. Flyer to talk about my grades and the possibility of paying for some extra help. She took one look at the woman and figured it out. The next thing I knew, she had arranged tutoring with a kid who lived down the street from us. He had serious hygiene issues and the worst breath."

I laughed so hard I snorted.

"Funny. Yeah, go ahead and laugh. My mom crushed my teenage dream of running away with Ms. Flyer. Promise me you won't do the same to Alex." Garrett set the iPad on the bar.

"Crush his dreams? Never. But I'm not going to encourage him to run away with Kat either. Your mom sounds hilarious, by the way." I rinsed a pint glass in the sink.

"Glad you think so, because you're going to have a chance to meet her soon."

A familiar rumble of butterflies erupted in my stomach. What did he mean by that? "Oh yeah, why?"

"My parents are coming to Leavenworth next week."

"They are?"

"Yep. Get ready for the invasion. We're going to have to set up some ground rules for dealing with my parents. My mom still thinks I'm twelve, so I'm already anticipating being smothered with her kisses and having her ask if I want the crusts cut off my sandwich."

"That sounds sweet." I didn't mean anything by my comment, but I could tell from the look of worry in Garrett's eyes that he thought he had offended me.

"Sorry, Sloan. I'm an idiot. I didn't mean . . ." He trailed off.

"Your parents are allowed to be sweet. I'm excited to meet them."

"They're excited to meet you too. I've been telling them about Nitro and the village, about you and Kat and, well, everyone. They've been in Australia for the last six months, so the first thing they're going to do after dropping off their stuff in Seattle is come out this way. Tess was my mom's aunt. She's dying to see the transformation."

Garrett had mentioned that his parents were traveling. They had retired a couple of years earlier and had set out on adventures in Africa and Australia.

"My sister is going to try to come up too," he continued. "She's trying to swap shifts with one of her fellow residents."

His sister was a doctor in Portland. Anytime Garrett

mentioned his family, I felt a twang of envy and felt intimidated by his family's success. His sister, Leah, was in her final year of residency. He had been an engineer before giving up his six-figure salary to start Nitro, and his parents were both retired professors. My two-year community college degree seemed feeble in comparison with Garrett's professional family.

"I can't wait for you to meet them. You're going to love them."

Maybe it was leftover angst from my past, but the thought of meeting Garrett's brilliant family sent a wave of anxiety through me.

"Great." I forced a smile. "Will they stay here?"

He frowned. "There's no way the guest rooms will be ready in time. I wish. That would have been cool, but I was going to see if there's space at the Hamburg. It's right around the block, and I think they would like a smaller, boutique-style hotel."

"Have you ever been inside?"

"No."

"You should check it out, it's beautiful." Then a thought occurred to me. "Actually, on second thought, maybe I'll go over and set up a reservation on your behalf. That will give me a chance to talk to Heidi."

"Killing two birds with one stone, as they say."

"Something like that."

Garrett's iPad buzzed. He stared at the screen for a minute. "Just got a weather alert. They're calling for damaging winds and snow later. We'll have to keep a close watch. Might have to stop pouring early tonight."

"Welcome to your first winter in Leavenworth." I dried my hands on a bar towel.

"It's early November," Garrett protested. "I thought winter didn't start until January."

"Not in the North Cascades. One year it snowed a foot on Halloween. We had to take Alex trick-or-treating in a sled."

"I guess it's time to start stockpiling firewood and flashlights," Garrett replied, turning off the iPad.

Kat and Alex came downstairs. Garrett tended bar while Kat and I chatted with Alex. His friend came to pick him up for soccer practice. "Watch the weather tonight," I called after him. "Go straight home if the storm hits, okay?"

"Mom, it's only snow. Don't freak out." Alex rolled his eyes.

The pub was slow. I had a feeling that everyone was loading up on groceries and supplies in case the storm came to fruition. Winter weather in Leavenworth was unpredictable. Sometimes the rugged Cascades served as a barrier, protecting the village from grueling winds, while other times the mountains trapped storm systems, dumping snow on us for days on end.

"I'm calling it an evening," I said to Garrett. "I'll stop by the Hamburg on my way home. How many nights will your family be staying?"

We went over the details, and I left the sanctuary of the quiet pub. Darkness was beginning to descend earlier and earlier. In this northernmost corner of the state, it would soon be dark when I woke in the morning and dark again by early evening. We would spend the winter months chasing the light. It was one of many reasons that villagers had petitioned the city council to leave Front Street illuminated all winter long.

For many years, the winter light festival kicked off the day after Thanksgiving and ran through New Year's. But a few years ago, a group of business owners put together a proposal to leave the festive lights on through March. The millions of tiny, dazzling lights were a draw for tourists during the slower winter months and helped take the edge off when we were plunged into months of darkness. I especially loved the lights after a fresh snowfall. They reflected off the white ground and made Leavenworth come to life in a magical glow.

I breathed in the cold evening air as I rounded the corner to the Hamburg Hostel. Soon my sweet town would be illuminated. I hoped that my visit with Heidi would shed some illumination on Kristopher's death.

The Hamburg lobby was empty. I went to the front desk and set up the reservation for Garrett's family.

"Is Heidi still here, by chance?" I asked after confirming the reservation.

The clerk nodded. "I think she's in her office. Would you like me to call her?"

"Please."

I waited while he made the call.

"She'll be down in just a minute," he said.

"Thanks." I took a seat in one of the oversized plush chairs. The one thing I hadn't considered was how to broach the topic of Kristopher's financial investments with Heidi. Jumping on her with accusatory questions wouldn't exactly lend itself to her opening up, so I quickly decided on another option— beer.

Heidi arrived in the lobby. "Sloan, two visits in one day. To what do I owe this pleasure?"

"I was wondering if you might be free to grab a beer at Der Keller."

"You bet. Let me go shut down my laptop and grab my things."

I was glad that Heidi hadn't asked why I wanted to get a beer with her. I hadn't thought my plan that far through. Hopefully, the conversation would naturally flow to Kristopher. I wanted to take her to Der Keller, a very public setting. On the off chance that my hunch was right and she had had something to do with Kristopher's death, I wasn't going to take any chances. I had learned that lesson the hard way.

"Ready." Heidi returned to the lobby with a broad smile. "I'm so happy that you stopped by, Sloan. A beer sounds wonderful. I could really use an escape from the office for the night. I've been working around the clock since Kristopher died."

Could this woman really be a killer? Her attitude didn't make me confident that I had the right suspect, but then again, I couldn't make any assumptions.

"I know. The entire village is on edge," I said as we walked along Front Street toward Der Keller.

"Tell me about it. I feel like there's a dark cloud hanging over us." She pointed to the starless sky. "And not just because they're predicting a major storm tonight."

The clouds above looked ominous. "Yeah, maybe the weather forecasters are right."

She followed my gaze. "You never know. It's so hit-or-miss. I feel like every time they predict something major, we end up without a trace of snow, and then when they don't, we end up buried in three feet."

We arrived at Der Keller and found a private booth. A waiter I had hired took our order and returned in a flash with two pints.

Heidi stared at her ornate glass Der Keller stein. "Do you miss it?"

"What? Der Keller?" I stared at my naked ring finger.

She nodded. "I don't mean to pry, but it must be such a change of pace to have gone from an operation like this to a start-up. I only say that because I know what a struggle it's been for me to try to keep the Hamburg afloat during our renovations."

"Yeah, you're right. Working in a small business is a different beast, for sure. There are lots of pros, but plenty of cons."

"Like money."

"Money is on the top of the list. It's strange after having a huge staff, marketing and distributing departments, human resources. Garrett and I are all of those things at Nitro."

"Exactly." Heidi lifted her stein and clicked it to mine. "Cheers to that."

"On that topic, I heard something odd today, and I wonder if you know anything about it."

"What?"

"There's talk that Kristopher had been privately investing in a number of small businesses in the village. Have you heard anything about that?"

Heidi choked on her beer.

"Are you okay?"

She coughed, trying to clear her airway. "I'm fine. I can't believe that's gotten out. Sometimes this place makes me crazy."

"So you've heard the rumors?" I didn't want to give Heidi any indication that I knew anything more.

She coughed again. Then she massaged the side of her head. "It's not rumors. It's true."

"How do you know?"

"Because I'm one of those rumors."

CHAPTER

TWENTY-FIVE

"YOU'RE ONE OF THE RUMORS?" I asked.

Heidi pounded her fingers under her eyes, as if trying to force out her frustration. "It's a long story."

"I have time, if you want to talk." I pointed to my full pint. "There's always more beer, and I don't know about you, but I could go for a bowl of Ursula's famous beer cheese soup."

"That sounds good," Heidi agreed.

We ordered bowls of the beer cheese soup and then returned to our conversation.

"It would be nice to talk about this," Heidi said, fiddling with her napkin. "I've been keeping it bottled up for so long now."

"I'm here to listen."

She reached for her stein and took a sip of her beer. "It started about a year and a half ago. If you remember, the Hamburg wasn't in great shape. I mean, we've done well in terms of staying booked through the busy season, but we haven't been able to compete with the bigger hotels in the village. We just don't have the same amenities—a pool, outdoor patios, suites. You know. And then there's a lot more competition with the vacation rental market these days. Everyone in the village is turning their spare bedrooms and basements into private vacation rentals."

I nodded.

"That's made it tough to stay competitive, and the hotel was in desperate need of modernization. Our guest rooms were outdated. We needed new electrical and plumbing systems and some ADA upgrades. All to the tune of tens of thousands of dollars. I didn't have that kind of capital on hand and went to a couple of banks to see if I could get a loan for the renovations. The local banks agreed to loan me the money, but the repayment costs were intimidating, and I'd be spending even more in interest over the life of the loan. I was complaining to another business owner, who suggested that I find someone with venture capital to invest in the hotel. That way I wouldn't have to worry about repaying a huge business loan. It would mean giving up a percentage of ownership, but that was fine by me. I'm not in this to make a fortune. I love the Hamburg, and I love being in the hospitality industry. I just want the hotel to continue to thrive."

She didn't sound like a killer.

"I wasn't sure where to start. I'd never sought out venture capital before. It sounded so out of reach. I mean, are there venture capitalists here? I figured I would have to go to Seattle and maybe hire an investment firm to help me, but then I learned that Kristopher was interested in partnering. It was like winning the jackpot. I'd known Kristopher for years, and

he was a respected member of the community—a city councilor. I should have done my due diligence, but I jumped at
his offer. He agreed to cover the renovation costs as well as
put some money into a marketing campaign in some regional
travel magazines. He didn't want any part of day-to-day operations, which was great with me. He wanted to be a silent
partner, so to speak, but in exchange for an influx of cash,
he asked for a substantial piece of ownership. I didn't think it
through. I'd always been a single owner since I purchased the
Hamburg two decades ago. The thought of having someone
like Kristopher as a sounding board and partner was appealing. I really thought it would take us to the next level."

"That sounds good to me."

"Yes, but you know what people say about things that
sound too good to be true?" Heidi massaged her temples.

I nodded.

"Well, they were. What I didn't realize was that Kristopher
had been investing in a number of other small businesses in
town."

"What's wrong with that?"

"He had a master plan to take over the entire village. He
wanted to create a German utopia of his making."

"Without alcohol."

"Among other things, yes. I guess he came from a very
wealthy family. His father died unexpectedly, and he inherited
a very large sum of money. He'd been using that to take a majority share in every business he invested in."

"What was his plan?"

She shrugged. "I tried to talk to him about it. He came to
me when he started his reelection campaign and explained his

stance on prohibition as well as informing me that once the campaign was over, the Hamburg was going to take a very different direction."

"Like what?"

"Honestly, I have no idea. I think maybe he was a bit crazy. His father had been killed by a drunk driver, and he went off the deep end. I can understand his grief, but he took such an extreme position. He was convinced that alcohol was the root of all evil. He didn't care about the businesses in Leavenworth and what banning alcohol might do to our livelihoods. He was on a singular mission, and if the village suffered, it didn't matter to him. He would be fine."

"I had no idea."

"No one did. It came as a complete shock."

Our soups and glistening buttered pretzels arrived at the table. Heidi broke off a chunk. "I didn't know what to do. I hired a lawyer, but there wasn't much she could do for me. I had stupidly signed a contract with Kristopher. He owned five percent more of the business than me, so he had all the power."

Knowing that Kristopher's motivation for canceling events like Oktoberfest stemmed from grief made more sense, but everything Heidi had told me so far made her motive for killing him that much stronger.

"I hate to admit this, Sloan, but I was kind of relieved when he ended up dead."

I plunged my spoon into the gooey, cheesy soup, trying to buy some time before I responded. This was my chance. I needed to craft my words carefully.

She continued before I could speak. "I didn't kill him, if

that's what you're thinking. Absolutely not. That's not me. I just mean that his death, while terrible, was also a relief. I wouldn't have to worry about what might become of the Hamburg or my job and income with Kristopher dead. I'm not the only one. I know there are plenty of other business owners who feel the same as me. They were in the same position. Which is why I'm sure that one of them must have killed him." She barely paused for a breath. "It makes sense, don't you think? That's why I've been so distracted and staying late at the Hamburg. I've been trying to figure out what other businesses he invested in and who might have gotten so desperate that they decided to kill him."

There was the possibility she was lying to me, but I wanted to believe her. She sounded sincere and equally stressed about who could have killed Kristopher.

"Do you know what other businesses he had a stake in?"

Heidi ripped off another piece of pretzel. "I've been replaying every conversation I had with Kristopher. He had mentioned diversifying his investments—wanting a combination of retail and restaurants. He claimed that the Hamburg was the only hotel he was investing in, but I have no way of knowing whether that's true."

"Have you mentioned this to Chief Meyers?"

Heidi shot me a strange look. "Multiple times. She was at the Hamburg for half of the day reviewing contracts and trying to help me jog my memory on anything else that could lead to his killer."

If Chief Meyers was already looped in on Kristopher's investment in the Hamburg, I felt even more confident that I wasn't sharing a beer with a killer.

"Do you have any other thoughts on who else in the village he was working with?"

"He was tight-lipped about his other investments, which makes sense in hindsight, knowing what he had planned. I have some speculations but nothing concrete."

"Like what?"

"I had heard a rumor that he approached Garrett about Nitro. Who knows, it could be nothing more than a rumor, but I guess Kristopher made him a very attractive offer to purchase Nitro's building and restore it back to a bed-and-breakfast. From what I heard, it sounded like Kristopher was successful with the offer."

I gulped. That couldn't be true. Garrett hadn't said a word to me about selling Nitro. "Are you sure?"

Heidi shook her head. "No. You know how the rumor mill works around here. Who knows."

"Have you heard of anyone else that Kristopher tried to buy out?

"No, but I heard that Conrad's nutcracker business hasn't been doing well."

"It hasn't?" Not that I was surprised. Everyone in the village had been slightly baffled when he opened his nutcracker shop.

"No. You didn't hear?"

"What?"

"He's probably going to have to close up shop. He hasn't paid his lease in months."

This was news.

"Conrad's shop hit all of the marks—small, new business that was having financial struggles."

"Right. I thought it was odd that someone would open a second nutcracker shop in town. It doesn't seem like there's a market for more than one."

"Me too. That makes it even more likely that Conrad might have jumped at the chance to partner with Kristopher."

She raised a valid point. The problem was that I had no idea what that meant in terms of Kristopher's murder. If Conrad needed cash to save his shop, he wouldn't have had a motive to kill Kristopher—would he?

Heidi pushed her soup around with her spoon. "Then there's Ross. He's the one who I personally think had the most motive."

"Really? Why?"

She lowered her voice. "We work out together. He and Kristopher got in a huge fight because Kristopher got him shut down."

"I heard that, but I also heard he was in danger of being shut down, not that he actually was shut down." I ran my index finger along the rim of my pint glass.

"No. He's been completely shut down. The state revoked his liquor license. He's trying to keep it quiet. That's why he's been painting and doing 'work' on the Underground. It's a smokescreen while he fights to get his license reinstated."

"Are you sure?"

"Positive." Heidi nodded. "I promised him I wouldn't say a word. Please don't share this information. He's worried that if people find out that the Underground is in trouble, regardless of whether it's true, that they'll boycott the bar and he'll lose the business."

"Of course I won't say anything." I sighed and took a

drink of my beer. "Except, I do feel like Chief Meyers needs to know this."

Heidi swirled her soup with her spoon. "She knows. Ross told me that he's been working with the police to prove his innocence. The only reason the state got involved was because Kristopher kept calling in fake complaints."

All the more reason he could have killed Kristopher, I thought to myself. The subject shifted to the upcoming light festival and the election. We finished our soups and beers and parted ways. I needed to get home to Alex. Heidi's revelation had sent me in a new direction. Was I closing in on a killer, or was I more lost than ever?

CHAPTER

TWENTY-SIX

THE STREET LAMPS CAST AN eerie glow on the sidewalk as I walked back to my car. Wind roared through the quiet streets. It was so loud that it sounded like a jet was flying overhead. I worried about the countless hours of work that the city crews had spent twisting twinkle lights into the trees as I sidestepped falling branches and shielded my face from an assault of flying debris. I wished I had a pair of gloves or a hat. Apparently, the weather forecaster had predicted correctly this time.

I had to fight to keep my balance as I pressed on. *Alex must already be home,* I thought. His coach wouldn't have let them practice in conditions like this. At least I hoped not.

"What are you doing out here?" Conrad shouted above the heavy din as I passed by his shop. He was trying to secure a sale banner that was whipping so violently I thought it might lash through his arm.

"Trying to get back to my car," I called.

"Haven't you heard the news?" He yanked one edge of the banner, which made it balloon out like a sail.

I tried to grab the other end. "No, what's going on?"

"They say we're going to get gusts up to a hundred miles per hour. No one is supposed to drive. They sent out an emergency alert. Didn't you hear it?"

"I was at dinner." I caught the edge of the loose banner.

We worked together to take it down.

"Thanks." Conrad pointed inside to his dark shop. "I already lost power. Not sure what I'm going to do. I guess sit inside and wait out the storm."

"Why don't we go to Nitro?" I had to yell over the wind. One hundred miles per hour didn't sound like an exaggeration. Gusts knocked over construction cones in the park and toppled two vintage rose bushes. "Maybe we still have power."

Conrad had to use every muscle to wrangle his front door open. He propped one foot against the base of the door and tugged as hard as he could. Once he got it open, he dropped the banner on the ground before the wind slammed it shut. "Doubt it. Looks like everything on Front Street is out."

I looked up to see the street lamps spark out. Every building and storefront went dark in an instant. "Well, at least we have gas in the kitchen. I can make us tea or something."

"No. I've got to stay and protect my products," Conrad said. "You go ahead."

"Okay, but if you change your mind, we're right around the corner."

I stayed to the far side of the sidewalk, hugging the shop fronts in order to stay as shielded as possible from the unrelenting wind. Carnage lined the streets. Broken strands of twinkle lights, loose tree limbs, garbage, plastic chairs and tables. I couldn't believe the storm had struck so quickly. I hadn't been at Der Keller that long.

Icy snowflakes pelted my face. At Nitro, our sidewalk bistro tables had been upended and our chalkboard sign was split in two. I unlocked the front door, using my cell as a flashlight.

"Hello! Garrett, Kat?" My voice echoed in the cavernous bar.

I scanned the blackness with the single strand of white light. There was a soft yellow glow coming from the back near the kitchen.

"Garrett," I called as I inched closer.

"Sloan? Is that you?" he answered.

Relief flooded my body. "Hey! It's crazy out there."

Inside the kitchen, Garrett had lit a dozen or so votive candles and placed them on the stainless-steel countertops. There was a pot of something simmering on the stove. The space looked like a beacon of warmth compared to outside.

Kat, who was scrolling on her phone, on the opposite side of the kitchen, clicked it off and ran over to hug me. "We were so worried about you. I saw your car still parked out front when we lost power and had to close the pub. Garrett went to look for you, but he couldn't find you."

Garrett stirred the pot. "Yeah, where did you go?"

"Der Keller. I met Heidi for a drink and dinner."

"We couldn't get you on your cell, so I tried calling over there, but the phone lines must be down too," Garrett said.

"I turned it off while I was at dinner."

Kat released me. "I'm just glad you're okay. Alex texted me a bunch. He's at your house with Mac. He wanted you to know. I told him that as soon as we found you, I would be in touch. Reception has been spotty in here. I'm going to run up to the bar and see if I can get a text through to him."

"Thanks so much," I said to Kat.

She held up her phone case; it was pale pink with white polka dots. "No problem. Don't worry, I'll get through to Alex."

"I feel terrible," I said to Garrett as Kat went to try and get better service. "I had no idea the storm would get so bad so fast."

"No one did. We saw a few gusts, but then it started blowing and wouldn't stop. The power kept flickering on and off, and then there was a huge boom." Garrett pointed to the dark lights above.

"It's starting to snow, too." I rubbed my icy fingers together.

Garrett lifted the wooden spoon. "Can I interest you in a hot chocolate? I'm making my mom's famous spiked peppermint schnapps recipe."

"That sounds divine."

Garrett measured the minty liquor and added it to his bubbling hot chocolate. It smelled wonderfully calming.

Kat returned, flashing a triumphant smile. "I got service. Alex says he's glad you're here and not to worry—he and Mac have a fire going and plenty of food and blankets. They say not to drive home. It's too dangerous."

I didn't reply. I wanted to get home to be with my son.

Garrett dished up mugs of steaming hot chocolate. We sat around the countertop listening to the wind pound the rooftop. "I hope we don't lose too many shingles. Those were custom clay tiles, and they aren't cheap to replace."

"Have they said how long the wind is supposed to last?"

Kat studied her phone. "I've been checking the weather up-date every few minutes. We're under a high-wind warning until two this morning. The police are asking everyone to stay inside. I guess it's going to be a slumber party at Nitro to-night."

"When Kat checked a few minutes before you got here, they were saying that the winds have toppled power lines and doz-ens of huge evergreen trees," Garrett replied.

"So I guess we're camped out here for a while."

"Yep," Garrett said. "We should be safe upstairs. There aren't any trees near enough to cave in the roof or anything."

I warmed my hands on my mug. "We get a big windstorm like this every few years. Once we lost power for a week. I re-member having to get really creative cooking in our kitchen fireplace."

"Let's hope that it doesn't last that long." Garrett blew on his hot chocolate.

"Don't get me wrong. I don't want it to last that long." I wished I was home with Alex now. "Do you think there's any chance if I left right now, I could get home safely?"

"That's a bad idea, Sloan." Garrett frowned.

Kat reached for her phone again. "I'm trying to preserve as much battery life as I can, but let me check the latest report. Nope. No service. But the last report I saw said that the high-way is officially shut down. I guess there are fallen trees and debris blocking it in both directions."

"Damn."

Garrett placed a strong hand on my shoulder. His touch was warm and comforting. "Don't worry, Sloan. It will be okay."

"Thanks." I smiled. "Hey, new subject to take our minds

off the storm. When I was having dinner with Heidi, she confessed that Kristopher invested in the Hamburg. Apparently, he had some kind of master plan to buy up every piece of property that he could in the village and turn Leavenworth into his own warped version of a new utopia."

"Whoa," Garrett replied.

Kat looked confused.

"She said that he'd been targeting businesses in trouble, like the Hamburg. He offered an influx of cash in exchange for a big stake in the business. She said she had heard a rumor that he made an offer to you? Is that true?"

"What?" Garrett scowled. "No. I never even met the guy."

I took a sip of the hot chocolate. It was the perfect balance of sweet with a spicy mint finish. "That's what I figured."

Kat held out her hand. "Wait, what's going on, guys? I feel like I'm totally out of the loop."

Garrett looked to me for direction.

"We've been helping Chief Meyers with the investigation," I said to Kat. "Nothing formal. She asked me to keep my ears open since Nitro is such a gathering spot for locals and since I've lived here for so long."

Kat's mouth hung open. "You guys have been working on trying to figure out who killed Kristopher without me?"

"Sorry." I gave her a brief rundown of everything I had learned in the past few days. We had nothing better to do while we waited out the storm.

Garrett added details every so often. Kat listened intently.

"You two are like a real detective team," she said when I finished. "I've been scraping wallpaper, and you're solving a murder case. Sloan, I bow down to you." She gave me a full bow.

"I wouldn't say solving the case. I'm not sure I'm any closer to figuring out who did it." I sighed. "Ross is covering up the fact that the Underground got shut down. Heidi, April, and Valerie all had motives, and Heidi also just told me that Conrad is about to go out of business. She thinks he made a deal with Kristopher too."

"That guy gives me the creeps." Kat shuddered. "He always has a nutcracker in his hand. It's like he thinks he's a ventriloquist or something. I bet he did it."

"But what's his motive?" I asked. "If his shop is floundering, which I don't doubt, getting an investment from Kristopher would be the best thing for him."

"Yeah, but then, maybe like Heidi, he realized Kristopher's bigger plan and wanted out of the deal?" Garrett surmised.

"That's a theory." I paused as a sketchy thought tried to take form. "Or . . ."

"Or what?" Garrett and Kat asked in unison.

"Or, what if Conrad approached Kristopher and Kristopher turned him down?"

"What do you mean?" Kat looked puzzled.

"Heidi mentioned that Kristopher was diversifying his investments. He was intentionally buying into every aspect of Leavenworth business—retail, pubs, restaurants, hotels. Let's assume that Conrad was having financial troubles and got word that Kristopher was investing. He approached Kristopher but got turned down."

"Like maybe Kristopher already had invested in a retail shop. The other nutcracker shop?" Kat interrupted.

I liked that she was getting into trying to piece together the clues.

"Exactly. Conrad needed the money, and when Kristopher turned him down, he turned violent."

Garrett tapped his fingers on his chin. "It's a possibility."

"It could be far-fetched, but it would give him a motive for murder, right?" I asked.

We all considered my latest idea.

Kat shrugged. "No idea. The guy is probably harmless. I shouldn't make assumptions. I'm just saying he gives me a weird vibe. That's all."

"You know what my mom always told me?" Garrett said, not waiting for either of us to reply. "Your instincts will never lead you astray."

"Agreed." I nodded. "Conrad might not be a killer, but I've thought there was something off about him, too."

I was about to expand on my theory when my phone vibrated in my pocket. "Hey, I have service."

"It's been spotty. I have it and then I lose it," Kat said with an almost wistful glance at my buzzing phone.

I recognized the number—the Underground. "Hello?"

A strange crackling sound came across the line.

"Hello?" I repeated.

An electronic piercing hum made me pull the phone away from my ear.

"What's wrong?" Garrett asked.

"Bad connection." I put the phone to my ear again. "Hello, Ross, is that you?"

The piercing hum had stopped. In its place I could have sworn I heard a scream.

CHAPTER

TWENTY-SEVEN

"SLOAN, ARE YOU OKAY?" GARRETT stepped toward me.

The phone went dead. I tried to dial the Underground, but there was no signal.

"What is it?" Garrett's gaze turned serious.

"I think something's wrong. I swear I heard a scream before the line went dead."

"Okay, let's go." Garrett didn't hesitate.

"Maybe it was just the wind." I tried once more to get service, holding my phone above my head and out in front of me.

"Exactly. Ross could be hurt." Garrett went into emergency mode. He turned to Kat. "You stay here and try to get in touch with Chief Meyers, okay? Keep checking for service. Maybe go upstairs and see if there's any better reception there."

Kat scratched her head. "What should I tell her if I can get through?"

"Tell her that we're at the Underground and to come or send

help as soon as she can. It might be nothing, but we might need an ambulance if someone is really hurt over there."

I twisted my scarf around my chin.

Garrett was already heading for the door with a flashlight in hand. He stopped and grabbed a coat. "Stick with me, Sloan," he said, using his weight to push the front door open against the wind.

I could barely see across the street with the blowing snow. It wasn't sticking yet, but rather swirling in gusty tornados.

"Careful," Garrett cautioned, tightening his grip on my arm, and maneuvering around a ten-foot branch that blocked the patio entrance. "Watch your step."

"I see it." I let him help me as I stepped over the branch.

The wind pierced my eardrums.

"Maybe this is a bad idea," Garrett called above the roar. "You should go back. I'll go on my own."

I shook my head. "No. It's just across the street. I can make it."

It was nearly impossible to stay upright. Each gust pushed my body to the side. I felt like I was moving through molasses.

"This is worse than a hurricane," Garrett yelled.

"I know. We call this a storm in the Pacific Northwest." I nearly slipped on a patch of snow.

"Careful." Garrett caught me with his free arm.

We trudged on. Without any streetlights, our only visibility was the tiny beam from Garrett's flashlight. It felt like we were moving through a tunnel of darkness.

Garrett stopped at the ramp that led to the Underground.

The closed signs had blown away. "You sure you want to do this? I can go on my own. I don't know what we might be walking into."

I nodded. "I'm sure."

He wrapped his hand over mine and placed it on the frozen railing. "Hold this tight. I'll go behind you with the flashlight."

"Okay." I clutched the railing. Was this a stupid idea?

"You good, Sloan?"

I realized I hadn't budged. "Yeah." I took one step, then another. Maybe it wasn't the brightest idea, but I didn't want to leave Garrett alone. Ross or someone else could be hurt and unable to move. Or it could be nothing. Maybe the scream I'd heard had been the wind.

Another thought invaded my head. What if the scream I'd heard had nothing to do with the storm? What if the killer was here? I shuddered.

Garrett turned. "You good?"

"Good." I gave him a thumbs-up. It wasn't entirely true, but I wasn't about to turn around now. And I was sure that as soon Kat got through to the chief, she would send help.

The descent down the ramp was precarious, but once we reached the bottom, we were shielded from the wind.

"Let me go in first, Sloan." Garrett moved in front of me. He went to turn the doorknob, but the door swung open.

I swallowed my fear and followed him.

He scanned the bar with his flashlight. It danced off shiny bottles of liquor behind the bar. We tiptoed farther inside. The chairs and tables had been stacked. A section of drywall on the far wall had been cut out. The hole in the wall was covered with thick plastic. Tools were piled on the bar, and another large piece of plastic had been secured to a doorway that I assumed led to the kitchen. It looked as if Ross hadn't lied about doing work.

A huge crash sounded.

I jumped.

"Ross? Is that you? It's Garrett and Sloan. We're here to help."

Was it from the wind, or was someone inside the bar?

Adrenaline pulsed through my body.

"This way." Garrett motioned, moving with intention toward the plastic barrier.

Another loud thud made me startle. It sounded like a pan or something heavy hitting the floor. There was definitely someone in the kitchen.

My mouth was completely dry. I could hear my pulse in my head.

Garrett held both hands low, signaling for me to stay behind him. "Something's not right, Sloan. I don't like this," he said in a low whisper. "Stay close to me."

He kept the flashlight on the floor. The floor was covered with photos of tourists toasting with pint glasses. The photos had been covered in multiple layers of lacquer, giving the surface a waxy finish.

Please hurry, Chief, I prayed internally as we stayed as quiet as possible.

What was Garrett thinking? Was he worried that we were in danger? Had he landed on the same thought as me? What if we were stuck in the dark with a killer?

When we made it to the door frame, Garrett made pantomime signs with his hands. I had no idea what he was trying to tell me.

He pointed to the floor and then to the plastic.

I realized he wanted me to lift it so that he could duck under it. I bent over and carefully lifted the corner of the plastic. Garrett went through and then waited for me to do the same.

We left a trail of dusty footprints.

The kitchen smelled of industrial cleaner. I pressed my fingers under my nose to try and block the chemical odor.

Garrett muffled a gag.

Ross had wiped the kitchen clean. I wondered if there was a reason.

We froze as a cupboard slammed.

"Who's here?" a man's voice called.

Garrett turned off the flashlight.

Another cupboard slammed. "Who's in here? I've got a knife, and I'm not afraid to use it."

Was it Ross?

Garrett stuck out his right arm and felt along the countertop. Was he looking for something to use to defend himself? I did the same thing.

"Whoever is in here, better show yourself." The man's voice was getting closer.

I felt something wooden and picked it up. It was a rolling pin. Garrett held a skillet. I wasn't sure how our weapons would stack up against a knife-wielding killer, but it was better than nothing.

"Get out!" the man shouted.

Garrett held his ground. He waited for another minute

and then just as the man came close to us, he clicked on the flashlight and shined it in the man's eyes.

It was a quick-thinking move. The light blinded our assailant. He reeled backward, shielding his face with the blade of his knife.

"Ross," I said aloud. "It's you?"

CHAPTER
TWENTY-EIGHT

"OF COURSE IT'S ME. WHO else would it be?" Ross kept the knife in front of his face. "Get that light off of me."

Garrett moved the light to the side, illuminating the cupboards. He kept frying pan positioned and ready to strike.

"Geez, I thought you two were intruders." Ross lowered the knife and blinked rapidly. "I almost had a heart attack. What are you doing here?"

I wasn't sure how to respond. Was Ross the killer? I didn't want to take any chances, so I stayed partially hidden behind Garrett. "You called me. I heard a scream, so we came right over."

"The call went through?" He set the knife on the counter.

That was a good sign.

"I didn't think you could hear me. I've been trying the cops and anyone I know in the village for the last thirty minutes." Relief flooded his voice.

"I heard a scream," I repeated, stepping out from behind Garrett's lanky frame.

"Yeah, that was me." He cracked his knuckles. "I came down to check on the bar. When I got here, I saw someone heading down the ramp. I thought maybe it was someone trying to take advantage of the storm and loot the place. That's when I tried calling the cops, Der Keller, you. No one would answer. I guess you must have, though, because I heard a huge crash, and I probably screamed."

Garrett let the pan hang in his arm. "Have you found anyone?"

Ross shook his head. "I was checking the walk-in fridge when I saw your light. It's hard to see down here, but I checked the bar and everywhere someone could hide in the kitchen."

"Is there any other exit?" I asked.

"Yeah, but it's in the back of the kitchen, and the door hasn't been touched. I checked." He pointed to the frying pan and rolling pin. "Why are you guys still holding those?"

Garrett turned to me and nodded. He was signaling that he didn't think we were in danger.

"Well, I've heard some conflicting reports about you," I said.

"Like what?" Ross squinted.

"That you lied about this construction work. I heard from a reputable source that this is a guise and that you've actually been shut down by the state."

The glow from the flashlight made his bald head appear shiny. "That's true, but this construction work isn't a guise. I'm using the opportunity to get some much-needed repairs done, and yeah, the state shut me down for a day, but it's all been cleared up. I can start pouring again tomorrow. I got the green light this afternoon." He moved toward the opposite side of the kitchen.

"What are you doing?" Garrett followed his movement with the flashlight.

"Getting this paperwork." Ross held up a piece of paper. "If you don't believe me, read this. It's my license."

Garrett traded the frying pan for the paperwork. He scanned it and then handed it to me. Ross wasn't lying. The state had given him the green light to reopen the Underground.

"You guys think I killed Kristopher, don't you?" Ross's voice was incredulous. He made an X over his heart. "I swear I did not touch the dude. I didn't have anything to do with his death. Like I said before, I'm not going to pretend that I'm upset that he's gone, because I'm not, but I didn't kill him."

"Sorry," I said, setting the rolling pin on the counter. "I guess we jumped to conclusions."

A siren wailed nearby. The police were here.

"Sounds like the troops have arrived," Ross said, motioning for us to head back to the bar.

Garrett turned and held the flashlight so that it illuminated the door frame. He waited for Ross and me to go through. As we reentered the bar area, I noticed the flap of black plastic that had been secured to the drywall was missing.

Then everything happened in a blur.

Someone sprinted through the bar, knocking tables and chairs in an attempt to escape. Ross and Garrett sprang into action. I watched in horror. It was impossible to make out the bodies thrashing around in the dark.

A chair raised in the air. The next thing I knew, it came crashing down and Garrett landed on the floor near me with a thud.

"Garrett!" I screamed, and ran toward him. "Are you okay?" I dropped to my knees.

He let out a low moan. "My shoulder. He hit my shoulder."

"Is it bad?" I couldn't see anything in the dark. Where had the flashlight landed?

Garrett tried to stand but fell to his knees. "I can't lift it."

Ross and the man struggled near us. I considered my options. I squinted, trying to get a better look at the man. It was too dark to see anything.

The man had knocked Ross off of him and pushed over another table. It landed with a crash that made me jump.

"We have to stop him." Garrett tried to move again, but the pain stopped him. He clutched his shoulder and keeled over.

"Don't move. I'll get help." I fumbled on the floor for anything I could use for a weapon.

In the corner of my eye, I caught sight of Ross, who was on his feet again. He swayed as he stood. Had he been hit in the head? Should I try to help him?

There's no time, Sloan.

The man was headed for the front exit. He had his back to me. I crouched behind a table and crawled toward him. The floor was ice-cold to the touch.

If I could sneak up from behind, maybe I could take him by surprise or grab a chair and whack him on the head. The question was, did he have a weapon? If he had a gun or a knife, why hadn't he used it?

I hedged my bets and crept closer. Adrenaline surged through my body. The sound of my heavy heartbeat and the raging wind muffled together. The blackness of the room engulfed me. I didn't dare turn around to see if Garrett or Ross was behind me.

The man was almost to the door. I had to make my move—now.

Carefully, so as not to make any sound, I pushed to my tiptoes and reached for the nearest chair.

At the same time, thudding footsteps pounded down the entrance ramp. The front door burst open, and light flooded inside. I dropped the chair and shielded my eyes. Two police officers holding massive flashlights came in, followed closely by Chief Meyers.

The escapee was tackled and cuffed in one blurry blaze of motion.

I blinked, trying to clear the tiny yellow halos in my vision, and stared in disbelief as one of the officers yanked none other than Conrad to his feet. The officer restrained him while Chief Meyers and the second uniformed cop began scanning the bar.

"Sloan, you good?"

Spots danced in front of my vision. I managed to nod and point behind me. "I'm fine, but Garrett and Ross are hurt."

"Sit," she commanded, picking up the chair that I had dropped. Then she motioned for one of the officers to come with her.

Conrad was silent. He narrowed his eyes and flared his nostrils. I turned my chair so I didn't have to look at him.

The chief attended to Garrett and Ross. She had her officer

get them both packs of ice and called for reinforcements. My hands shook so fiercely that I stuck them underneath my thighs. The adrenaline was wearing off.

Conrad was the killer. I couldn't believe it—my instincts (and Kat's) had been right after all. Garrett's mom's advice seemed most profound at the moment—always trust your instincts.

An EMS crew arrived and immediately began to bandage Garrett's shoulder. Once the medics took over, the chief returned to me. She crouched next to me and patted my knee. "I know you've been through the wringer tonight, so I'll keep it as short as I can for the moment. Anything you can tell me about what went down while your memory is fresh will be helpful."

"Yeah, no problem. I'm fine."

"Your body language tells me otherwise, Sloan." She nodded to my left foot, which was bouncing on the cement floor.

I tried to smile. "Are Garrett and Ross okay?"

"They'll both be fine." Chief Meyers stood. She held her flashlight to the ceiling and moved the spotlight toward the opposite side of the room. "Where did you find Conrad?"

"I think he might have been hiding in there." I pointed to the section of missing drywall.

She motioned to the police officer, who immediately went to check out the area. The officer searched the cutout section with his flashlight. "We got them, Chief. You were right."

Got them? I was confused. Was someone working with Conrad?

I waited with bated breath while the officer set his flashlight on the floor and put on a pair of gloves. Then he proceeded to reach into the area and pull out April's ceremonial ribbon cutting scissors.

"Trying to stash the evidence, and frame Ross?" The chief turned to Conrad.

He closed his eyes and refused to answer her.

"Get him out of here. Put him in the car," she directed the officer guarding Conrad.

"That's the murder weapon?" I asked the chief after Conrad had been led away.

"Looks like it." Her walkie-talkie buzzed with storm reports. "I need you to clear the premises. We need to do a sweep and then get back out there. It's blowing like crazy. I'll be in touch to take your statements when I can."

She dismissed me and went right to work. The medics had finished triaging Ross and Garrett. I went to join them. Garrett's left arm was tied in a sling. Ross had two butterfly bandages on his forehead.

"How are you guys?"

Garrett gave a pained attempt at a smile. "My shoulder was dislocated, but they got it back in place. I'll be fine, but you might be lifting bags of grain for the next couple of weeks."

"Dislocated?" I winced.

"It doesn't hurt. They told me to take some Advil and take it easy with any heavy lifting. It could have been worse."

"Me too." Ross rubbed his temple. "No sign of a concussion, but they did warn me that I might have a doozy of a headache tomorrow."

The three of us walked outside together. In the short time we'd been in the bar, more debris and snow had fallen.

"You want to come have a pint?" Garrett asked. "Consider it an apology for accusing you of murder."

Ross clapped him on the back.

Garrett flinched.

"Sorry, man. I'll take a rain check." He pointed to the apartments above the bar. "My place is upstairs, and after what went down, I think I need something stiffer than a pint. A shot of scotch has my name on it. Followed by an Advil chaser. I'll catch you guys later."

We left him and pushed through the storm to Nitro. Kat was pacing in the kitchen. "I was so worried about you guys." She threw her arms around me again. "My phone died and then I heard the police sirens." Then she noticed Garrett's sling. "What happened to you?"

"We're okay," I assured her, and then we filled her in.

When we finished, she let out a long sigh. "I'm so relieved, but now I have a bigger problem."

"What's that?" I asked.

Kat intentionally shook her hands as if she was having withdrawal symptoms. "This is going to sound pathetic, especially since you two just came face-to-face with a killer and you have a bad shoulder, Garrett. But how am I going to live without my phone for the night?" She grinned and pretended to choke herself. "I'll totally die without it."

"Let's hope that doesn't happen." Garrett laughed. "You know, I just thought about the fact that my family is coming next week. I hope they can get through the passes."

"I'm sure they'll get here fine." I didn't want Kat or Garrett to worry, but I suspected the visit might have to be delayed.

I knew from experience that one of the cons of living in a remote location high in the Washington mountains was that it took longer to get support and restore services after a storm or major weather event. Kat might have to last without her phone for a while. Floods in the 1990s had sent rivers of mud and water gushing from the mountain, flooding the village and cutting us off from the outside world. Floodwaters threatened the dam, causing over fifty homes to be evacuated.

"Now that I know you guys are okay and I'm phoneless, I guess I'll go to bed." Kat left us with a yawn.

"So," Garrett said, eyeing me. "Should I make another batch of my hot chocolate while we wait for the chief?"

"I've had enough hot chocolate for one night. Not to mention, you're not doing anything with that arm. Although I might need a coffee. I'm running on fumes at the moment, but once the shock of what we just went through wears off, I have a feeling I'm going to crash. Can I make you a coffee or get you anything else?"

"I could go for a coffee."

We replayed every detail of the evening over strong cups of coffee. I lost track of time as I watched the candles flicker.

I must have dozed off, because the next thing I remembered was waking to the sound of footsteps echoing on the brewery's cement floors.

"Sloan, Garrett, you in here?" Chief Meyers's voice reverberated in the brewery. Next, I saw a beam from a flashlight illuminate the cement floor.

"In here, Chief," Garrett replied. "You're awake," he said to me with a half grin. Three of the candles had burned out. He appeared to be working on something on his iPad.

"How long was I out?"

"Not long. Maybe a half hour."

I stretched. My neck felt stiff. Probably because I had fallen asleep on the stainless-steel countertop.

"I was going to grab you a pillow," Garrett said sheepishly. "But I didn't want to wake you."

Chief Meyers barged in. "Glad you're both still awake. I need to take your statements while everything is still fresh." She whipped out a notebook.

My mind was still fuzzy. "Did he confess?"

She clicked a pen. "Statements first, then we'll discuss what I know."

CHAPTER

TWENTY-NINE

I POURED CHIEF MEYERS a cup of coffee while we recounted what we remembered with as much detail as possible. She took rapid notes, stopping us every once in a while for clarification.

When she was finished with her list of questions, she pushed the notebook aside and relaxed her body language. "Back to your original question, Sloan. Conrad confessed everything."

Her flashlight danced off the ceiling as she spoke. "We'd been closing in on him. Got ahold of his financials. The shop was in terrible shape. Conrad already filed for bankruptcy. He was going to lose the business."

"Do you think he went to Kristopher for help?" Garrett asked. He cradled his left arm as he spoke. I wondered if he was in more pain than he was letting on.

The chief nodded. "Yep. We found a moving van behind his shop loaded with valuable nutcrackers. If it hadn't been for your tip, he might be halfway to Seattle by now. He probably figured he could get far enough away and then buy himself some extra time while we dug out from the damage. It's not a bad plan."

"But aren't the highways closed?" I was slowly starting to come out of my fog. What time was it? I checked my watch. It was almost five in the morning. Garrett had lied. I had obviously slept for more than a half hour.

"Yep. Many of them are shut down, but that doesn't mean he couldn't have found an alternate route or blown past the detours. This was a man with nothing left to lose, remember."

I nodded.

"He told us that he had approached Kristopher about investing in the shop. Kristopher took a look at his books and declined. Conrad was furious. Kristopher was an astute businessman. He knew that the nutcracker shop was a losing venture. Apparently, he went to Conrad's competitor, Stan, and offered him a chunk of money. This sent Conrad over the edge. He had poured his life savings into the shop. He didn't have a dime to his name, and he was convinced that Kristopher was toying with him. He went to talk to Kristopher. He and Kristopher argued, and the built-up stress and rage reached critical mass. He says he didn't intend to kill Kristopher. That things took a bad turn."

"Do you believe him?" Garrett asked.

Chief Meyers rested her flashlight on the counter. "I do. He said he was at his shop early the morning of the murder, unloading a new shipment. He saw Kristopher heading to April's office and seized the opportunity. He followed after him and confronted him about offering Stan a partnership. Kristopher was smug about it, and Conrad snapped. There was a struggle and then he grabbed the scissors from the wall and stabbed Kristopher."

"That means April is in the clear?" I said, already knowing the answer.

"She is, and it sounds like she has you to thank for that, at least in part." Chief Meyers smiled ever so slightly. "If I were you, Sloan, I wouldn't let her forget that."

Garrett laughed. "Imagine the power. Maybe you should let her sweat it out a while longer."

"I can't condone that," Chief Meyers said. "It won't matter anyway. The news of Conrad's arrest will quickly surpass any news about the storm by sunrise. Mark my words."

"What about Heidi and Valerie? They're both in the clear, right?"

"Yes. Both of them had their own motives for killing Kristopher, but neither of them acted on their anger. We've got our killer in custody with a full confession. This should be enough for the DA. We'll continue to follow up by matching DNA evidence found at the crime scene to Conrad and sorting through Kristopher's financials. Plus, we found Conrad trying to dispose of the murder weapon. He hasn't admitted it, but I'm sure his intent at the Underground tonight was to frame Ross. He knew that Ross was on our radar and figured if we found the murder weapon at his property it would implicate him. The DA is going to love me. It should be an open-and-shut case."

I couldn't believe Conrad had been so desperate that he had actually killed Kristopher. I was glad to know that the real killer was behind bars and that life in the village could return to normal, but I also felt sad for Conrad. I loved our village and Nitro too. I could imagine Conrad's desperation. It didn't give him the right to take Kristopher's life, but I understood his motivation.

"I need to get back to the office. We're coordinating storm cleanup now that the bulk of the high winds are behind us. I wanted to thank you and make sure that you heard the news first." She picked up her flashlight. "Be careful out there."

"Chief." I called for her to wait. "Do you think it's safe to go to the farmhouse to check on Alex?"

"It's looking better out there, but watch your speed and keep an eye out for debris. The crews have already cleared two large oak trees from Front Street. I don't know what the highway is like, though, so use caution."

"Okay. Thanks."

After she left, Garrett ran his fingers through his already disheveled hair. "I never imagined that starting a nanobrewery here would lead to such excitement and danger."

"I know. I didn't see that coming. My theory sounded crazy, even to me, but at the same time, it makes sense. I feel sorry for Conrad. Is that wrong?"

He shook his head. "No. I get it. I would probably feel desperate if I was about to lose Nitro. Not that I would kill anyone, but if he felt like he didn't have any other options or support, I can see how it might have led him down that path. It's too bad."

"For nutcrackers."

Garrett gave a low whistle. "For nutcrackers."

"The good news is that, hopefully, April will back off for a while. I mean if Conrad killed over losing his nutcrackers, that alone should give the woman pause."

"That's really wishful thinking, Sloan."

"True. Very true." I took the empty coffee cups to the sink. "I'm going to go check on the house and Alex. You're sure you don't need anything?"

"No. I'll take some Advil and try to sleep." He walked with me to the front. "Don't come in until later. Who knows if we'll even have power."

"I'll check in later."

He locked the door behind me. The sky was a light shade of purple, allowing my first view of the storm's aftermath. Tree branches and other debris lined the street. I had to pull two huge tree branches from my windshield, but fortunately my car hadn't sustained any damage. Snow continued to fall and had begun sticking in earnest now that the winds had died down.

Front Street was a sea of flashing yellow lights and work crews. There were strands of Christmas lights littering the sidewalk. *Those poor work crews,* I thought as I slowly drove up the street. Not only did they have to clean up the storm damage, but then they would have to put up all the lights again.

It took an extra twenty minutes to navigate to the farmhouse. I had to steer past obstacles like a shattered plastic chair. Twice, I had to detour because of trees fallen across the roadway.

When I pulled into our long gravel driveway, I was relieved to see the house intact. All of our sturdy evergreens were still standing. Thank God. With their dusting of snow, they reminded me of the pine tree shortbread I had made.

I parked and went inside. Mac and Alex were both snoring on the living room floor. They had taken all of the couch cushions and pillows to make a pile on the floor and covered themselves with blankets. It reminded me of when Alex was in preschool and we would have "campouts" in the living room. I had a feeling Mac had suggested sleeping in the living room because it was the most central and hence safest room in the house.

I blew Alex a kiss and tiptoed down the hall. My family was safe, and Kristopher's killer had been apprehended. There was going to be much to do today, but as I slipped into bed, I said a prayer of thanks and gratitude. Regardless of my strained relationship with Mac, I was surrounded by people I loved and people who loved me. I couldn't ask for anything more.

CHAPTER

THIRTY

WHEN I WOKE UP A few hours later, I got a better glimpse of the full extent of the storm's damage. We'd lost an entire row of hop trellises. One of my favorite pots had been shattered. Some of the fencing around the perimeter of the property had been knocked over by the winds. None of it mattered. Snow blanketed the farm. It fell in fat, puffy flakes. There was nothing more beautiful or calming than the first snow. I wrapped myself in my plush cashmere robe (another present from Mac) and tiptoed down the hallway.

The scent of a crackling fire and the sound of Mac's and Alex's voices greeted me. Lately, it had been hard to differentiate their voices when talking to Alex on the phone. His deepening voice sounded more and more like Mac's every day.

"How was the slumber party?" I asked, entering the kitchen and attached dining room to find Mac and Alex camped in front of the fire under a pile of blankets.

"Sloan, you're wearing the robe I got you. It looks good." Mac gave me a suggestive smile.

If Alex hadn't been there, I would have smacked him, but instead I ignored his blatant attempt to get under my skin. "Is the power still off?"

"Last time we checked it was." Alex held up a box of granola bars. "Hungry? We raided the pantry."

He wasn't kidding. Cereal boxes, marshmallows, chocolate bars, bagels, and a package of cookies lined the hearth.

"I see that." I walked to the fireplace and reached for a cookie. Then I made room on the floor near Alex. "How long have you guys been up?"

Mac stared at the cuckoo clock on the wall. Ursula and Otto had given it to us on our wedding day. "Not long. Maybe a half hour or so. When did you get home last night? We didn't hear you come in."

I munched on the dry cookie, wishing that it was a pine shortbread instead. "Late, well actually early, I guess," I replied and then I launched into a recap of last night's events. It was strangely cathartic to allow the details and the pent-up anxiety to spill out.

"Sloan, you could have been killed." Mac's face was as white as the snow falling out the window.

"No. We had Conrad outnumbered." I crunched another cookie.

Mac scoffed. "What would you say to Alex if he told you that he snuck off after a killer in the middle of a massive storm?"

"Yeah, Mom, Dad has a valid point. You would kill me." Alex made a slicing motion across his throat. "I'm going to

263

have some serious cred with everyone at school. The other moms are making peanut butter and jelly sandwiches and my mom is tracking down a killer in the middle of a blizzard."

The power flickered on. Talk about synchronistic timing. The return of lights saved me from Mac's and Alex's reprimands.

Alex threw off the covers. "I've got to go get online and see if anyone's up yet. Fresh powder means snow day!" He ran to his room.

"Thanks for staying with him last night, Mac. I was worried." I picked up a couple cereal boxes. "You want a cup of coffee?"

When we were married, Mac rarely helped with housework, but to my surprise, he got up and helped me gather the remains of their breakfast snack feast. "Coffee would be nice."

I made coffee while Mac folded the blankets and stoked the fire.

"We were worried about you, Sloan." His voice was thick with emotion. "I know things haven't been great between us, but I don't know what I would do if anything happened to you."

Every so often in moments like this, I saw flashes of the Mac I had fallen in love with. "Thanks. I swear, I'm fine."

I poured us coffee and joined him at the dining room table. Maybe it was because of our brief emotional connection, but I found myself asking him about my past. "Can I ask you something, and when I do, will you promise to tell me the truth?"

"Anything." Mac's brow creased ever so slightly. I had a feeling he was nervous that I was going to ask about his infidelity.

"Do the names Forest or Marianne mean anything to you?"

Mac's face drew a complete blank. "No, why?"

"You never heard your mom or dad mention them or anything about my past?"

His round cheeks scrunched. "No. I don't know anyone by those names, and I definitely never heard Mama or Papa talk about your past, other than the occasional mention of being worried about you. Why?"

If there was one thing I could count on from Mac, it was his inability to lie. When he lied, his already ruddy cheeks would turn crimson. He would slur his words together and talk in rapid-fire speech. I knew he was telling the truth.

"Honestly, I'm not ready to talk about it yet. I promise I will once I've had some more time to figure this out myself, and I might need your help."

He reached across the table and squeezed my hand. "Whenever you're ready to talk about it, I'm here."

I appreciated the gesture. The old Mac would have pressed me until I relented. For the first time ever, I thought maybe Mac and I could end up friends.

"How's the condo search coming along?" I pulled my hand away and drank my coffee.

"Good. I like the Blackbird Island place, but I want Alex to come see it with me before I sign a lease."

I wanted to broach the subject of selling the farmhouse, but it didn't feel like the right timing, especially since I had yet to tour the A-frame I was interested in seeing. April owed me a favor. Maybe I would drop by her office and see about arranging a showing.

Alex returned from his bedroom with a duffel bag of his snow gear. "Can one of you take me into town? I'm going to meet my friends, and we're going to hit some of the cross-country trails since the lifts aren't open yet. My skis are in the garage."

"I'll take you," Mac offered, not only picking up our coffee cups, but washing and then drying them in the sink.

Alex went to get his skis from the garage.

"Why are you staring at me like that, Sloan?" Mac returned the coffee cups to the cupboard and wiped down the countertop.

"I don't know if I've ever seen you wash a dish."

He looked injured. "That stings, but it's probably fair. I'm finally realizing how much you did to hold this family together now that I'm on my own. I'm sorry." His sapphire eyes welled with emotion.

"Come on, Mac, I'm being glib." I decided to change the subject before things turned more serious. "Can I catch a ride with you? I'd like to stop by April's office, and your beastly machine can probably maneuver over any debris."

We piled into Mac's hummer and drove into the village like old times. I caught Mac staring at me in the rearview mirror, so I kept my gaze on the winter wonderland out the window. Mac and I were going to have to sit down and work through some painful conversations about the house, finalizing our divorce, and his parents' involvement in keeping me from my past. For now, though, it could wait.

CHAPTER

THIRTY-ONE

MAC DROPPED ALEX AND ME off at Front Street Park, where kids were sledding and rolling giant balls of snow into snowmen. It continued to dump fluffy flakes from the sky. The village was bustling with activity. Shop owners were assessing damage, while snowplows tried to keep up with the blizzard of white. City crews had already made a large dent in clearing tree branches and refastening twinkle lights in the trees. If the snow continued like this, we might have five or six inches on the ground for the lighting ceremony.

I left Alex with his friends and tromped through the powdery snow to April's office. There was a lightness about the village that had been missing for the last few days. I smiled as I passed the Café Haus, where the owner had set up an outdoor hot chocolate and cider stand with peppermint stir sticks and gingerbread cookies.

"Cider, Sloan?" he asked as I passed. "It's free. A snow day special."

"That's so thoughtful," I replied. "But save it for the kids."

"Everyone's a kid on a snow day." He winked.

I continued on to April's. Her receptionist greeted me with a smile. "April's been expecting you, go on back."

Expecting me? We didn't have an appointment, did we?

April's office was a tribute to her. A photo gallery on the wall opposite her imposing walnut desk with brass handles displayed photos of April in a variety of costumes and poses. "*Guten Morgen,* Sloan." April waved her fingers in the air. She was dressed in a puffy black ski jacket and matching pants with German flag patches plastered all over them. Her garish red hair was tied in two long braids and covered with a striped German flag ski hat. Any trace of her freckles had vanished under a thick layer of makeup.

"You look like . . ." I tried to think of something nonoffensive. "Like yourself."

"Thank you." She pointed to the chair. "Sit, sit. We have much to discuss."

"How did you know that I was stopping by?"

April flipped her braids. "Why wouldn't you come? I figured you want to rehash the tragic events, and we simply must go for a celebratory cup of mulled spice *Wein*. I'm a free woman again."

Yep, April was back. Great.

"Do tell." April rubbed her hands together. "I must know every detail about how Conrad was apprehended—that little rat. Chief Meyers was less than forthcoming, despite my reminders that everyone in the village will be coming to me for news and insight."

I tried not to roll my eyes.

"Vell, Vell, out vith it." April spun her hands in circles.

Oh no. Not the fake accent, too. I gave April the condensed version.

When I finished, she stood and walked to the spot on the wall where the scissors had been. "I knew it. I knew that Conrad was no good. I should have done something about it sooner and saved myself a splitting headache. Jail is absolute torture, Sloan. I've warned the chief that I could sue."

"It's not the chief's fault, April."

She traced the outline of the scissors. "Sloan, you know as well as I do that Leavenworth would implode without me. The chief had a duty to uphold civility. She could have been much more discreet."

"You should blame Conrad, not Chief Meyers. She was doing her job. The initial evidence pointed to you."

"Oh, mark my words, I will be suing the pants off of Conrad, too." She brushed imaginary dust from the wall. "And the chief owes me a new pair of scissors."

In the grand scheme of things, ceremonial scissors sounded trivial, but this was April I was talking to.

"Come on, let's go." April tugged on a pair of red, yellow, and black striped gloves. Where did she shop? Germans R Us?

"Where are we going?"

"You'll see." She yanked me outside into the snow. She was on a mission. I had a hard time keeping up with her, even though my legs were much longer.

"April, what's the rush?" I huffed as we practically ran past the gazebo and up the hill to where Front Street curved and merged onto Highway 2.

We stopped just before we made it to the highway. "Look." April pointed to an adorable cottage next to the grange.

"What am I looking at?"

"The cottage." She yanked me closer. I had always admired the cottage, with its white stucco exterior and thatched roof. The roof wasn't literally thatched, but it was designed to resemble a farmer's cottage. "Want to take a look inside?" April unzipped her ski parka and dangled a key ring in front of me.

"Why?"

"Because it's yours if you want it. I owe you one, Sloan, and I have it on good authority that the property is coming up on the market. I've told the owner that we want first dibs, and using much discretion, as I always do, when the owner learned that you might be interested in the cottage, they are willing to make you a very good deal."

"But I've never said anything about wanting this cottage. We talked about looking at that A-frame outside of town."

April stuck her hands on her hips. "Sloan, if you want to pine away and feel sorry for yourself in a remote cabin in the forest, go for it, but you've been there and done that. You're starting a brand-new life. Do you really want to be miles from the village, or do you want to be in the heart of the action? You can walk to Nitro. You can walk everywhere."

She had a point.

"Take it from me, the single life can be rewarding, but also very lonely." There was a vulnerability in her tone that I had never heard before. "If you have your heart set on the A-frame, I'll show it to you, but it's the wrong choice. You don't need to isolate yourself more. You need to embrace this village and everyone in it who cares about you."

Her words almost made me teary. Could it be that April Ablin really had my best interests at heart?

She clinked the keys. "You want to see inside?"

"Okay."

The minute we were inside, I fell in love with the cottage. It was cozy, with rustic wood floors, slanted windows, a red brick fireplace, and an updated kitchen. There were two bedrooms and a small den with a wood-burning stove. It was the perfect size for me and Alex.

"Do you love it?" April asked when we finished the brief tour.

"I do." I could hear the surprise in my voice.

April was smug. "I knew it. Shall we go back to my office and write up an offer?"

"Wait." I motioned for her to slow down. She was already halfway out the door. "I don't know that I'm ready to make an offer. I should probably think about it. I haven't even looked at any other properties."

April pursed her lips. "I will gladly show you every property on the market from here to Wenatchee, but I'm an expert, Sloan. This is your house. I know it. You know it. Think about it if you want, but you're going to come to the same conclusion, and you only suffer by spending hours agonizing over your decision."

"But I haven't even talked to Mac about selling the farmhouse yet."

"Your point is?" April swept her arm around the cute front entrance with a built-in mail slot. "This is not a multimillion-dollar property, and it's hardly as if you're broke. The Krauses are some of the most successful business owners in the village.

You're going to come out ahead in the divorce, and I guarantee that the numbers I discussed with the current owner will allow you to buy this with cash."

For my every hesitation, April had a compelling counter-point.

"Let's go." April held the door open for me. "I'm not going to force you into this, Sloan. The property hasn't even listed yet. But don't take too long on this one. Someone will scoop it up fast."

I took one final look at the cottage. In my heart, I knew April was right. I belonged here.

CHAPTER

THIRTY-TWO

AFTER THE COTTAGE TOUR, APRIL suggested we have a celebratory *"Wein"* at the Alpen Winery. The windows of the winery steamed from the heat of warm bodies and warm mulled spice wine.

"Prost!" April toasted to me. "To freedom and new adventures."

"To freedom and new adventures." I returned her toast.

"Do you mind if we join you?" someone asked. I turned to see Valerie with a group of her campaign team standing next to the family-style table we were seated at.

"Sure." I scooted down the bench to make room.

"I don't mean to interrupt, but I have some news to share." Valerie blushed.

April perked. "News? Do tell."

Valerie was drinking a deep merlot. She held her glass up to the light and swirled the deep-red wine. "I've had confirmation from the mayor and current council members that

Kristopher's name will not appear on the ballot. I'm running unopposed, so the election next week is a formality."

"Congratulations!"

"*Ich gratuliere!*" April raised her mulled wineglass. "That's proper German, Sloan. I'm surprised you didn't know that."

Valerie reddened more. I wasn't sure if it was from the wine. "Thanks. I'm looking forward to serving Leavenworth, and I hope you'll come to me with any suggestions or feedback for making our town even stronger."

"I have a list," April said.

One of Valerie's campaign volunteers laughed. April shot daggers at him. "I'm serious. I've taken it upon myself to craft a list of critical policies that need to be implemented immediately."

"Excellent." Valerie forced a smile. "I look forward to it."

"I'll be by your office first thing tomorrow morning. Shall we plan on a couple hours to review my input?"

Valerie gulped her wine. "Great."

Poor Valerie.

I spotted Heidi ordering a drink at the bar. "Thanks for the wine, April, and congratulations, Valerie. I see a friend I want to say hi to and then I should get over to Nitro and see how things are there."

April caught my eye and then tapped her wrist. I got the hint. I walked over to where Heidi was sitting. "Heidi." I tapped the back of her shoulder.

She let out a little scream.

"Sorry. I didn't mean to scare you."

"Oh, it's you." She fanned her face. "I've been so jumpy today after the storm. I couldn't sleep. I was so sure the roof was going to cave in at the Hostel. After all that money and work, can't you just imagine? And then I was worried about our guests when we lost power. I went over and made sure the flashlights were working and had the night manager light candles. I'm so glad I live in the village. I can't imagine what I would have done if I lived out of town."

"How is the Hamburg?"

Heidi took her glass of white wine from the bartender. "I'm happy to report that, unlike me, she weathered the storm without any major damage." She nodded to her wineglass. "I thought I would have a quick drink to help settle my nerves and then I'm going to assess some broken yard art and a couple of windows with my handyman."

"I'm so glad to hear that."

"What about Nitro?" Heidi asked, taking a long sip of her wine.

"That's where I'm headed now. Fingers crossed. When I left late last night—or, I guess, early this morning—the building was still standing."

"Did you hear about Conrad?" She tucked her hair behind her ears. "I guess we were right, but it's one of those times I wish I was wrong. I feel terrible for Kristopher."

"Me too."

Heidi patted my forearm. "Thanks for always being such a model of calm. You're so grounded, Sloan. I need to learn from you."

"If you only knew." I smiled. "I'm a mess internally, trust me." I couldn't believe I was admitting my weakness to Heidi. Maybe Mac wasn't the only one changing.

"No way." Heidi shook her head. "I don't buy it."

"It's true."

"Well, then we should get a glass of wine soon, so I can get to know the real Sloan. I enjoyed our dinner, and I'd love to spend more time with you." She made a goofy face. "Now I sound like I'm in grade school and asking if you want to come over for a playdate."

"A playdate sounds great." We agreed to meet up for dinner in a few days. I left the winery with a broad smile.

Front Street Park was a sea of colorful sleds. Teens amassed snowballs for an epic battle while the younger villagers made snow angels. The snowfall had let up a bit. Thick, wet flakes had been replaced by dainty snow floating to the ground in beautiful wisps. I paused and took in the picturesque scene. Smoke puffed from chimneys. Rooftops were laden with marshmallow-like drifts of fresh snow. A horse-drawn carriage cut tracks down the middle of the street. Silver bells jingled as the blanket-clad horses trotted past me.

This is utopia, I thought as I kicked snow on my walk to Nitro.

As I had said to Heidi, Nitro had indeed been spared from any major damage. A string of Edison-style outdoor lights had been ripped from the exterior door frame, and the wooden Nitro sign hung crooked, dangling by a single nail. Fortunately, Kat had managed to set our bistro tables and chairs back up. Short of a few minor repairs, the building appeared to be structurally sound.

Someone had shoveled a path to the front door. The broken sandwich board was propped against the entryway. It read HOPPY SNOW DAY. Someone, I guessed Kat, had drawn snowflakes landing on the top of frothy steins.

I went inside to find Kat pouring pints. Every table was packed, and there was a crowd gathered at the bar. "When did you open?" I asked, tugging off my coat and gloves and stashing them under the bar. "And how is Garrett doing?"

Kat delivered two pints of our Cherry Weizen to a couple at the end of the bar. "An hour ago. He seems fine. He's like a superhero or something. He just took a tray with four taster flights over to that table with one arm." She paused and motioned to the bar. "Can you believe this? It's like everyone came out for the snow."

"Yeah, snow days aren't just for kids." I washed my hands in the sink. "Put me to work. What can I do?"

"Garrett's delivering the first round of taster flights for that big group up front. Can you pour three more trays?"

"I'm on it." I reached for three paddles and started filling two-ounce glasses. It felt good to have Nitro buzzing. We hadn't been this busy since Oktoberfest. Once I had the taster flights finished with our beers in order from the lightest pale ale to the darkest stout, I delivered them to the waiting table and was greeted with a round of applause and cheers.

That was one of the best things about working in a craft brewery. Beer brought people together in celebration and in times of sadness. I was grateful to get to be a small part of our customers' lives.

The next hour or so was a frantic frenzy of pouring pints and washing glasses. The pine shortbread was a hot seller. We sold out of the batch that I'd made earlier in a matter of minutes. We went through bags of Doritos and peanuts. No one expected anything more since everyone was in the same boat of recovering from the storm and subsequent power outage.

When things slowed a bit, I spotted Ross at the far end of the bar. He and Garrett were chatting like long-lost friends.

"Hey, Sloan," Ross said, raising his glass of honey wheat ale when I joined them. "I had to take you guys up on your offer from last night. I was just saying to Garrett that I'd love to get a keg of this on tap at the Underground. I know you guys don't have many kegs to spare, but if you'd be willing to send one to me, I'll make sure my bartenders tell customers to come across the street to try more of whatever you have on tap."

Garrett pushed up the right sleeve of his Nitro sweatshirt. "What do you think, Sloan? We can spare one keg, can't we?"

"Absolutely." I glanced behind us to the menu board and did some quick calculations. Our holiday line would be ready to keg in a week. The current line of fall beers we were pouring were going quickly, but I had a feeling the snow day was an anomaly. We still had a few kegs in the back, and things shouldn't heat up again until the Christmas lighting, when we would debut our holiday ales. "That would be great."

Ross reached over and shook both of our hands. Then he raised his glass again. "To new partnerships."

Garrett and I had discussed partnering to get Nitro on tap at other bars and restaurants in the village, but thus far we hadn't had the capacity. One keg at the Underground seemed like an excellent starting point.

"Have you recovered from last night?" I asked. "How's the head?"

Ross gently tapped the butterfly bandages on his forehead. A hint of a bruise had begun to form on his skin. "The EMS